A Nurse's Story
and Others

A Nurse's Story

and Others
by Peter Baida

University Press of Mississippi   *Jackson*

www.upress.state.ms.us

These stories appeared in the following publications, some of them
in slightly different form: "A Nurse's Story" in *The Gettysburg Review* and
The O. Henry Awards Prize Stories 1999; "Mr. Moth and Mr. Davenport" in
The Gettysburg Review; "The Rodent," "Class Warfare," and "The Reckoning" in *The Free Press*; "No Place to Hide" in *American Literary Review*;
"Points of Light" in *Western Humanities Review*; "Family Ties" in *Confronta-
tion*; and "A Doctor's Story" in *The Missouri Review*.

06 05 04 03 02 01   4 3 2 1

Library of Congress Cataloging-in-Publication Data
Baida, Peter.
  A nurse's story, and others / Peter Baida.
    p. cm.
    Contents: A nurse's story—The rodent—No place to hide—Points
of light—Family ties—Class warfare—Mr. Moth and Mr. Davenport—A
doctor's story—The reckoning.
    ISBN 1-57806-318-3 (alk. paper)
      1. United States—Social life and customs—20th century—Fiction.
I. Title
    PS3552.A3625 N87 2001
    813'.54—dc21   00-049525

British Library Cataloging-in-Publication Data available

Contents

Preface: Remarks Made at the O. Henry Awards Presentation

Peter Baida was in the hospital and too ill to attend the O. Henry Awards presentation for "A Nurse's Story," which had won first prize. The comments that he wrote for the occasion were delivered by his wife, Diane Cole, on the evening of October 21, 1999.

Thank you. Peter regrets that because of illness he cannot be here tonight. He asked me to read the following remarks:

I am happy to accept this prize in the 1999 O. Henry Awards. Of course, anyone with any sense knows that the same three judges, on a different day, or even at a different time on the same day, might have chosen a different story. Nevertheless, if prizes are given, someone must win, and I am glad to have won this prize. It is especially gratifying to know that the judges made their selection after reading "blind" copies of the stories, with the names of the authors and magazines omitted.

In the note about "A Nurse's Story" that I wrote for this volume [*The O. Henry Awards Prize Stories 1999*], I mentioned that twenty-two editors rejected the story before Peter Stitt accepted it for *The Gettysburg Review*. While the rejections were rolling in, I said to my wife, "You know, if I can't sell this story, I think I might as well give up, because I don't think I can write a better one." I sometimes see editors quoted as saying that every really good manuscript eventually finds a place to be published. I don't believe this for a second. In that same note, I asked, "What are editors looking for? How good does a story have to be to get published in the 1990s?" I still think that these are good questions.

This prize is dedicated to my parents, Lillian and Erwin Baida, to my wife, Diane Cole, and to my son, Edward. In the tradition of the Academy Awards, I also would like to thank everyone I have ever met, but not by name. I am very grateful that the 1999 O. Henry Awards have brought my story to a much larger audience than it ever would have reached otherwise. Thank you.

A Nurse's Story
and Others

A Nurse's Story

The pain in Mary McDonald's bones is not the old pain that she knows well, but a new pain. Sitting in her room in the Booth-Tiessler Geriatric Center, on the third floor, in the bulky chair by the window, Mary tries to measure this pain. She sits motionless, with a grave expression on her face, while the cheerless gray sky on the other side of the window slowly fades toward evening.

Mary McDonald knows what this pain comes from. It comes from a cancer that began in her colon and then spread to her liver and now has moved into her bones. Mary McDonald has been a nurse for forty years, she has retained the full use of her faculties, and she understands perfectly where this pain comes from and what it means.

"Union?" Eunice Barnacle says. "What do I want with a union?"

"Miss Barnacle," Mary McDonald says, looking at her from the chair by the window, "do you think you're paid what you're worth?"

Miss Barnacle is a lean, sharp-featured black woman in her middle twenties, with a straight nose, small teeth, wary eyes, and a straightforward manner, who joined the staff at Booth-Tiessler about a month ago. "This place can't afford to pay me what I'm worth," she says.

"That's certainly what they want you to believe, Miss Barnacle. May I ask a nosy question?"

"I suppose."

"What do they pay you, Miss Barnacle?"

"That's my business."

"Eight-fifty per hour. Is that about right, Miss Barnacle?"

Miss Barnacle, in her white uniform, turns pale. She has paused with her hand on the doorknob, looking over the neatly made bed to the chair where Mary McDonald is sitting. Pearl-gray light falls on a walker near the chair. Mary McDonald's hands are closed in her lap, over a green-and-gold quilt. Her face is solemn.

"Do you think this place *knows* what you're worth, Miss Barnacle?"

• • •

A good death. That's what everyone wants.

Mary McDonald still remembers, from her first year as a nurse, well over forty years ago, a little old woman named Ida Peterson, with a tumor in her neck near the carotid artery. The call bell at the nurses' station rang, and Mary McDonald walked down the hall, opened the door, and was struck squarely in the face by something warm, wet, and red.

Blood from a ruptured artery gushed out of Mrs. Peterson's tracheotomy opening, out of an ulcerated site on her neck, out of her nose, out of her mouth. Mary was stunned. She saw blood on the ceiling, on the floor, on the bed, on the walls.

Mrs. Peterson had wanted to die a peaceful, dignified death, in the presence of her husband. She had wanted to die a "natural" death. Now, as the life poured out of her, she lifted her hand to wipe her nose and mouth. With wide eyes, she looked at the blood on her hand.

Ida Peterson had wanted a natural death, in the presence of her husband, and she was getting one, in the presence of Mary McDonald, a nurse she had known for five minutes.

Mrs. Peterson's blue, terrified eyes looked into Mary McDonald's eyes for the full fifteen minutes it took her to bleed to death. Her hand gripped Mary's hand. Mary did nothing. Her orders were to allow Mrs. Peterson to die a natural death.

Mary had never before seen an arterial bleed. She still remembers the splash of blood on her face when she stepped into Mrs. Peterson's room. She still remembers how long it took Mrs. Peterson to die. You wouldn't think that a little woman could have so much blood in her.

• • •

"They tell me you were some good nurse," Eunice Barnacle says, taking Mary's blood pressure.

"I'm still a good nurse," Mary McDonald says.

"They tell me you helped start the nurses' union, over at the hospital."

"Who tells you?"

"Mrs. Pierce."

"Ah."

"Mrs. Pierce says those were the days."

"Maybe they were."

Eunice loosens the blood pressure cup from Mary's arm. "Mrs. McDonald?"

"Yes?"

"That union—" Eunice hesitates, looking at the floor.

"What about it?" Mary says.

"You think it helped you?"

• • •

Booth's Landing is an unpretentious town with a population of nearly nine thousand, located among gently rolling hills on the east side of the Hudson River, fifty miles north of New York City. In every generation, for as long as anyone can remember, the Booths and the Tiesslers have been the town's leading families. The Booth family descends from the town's founder, Josiah Booth, a merchant of the Revolutionary War period whom local historians describe as a miniature version of John Jacob Astor. The Tiessler family descends from Klaus Tiessler, an immigrant from Heidelberg who in 1851 founded a factory that makes silverware.

"A nice town," people who live in Booth's Landing say. "A

nice place to bring up a family." That's how Mary McDonald has always felt, and that's what she has always said when people asked her about the place.

In every generation, for as long as anyone can remember, one member of the Booth family has run the town's bank, and one member of the Tiessler family has run the silverware factory.

The town also supports two movie theatres, three sporting goods stores, three opticians, three auto repair shops, one synagogue, and nine churches. Most of the people who die in Booth's Landing were born there. Many have died with Mary McDonald holding their hands.

Oh, not so many, Mary thinks, pursing her lips. Not that she has kept count. Why would anyone keep count?

You can do worse than to live and die in a place like Booth's Landing. The air is fresh. The streets are clean and safe. The leading families have paid steady attention to their civic and philanthropic responsibilities. If you're sick in Booth's Landing, you go to the Booth-Tiessler Community Hospital. If you want to see live entertainment, you buy tickets for the latest show at the Booth-Tiessler Center for the Performing Arts. If you can no longer take care of yourself, you arrange to have yourself deposited in the Booth-Tiessler Geriatric Center.

At the Booth-Tiessler Community College, nearly fifty years ago, Mary McDonald fulfilled the requirements for her nursing degree. Now, sitting by her window on the third floor in the Geriatric Center, looking over the cherry tree in the yard below toward the river, with the odor of overcooked turnips floating up from the kitchen on the first floor, she finds her mind drifting over her life, back and forth, here and there, like a bird that hops from place to place on a tree with many branches.

• • •

"I've never been a troublemaker."

That was what Mary McDonald said to Clarice Hunter when Clarice asked her to help form a nurses' union at the Booth-Tiessler Community Hospital in 1965.

"Hon," Clarice Hunter said, "do you know what the nurses get paid in New York City?"

"I don't live in New York City," Mary said.

"You know what the nurses get paid in Tarrytown?"

"I don't live in Tarrytown."

"It's only ten minutes' drive."

"Okay. What do they get paid in Tarrytown?"

Clarice told her.

"Holy moly," Mary McDonald said.

"Will you help me?" Clarice said.

"Clarice, don't pester me."

"You call this pestering?"

Mary did not answer.

"What's the problem, Mary?"

"I'm not a big believer in unions."

"Being a doormat—is that what you believe in?"

Mary pursed her lips.

"It's your Catholic upbringing," Clarice said.

"What about it?"

"Mary, they *programmed* you. They programmed you to bow down to authority."

No doubt about that, Mary thought. Call me Bended Knee.

"Mary, your help would mean a lot to us."

"I've never been a troublemaker."

• • •

"I don't think I'll ever make much money."

That was what George McDonald told Mary, a long time ago.

Well, George, you were right about that.

Mary was twenty-one when she met him, in 1948. She had just taken her first job at the hospital, as a nurse in the emergency room.

George was twenty-seven. In the Pacific, he had fought in the Battle of the Coral Sea and in the Battle of Midway.

The first time Mary saw him, George was helping his father carry a sofa up the stairs into the apartment his sister had rented, on Jefferson Street. Mary was friends with the sister, Eleanor, a nurse at the hospital.

He was a big man, six foot three, with hair the color of fresh corn and a big boyish smile. The war had left him with a scar six inches long, an angry pink dent, on his left shin.

Mary herself was a heavyset young woman, with a figure that lacked curves. Even in her twenties, she looked as if she had been carved from a block of wood. As she aged, she looked as if she'd been carved from a larger block.

I was stout, not fat.

On their first date, George took Mary to see a movie called *Johnny Belinda*. Then they went over to Krieger's, the luncheonette on Main Street. Mary had a hot fudge sundae.

George taught at the Booth's Landing high school. He played the clarinet. He thought he would be satisfied teaching music and living in Booth's Landing for the rest of his life.

"I guess I'm not too ambitious," he said.

On the second date, George took Mary on a picnic, in Dabney Park. After lunch he took her rowing. At the far end of the lake, they paused in the shadows under tall trees. Kiss me, Mary thought. George crossed his hands over his knees.

"I don't think I'll ever make much money," he said. "I've never cared much about it."

"There's more to life than money," Mary said.

On the third date, George took Mary to see a movie called *The Snake Pit*. Would you like to go to Krieger's for a sundae, he asked when it was over.

"I don't want a sundae," Mary said. "Let's go walk by the river."

She took his hand as they walked down Tremont Street. The night was cool. His fingers were as thick as cigars.

Six months later they were married.

Mary still remembered the way his fingers felt, laced in hers.

Thirty-nine years together. Three kids, all of them grown now and moved away. No other women in his life, no other men in hers.

He died of kidney failure in 1988. A man who rarely lost his temper, a father who taught his sons how to scramble eggs and his daughter how to throw a baseball, a small-town music teacher who loved the clarinet.

Oh, George, I miss you. You can't imagine.

Maybe you can.

• • •

"How you feeling today, Mrs. M?" Dr. Seybold says. He is a large man with a friendly face, pink skin, and paprika-colored hair. His breath smells of peppermint.

"Well enough, Tom. How you feeling?"

"I'm fine, ma'am. Thank you."

"How's your family?"

"My mother broke her toe."

"Broke her toe? How'd she do that?"

"Bowling."

"Dropped a bowling ball?"

"No. Dropped a coffee mug. She tried to hop away, but she couldn't hop fast enough."

"None of us hop as fast as we used to."

"That's the truth, Mrs. M."

"You tell her I hope she feels better. Don't forget."

Forty years ago, in the years before Tom Seybold was born, his mother had two miscarriages. Mary still remembers the look in Laura Seybold's eyes after the second one. She had carried the child for six months, the happiest months of her life, and when she lost it, the life went out of her eyes, the spring went out of her step, and for a full year she wandered through town with a bleak, dazed, shell-shocked look on her face. Mary still remembers taking care of Laura Seybold during the three days she spent in the hospital after the Saturday night when she swallowed every pill in the house.

Tom Seybold puts his hand gently on Mary's shoulder.

"You sure you're feeling fine, Mrs. M?"

A coffee mug. Broke her toe with a coffee mug.

"Tom, how long have you known me?"

"As long as I can remember."

"May I ask you an honest question?"

"Why sure, Mrs. M."

"Considering I've got a colon cancer that's chewing up my liver, just how well do you expect me to feel?"

• • •

Meat loaf.

If this is Monday, that gray-brown slab on Mary McDonald's plate must be meat loaf.

"What I want to know is where the money goes," Lucy Heywood says. "We *pay*. It's not as if we don't pay."

"What I want to know," Penny Mack says, "is what happens to us when the money's all gone."

"Moneymoneymoneymoney," Roy Quigley says. "If I had a dollar for every day I've spent worrying about money, I'd be a rich man."

"I'm tired of meat loaf," Barbara Collins says.

"Did you read in the paper about Frank Sinatra?" Lucy Heywood says.

"You're not tired of meat loaf," Mary McDonald says.

"I am," Barbara Collins says. "I certainly am."

"What happened to variety shows?" Penny Mack says. "Remember Garry Moore?"

"That man has no shame," Lucy Heywood says.

"Garry Moore?"

"Sinatra."

"Did you see those photos of Princess Di?"

"Whatever happened to Carol Burnett?"

"You're not tired of meat loaf," Mary McDonald says, leaning toward Barbara Collins. "You're tired of life."

"I'm *not*," Barbara Collins says, holding up a fork with a gravy-smeared piece of meat loaf on the end of it. "I'm *not* tired of life."

• • •

Mary McDonald's grandmother also died of colon cancer. "Also" is the word that comes into Mary's mind. Her grandmother died in 1957, or maybe 1958. If you lived long enough, Mary had noticed, you forgot when things happened. The only years she remembered were the years her kids were born.

Mary's parents took her grandmother down to New York City, to Columbia-Presbyterian, so a famous surgeon could operate. Mary could remember the look on the surgeon's face, after the operation, when he came into the room where Mary and her parents were waiting.

Mary sighs, sitting by the window in her room. Outside, in the yard below her window, a breeze stirs the leaves of the cherry tree. The sky is white today. Poor Grandma! The famous surgeon cut her open, looked inside, and sewed her up. Nothing he could do. Just as, nine months ago, a different surgeon had sewed up Mary.

My goose is cooked.

At Booth-Tiessler, in Grandma's final days, Clarice Hunter was the nurse on the day shift. Mary remembers her grandmother telling her how Clarice had bathed her, and combed her hair, and talked to her. Mary's grandmother was a plain-looking, plain-talking woman, with only an eighth-grade education, who expected nothing from life and generally got what she expected. But then, in the last days of her life, she got Clarice Hunter as her nurse.

"This woman is a jewel," Mary's grandmother said to Mary, while Clarice blushed. "This woman is a blessing."

"Just doing my job," Clarice said, checking Grandma's pulse.

At one o'clock in the morning on the night Mary's grandmother died, she insisted on seeing her family. The night nurse called Mary's parents, who came to the hospital with Mary.

"Where's Clarice?" Mary's grandmother said. "I want to see Clarice."

"It's the middle of the night," Mary said. "She'll be here in the morning."

"I need her *now*," Mary's grandmother said, turning on Mary a look so fierce that Mary still remembered it.

Mary called Clarice, who came to the hospital at two in the morning. At three, Mary's grandmother fell asleep with her mouth wide open. At six, with a terrifying snort, she woke and died. Clarice helped the night nurse wash the body. Then she worked the day shift.

• • •

"Little stick," Eunice Barnacle says, leaning over. She pushes a tiny needle into a vein in Mary's hand. Blood flows back through the needle, into the tubing.

"Good shot," Mary said.

"Tell me about that strike. When was it?"

"1967."

"What was it made you want a union?"

"I didn't want one. Not at first."

"So what happened?"

• • •

At a sink in the nurses' lavatory, Clarice Hunter is crying. The year is 1965, ten years after the death of Mary McDonald's grandmother. Mary is thirty-eight; Clarice is ten years older. Mary walks over to the sink and, carefully, puts one hand on her friend's shoulder.

"You okay?" Mary asks.

"I guess." Clarice blows her nose. "Thanks."

Mary waits.

"Mary?"

"Yes."

"They're driving me crazy. They're running me off my feet."

"They're running all of us, dear."

"But it's making me crazy, Mary. I lost my temper with Mrs. Grbeck, I nearly got into a fight with Mr. Palermo's daughter, and I forgot all about Mr. Howard's pain medicine. That poor man waited *fifty* minutes for his pain medicine."

"We're all rushing, Clarice. We're all making mistakes."

"Mary, I have *twenty* patients."

"I know, dear."

"I can't take care of twenty patients."

"I know, dear."

"Mary?"

"Yes."

"You know how hard a nurse has to work."

"Of course."

"What'll I do, Mary? I can't take care of twenty patients. I can't. I just *can't*."

• • •

"How about you, Mary?"

In the nurses' lounge, back in 1965, that was the question Ruth Sullivan asked, a few days after Mary McDonald had found Clarice Hunter crying at the sink in the nurses' lavatory.

In three weeks, the nurses would vote on whether to form a union. Mary had always expected to vote no.

"I think maybe I'll vote yes," Mary said.

"You'll vote yes?"

"I think so. Maybe."

"I thought you didn't believe in unions."

"I don't. But I think—oh, I don't know. I think I changed my mind. Maybe."

It hadn't occurred to Mary McDonald that anyone would care how she voted. But if you talked to other nurses, you found out that Mary's opinion made a difference.

"I hear Mary McDonald's voting yes," a nurse would say.

"Really?"

"That's what I heard."

"I thought she didn't want a union."

"She changed her mind."

"Really?"

"That's what I heard."

The vote drew near. Arguments were made, pro and con. Tempers flared. In September 1965, the nurses voted in favor of a union.

    • • •

In the nurses' lounge, Pam Ryder is leafing through a copy of *Family Circle* magazine.

"Well, it won't be long now," Eunice Barnacle says.

"What?" Pam Ryder says.

"Mrs. McDonald," Eunice Barnacle says.

"Poor woman," Pam Ryder says.

"She told me about that union, over at the hospital."

"We need one here," Pam Ryder says.

"You think so?"

"You don't?"

Eunice does not answer. Pam Ryder turns the page in her magazine. Eunice stirs her coffee.

"I know one thing," Eunice says.

Pam Ryder looks up, brushing a hair off her forehead.

"That union can't help her now," Eunice says.

"May I have this dance?"

Brad, her youngest, bends over Mary with his hand out-stretched. Mary struggles to her feet. Brad takes her right hand with his left. His other hand settles on the small of her back. Barely moving, they dance.

In her chair, half dozing, Mary remembers that dance.

It was two months ago, on Mary's sixty-ninth birthday. All three of her children had come to Booth's Landing, with their families.

They know what's up.

George, Jr., offered, again, to take her to Chicago.

"I want to die here," Mary said.

"But Mother—"

"No but."

A gangling, loose-jointed, long-armed boy, a star athlete, George, Jr., has grown up to become an earnest, quiet-voiced man who dresses in rumpled suits. He's an attorney, but, of course, he can't win an argument with his mother. Who can? Though he's tall and moves gracefully, he's no longer slim. His face has grown puffy. His belly bulges over his belt.

"George," Mary said, on her birthday two months ago. "You need to lose weight."

"Yes, Mother," George said. The look in his eyes told her how sad he was to see her dying.

Oh, George, I'm sorry I nagged you. But it's true, you *should* lose weight.

Jane came from Boston, with her two little girls, cute as could be, but bored, and who could blame them? They didn't understand why Mommy had dragged them to see their grandmother.

"Jane, you look tired."

"Mother, I'm a *nurse*. You know what that means."

Three years ago, Jane had a drinking problem. Now she's licked it—maybe. But she bites her fingernails and smokes.

Jane, do you think I didn't notice?

Brad came all the way from Seattle, where he's worked for a decade. Everyone laughed again at the story about the phone call when he'd told his parents about the job.

"Microwhat?" Mary had said.

"Microsoft, Mother."

"You couldn't get a job with IBM?"

"Mother, I'm working for Bill Gates."

"Bill who?"

Mary turned a happy pink while Brad told the story.

"Look at Mom! Look at her face!"

Brad, my baby. That time when you ran full speed into the clothesline, and busted your head open, and I held you while Dad drove us to the emergency room—I know you can't remember, but no one will ever love you the way I loved you on that ride to the hospital.

•   •   •

"Enough about me, Eunice. Tell me about yourself."

"I was born in Virginia, in Richmond," Eunice says. "My father was no good. My mother brought me up."

Outside, three black birds are flying toward the river.

"I don't like to talk about my family, Mrs. McDonald."

"That's all right. You don't have to."

Two days later, while Eunice gives Mary a back rub, the conversation resumes. The smell of rubbing alcohol makes Mary feel drowsy. Rain is drizzling from a bleak sky.

"My mother—she's in jail."

"Oh?"

"She had a boyfriend, Jethro, who beat her when he got drunk. So, about six years ago, Jethro got arrested, and she bailed him out. But then, when they got home, she killed him."

"Oh!"

"They gave her life in prison. I guess maybe they had to."

"Why did she bail him out?"

"That's the thing. She bought a shotgun. She bailed him out to kill him."

"Hmm."

"She's in Sing Sing. It's only thirty minutes' drive. I visit every Sunday. You know what's funny?"

"What?"

"Sing Sing. It's in a town called Ossining. I never knew that before."

Mary feels Eunice's fingers on her back.

"She's a good woman, my mother. But she did wrong. I know that."

Mary feels Eunice's fingers on her shoulder blades.

"That fellow Jethro, he pushed her too far."

George would give her a back rub, and then a front rub, and then—well, what's marriage for?

"My mother, she's only thirty-nine. She was sixteen when I was born."

• • •

A football, thrown with a perfect spiral, thrown forty yards through the gray November air, beneath a sky like the sky outside this minute, a football hurled forty yards and falling into the hands of the receiver, glancing over his shoulder at exactly the right moment, reaching up at exactly the right moment, making the catch, and sprinting into the end zone.

It was the winter of 1967. George, Jr., threw the football, Warren Booth, Jr., caught it, the Booth's Landing football team won the county championship, and life was as good as it gets.

Except for the strike.

The strike had begun in September, two years after the nurses organized their union.

What did the nurses want? That was the question that Richard Dill, a reporter on the Booth's Landing *Gazette*, asked

Clarice Hunter, who was the head of the strike committee. Clarice told him.

Money.

Job security.

Some say in decisions relating to staffing levels.

No, no, no. That was what management said. So Mary McDonald, who never in her life, before or after the strike, ever voted for anyone but a Republican, found herself on a picket line.

• • •

Sister Rosa, the executive director, was a short, no-nonsense woman who made it her business to be seen, striding through the halls of Booth-Tiessler Community Hospital, waging war on dust, dirt, and disorder, encouraging nurses and nurses' aides, keeping doctors in line, looking for inefficiences to eliminate, attacking problems, pushing for improvements.

"Mr. Dill," Sister Rosa said in the first interview that she gave after the strike began, "our nurses are wonderful, all our employees are wonderful, but we cannot let employees set their own salaries. We cannot let employees define the terms and conditions of employment. We cannot let employees set staffing levels."

Remembering, Mary McDonald sighs.

Oh, Sister Rosa, how I admired you! How I hated doing anything that might displease you. How I wanted you to *like* me. How I wanted to hear you say, "Good work, Mary . . . Nice job, Mary."

"Mr. Dill, management must not run away from its responsibilities."

Five years before the strike, Mary McDonald worked with Sister Rosa on a project to improve the patient scheduling system in the radiation department. With Sister Rosa guiding the project, staff members collected and evaluated treatment time data. Then Sister Rosa designed a system that matched the time allotted for an appointment to the complexity of the treatment. A more flexible scheduling system was put in place. The result: a 20 percent decrease in patient waiting time, and a 15 percent increase in physician and hospital revenue. Mary later used what she had learned from Sister Rosa to improve the patient scheduling system in the chemotherapy department.

"Mr. Dill, management must *manage.*"

• • •

One week before Thanksgiving. Outside, a nasty sky. Inside, the radiator clanks and rattles. Eunice has brought Mary McDonald a tiny white pill in a tiny white cup.

"You visiting your family for Thanksgiving, Mrs. McDonald?"

"No." Mary swallows her pill. "I'm too tired."

"Your family coming here?"

"They came for my birthday. That was enough. How about you, Eunice?"

"Guess I'll take my little girl to see my mom." Eunice has a daughter, three years old, in day care.

"That's nice." Mary looks at Eunice, who is looking at her watch while she checks Mary's pulse. Mary feels the pressure of Eunice's fingers—a nice feeling.

You're a good nurse, Eunice, but the two-year degree isn't enough. You should go back to school. Do it now, while you're young.

Mary hears those words in her head, but she does not say them aloud. Mary and Eunice often talk about Eunice's future, but Mary does not feel like talking today.

"I've got a new picture." Eunice opens her wallet, takes out a photo, and holds it out for Mary to see. The photo shows a bright-eyed little girl with twin pigtails sitting on a mechanical rocking horse, outside Tyler's Pharmacy.

"I heard from her daddy."

"Oh?"

"He lost his job, out in San Diego. Asked if I could send him some money."

Eunice is staring at the photo of her little girl.

"That man," Eunice says, shaking her head. "That man needs a brain transplant."

• • •

For six months, the nurses carried picket signs outside the hospital. Twenty nurses, on the picket line, every day and into the night. Mary still remembers the looks people gave them. Friendly looks, hostile looks, curious looks. She still remembers the sign she carried:

TOGETHER WE WILL WIN

The hospital hired a company that specialized in fighting strikes. The company flew in scab nurses. On the picket line, Mary sang:

UNION BUSTING, IT'S DISGUSTING

In Booth's Landing, people took sides. Millie Tolliver said to Mary at a PTA meeting, "Mary, I'm surprised at you." Carl Usher, the plumber whose son took clarinet lessons from George, said, "Mrs. McDonald, I just don't see how you girls can walk out on your patients." In an interview on TV, Cheryl Hughes, a woman whom Mary had always liked, whose husband prepared Mary and George's tax returns, said, "If you ask me, it's an outrage. Let's just hope nobody dies. Those women ought to be ashamed."

• • •

The web that connects people in a small town is more tightly spun than the web that exists in a large city. In Booth's

Landing, the man who will write Mary McDonald's obituary for the local newspaper is the son of the reporter who covered the nurses' strike of 1967.

Richard Dill, the father, lives on the same floor as Mary McDonald at the Booth-Tiessler Geriatric Center. Richard Dill sees that Mary has lost twenty pounds in the last six months, sees that her step is weaker each time she comes out of her room, sees that she comes out less and less often, and sees that her skin grows paler and paler, grayer and grayer, with every week.

Watching Mary fade away, Richard Dill remembers her as a sturdy woman carrying her picket sign, thirty years ago. He remembers her twenty years ago, nursing his wife after her surgery.

Roger Dill, the son, sometimes sees Mary in the hall with her walker when he visits his father, and he nods amiably in her direction, but he does not remember the nurses' strike of '67 because he was only three years old when it took place. Roger Dill does not remember that, when he was six, Mary's daughter, Jane, was one of his camp counselors. He remembers the surgery his mother had when he was twelve, but he does not remember any of his mother's nurses.

"A nice boy," Mary thinks when she sees Roger Dill, though she merely nods as he walks with his father in the hall. Mary remembers Roger at the age of twelve, a skinny kid carrying a football helmet, visiting his mother in the hospital. Poor woman. What was her name? Jennifer. From a town called Mistletoe, in Mississippi. Mary taught her how to care for the colostomy bag that she needed after her surgery.

• • •

Two months into the strike, the hospital withdrew recognition of the union.

"Withdrew recognition?" Mary said to Clarice Hunter. "How can they do that?"

"They can't," Clarice Hunter said. "Not unless they've hired those scabs as permanent replacements."

"Sister Rosa wouldn't do that."

In fact, that was exactly what Sister Rosa had done.

"What'll we do?" Mary asked Clarice.

"We'll move into phase two."

Phase one: the nurses carried picket signs outside the hospital.

Phase two: the nurses took their fight up to the top of Mountainview Drive.

Why Mountainview Drive? Because that was where Warren Booth, the chairman of the board, lived with his wife and children.

Mary McDonald remembers Warren Booth, with a big frown on his broad, well-scrubbed face, when he came down the driveway from his mansion to confront the strikers. She remembers the tone of his voice, and the look in his eyes, and the way his jaw worked, and the way he turned on his heel and strode back up the driveway and into the house.

George, Jr., said, "But, *Mom*, don't you see what you're doing? I'm the *quarterback*, and Warren, Jr., is my best receiver."

In Booth's Landing, back in 1967, the public schools were good enough that the son of the richest man in town and the son of George and Mary McDonald could go to the same school and play on the same football team.

"Mom, Warren's my *teammate*."

"Yes, George. I understand. But out in the world, where I work—well, let's just say that Warren's dad isn't my teammate."

• • •

Frank Gifford.

"If Frank Gifford ever comes to town," George used to say, "I'll have to lock Mary away from him."

Well, George, you may have been right about that.

Mary and the Giants. Everybody who knew Mary McDonald knew about her love affair with the Giants.

She was a knowledgeable fan. When the announcer said that the Giants had gone into their "prevent defense," Mary would shout, "No! Not the prevent! Anything but the prevent!" She'd seen the Giants lose too many games when the prevent defense failed to prevent anything.

Her other great love was beer, the darker the better. "I can't stand that piss-colored beer," she would tell people. Once she discovered Guinness, she never drank anything else.

It's true. I could use one right now.

She didn't like games. She didn't like to travel. She didn't have any hobbies. What she really liked was—nursing.

That's also true. I loved it from day one.

She knew things that only nurses know. If you smell an unpleasant odor coming from a patient's urine drainage bag, add ten milliliters of hydrogen peroxide to the bag when you empty it. If a nasogastric feeding tube becomes clogged, use diet cola to flush it. If you need to remove oil-based paint that is close to a patient's eyes or mouth, use mineral water, not turpentine.

In the neighborhood where George and Mary lived, phone calls to physicians were rare. People called Mary first, and Mary told them what to do.

• • •

"So they hired permanent replacements," Eunice Barnacle said. "Then what?"

"What you have to remember," Mary said, "is that Booth-Tiessler is part of a chain of hospitals. And it's a chain of *Catholic* hospitals. That's why nuns run the place."

"What difference does it make who runs it?"

"A big difference. Maybe all the difference."

Most of the striking nurses also were Catholic. They didn't merely picket outside the hospital. They prayed:

> *Give us this day our daily bread,*
> *And forgive us our trespasses,*
> *As we forgive those who trespass against us.*

And they chanted:

> *United we bargain,*
> *Divided we beg!*

And they sang:

> *I dreamed I saw Joe Hill last night,*
> *Alive as you and me . . .*

On TV in those days, in and around Booth's Landing, people saw nurses on strike, with their picket signs lowered and their heads bowed in prayer. When people remembered the strike, years later, what they remembered was nurses praying on the sidewalk outside the hospital.

"If the hospital hadn't been run by an order of nuns," Mary McDonald said to Eunice Barnacle, "I think we'd have lost. But we hit those nuns where it hurt. We appealed to their consciences."

The Sisters of Mercy—that's what the nuns were called. Somebody looked up their mission statement. It said that they were committed to act in solidarity with the poor, the weak, the outcast, the elderly, and the infirm.

On the chilliest day that winter, with her cheeks freezing and her breath visible in the air, Mary McDonald read the Sisters of Mercy mission statement out loud, while TV cameras rolled.

Then Beverly Wellstone began a fast. A nurse who had

once been a nun, she was five feet tall, trim and intense, with bright blue eyes and cinnamon-colored hair. She fasted for thirty-three days, her eyes growing brighter and brighter as the flesh fell from her face. Other nurses fasted in support, usually for twenty-four or forty-eight hours. The TV cameras kept rolling.

"I am fasting in an effort to bring this strike to the attention of higher authorities," Beverly Wellstone said. The look in her eyes was the look you see in paintings, in the eyes of martyred saints.

Other strikers begged her to stop, but Beverly Wellstone declined with a nearly invisible movement of her parched lips.

"To represent the women on this picket line," Beverly Wellstone said, "is an honor and privilege I will never know again in my life."

A camera crew arrived from New York. One of the national networks had picked up the story. That night, millions of people learned about the striking nurses of Booth's Landing. From her cot in the basement of a local church, Beverly Wellstone whispered a few words about the role of faith in her life. Warren Booth, Sr., entering the hospital for an emergency meeting of the board, declined to comment. He looked haggard and distracted.

The next day, according to newspaper reports published later, a stranger arrived in Booth's Landing. Three days later, the strike was over.

• • •

"A stranger?" Eunice Barnacle said.

"An emissary of the cardinal," Mary McDonald said.

"What did he do?"

"He carried a message to Sister Rosa."

"A message from the cardinal?"

"Yes."

"Then what happened?"

"Talks resumed, but in a different spirit."

Eunice was leaning against the windowsill in Mary McDonald's room. The light that poured through the window from a clear winter sky made her skin shine. Mary McDonald, as she told the story, was sitting up comfortably in bed, her back supported by two pillows set on end.

"So you won?" Eunice Barnacle said.

"The scab nurses were dismissed," Mary said. "The striking nurses were rehired. The effort to decertify the union was abandoned."

"You got the salary increase you wanted?"

"No. We got about half the increase we wanted. But we also got something we wanted for our patients."

"What was that?"

"More staff on the medical and surgical floors. For the next three years, after we signed that contract, we had the staff to give the kind of care we wanted to give."

• • •

Thirty thousand dollars—that was what Sister Margaret calculated that Booth-Tiessler Community Hospital would save annually by buying less expensive surgical gloves. Sister Margaret's expertise in materials management dazzled everyone who worked with her at Booth-Tiessler. It was an expertise she had honed in years of hard work under the eye of her mentor and predecessor, Sister Rosa, whom she had succeeded as executive director in 1984.

Sister Margaret had turned on her dictaphone, with the intention of dictating a memorandum on the subject of surgical gloves, when Sister Celia softly entered the office with the latest pile of papers and reports for Sister Margaret's in-box. Something in Sister Celia's eyes—a flicker that suggested the desire to speak—led Sister Margaret to lift her own eyes with an inquiring look.

"Mary McDonald died this morning," Sister Celia said.

"Ah." The word came out of Sister Margaret's mouth as a

sigh. When Mary McDonald was transferred from the Geriatric Center to the hospital, three days ago, Sister Margaret had suspected that the end was near. Now, memories of Mary McDonald mixed in Sister Margaret's mind with the thought that the time had come to take another look at soap prices.

What Sister Margaret said, looking at Sister Celia, was, simply, "A good nurse . . . A *damned* good nurse." The word "damned" was pronounced with an emphasis that verged on audacity. Sister Margaret remembered the nurses' union, and the strike of '67, and the look on Sister Rosa's face in the days after the cardinal had sent his emissary to Booth's Landing. "Of course," Sister Margaret said, "we had our differences."

• • •

Roger Dill, at his old-fashioned desk in the old-fashioned offices of the Booth's Landing *Gazette*, took a long sip of coffee, paused to savor the taste and the warmth in his stomach, and typed: "Mary McDonald died at the Booth-Tiessler Nursing Home on December 16. She was sixty-nine."

Roger closed his eyes. When they opened, his fingers moved swiftly: "A graduate of Booth-Tiessler Community College, Mrs. McDonald worked for many years as a nurse at Booth-Tiessler Community Hospital . . ."

Roger closed his eyes again. People of no great consquence died every week in Booth's Landing, and Roger Dill was required to write three to five paragraphs about them. It was not a task that he resented, but it was not one that excited or inspired him. How much could he say about a nurse he had never met?

"Mrs. McDonald is survived by three children . . ."

Roger Dill suppressed a yawn, and thought about the legs of his son's piano teacher. Even with coffee, he found that it was sometimes a challenge not to fall asleep with his fingers on the keyboard, the computer humming gently on his desk, and the conventional sentences taking shape in his head.

• • •

From his office on the top floor of the Booth's Landing Savings and Loan Association, a sturdy stone building at the intersection of Tremont and Main streets, Warren Booth, Jr., could see the blue shimmer of the Hudson, sweeping south, and, beyond it, the fields and meadows of New Jersey. Though it had rained a few hours ago, the day had brightened. Warren Booth allowed his gaze to linger on the river, beneath the sparkling blue of the mid-afternoon sky.

The Booth's Landing *Gazette* lay open on Warren Booth's desk. Looking out over the river, the town's leading banker found himself falling into a strangely agitated mood. Nearly thirty years had passed, yet he still remembered the days when nurses picketed his family's house, while he tried to prepare for the biggest football game of his life.

In those days, nothing in the world had seemed more important to Warren Booth than the Booth's Landing football team. George McDonald had been the team's quarterback. Warren had been the team's primary receiver. The team itself had been outstanding—the best that anyone could remember. Yet Warren remembered the winter of 1967 as a painful and confusing time, because a group of nurses, including George McDonald's mother, had made made life miserable for Warren's father. Why? *Why?*

With an exasperated sigh, Warren Booth shifted in his chair. He had inherited not merely his father's position in life but also his attitudes on matters pertaining to civic and business affairs. The nerve! The nerve of those women. What great enterprise had they ever managed? What did they know about worldly affairs?

Something that resembled a grimace appeared on the face of Warren Booth. The fact that he himself had never managed any great enterprise did not occur to him. Those women had made Warren's father out to be some Scrooge, and the press, the damned press—well, better not to think about the press.

Warren Booth took a deep breath. He would send a condolence card to George McDonald, in Chicago. Yes, he would do that. Hell, he would go to the funeral. Why not? Go to the funeral. Pay his respects. See old George . . . Talk with old George? What would they say to one another? What could they possibly say to one another?

Sighing, Warren Booth leaned back in his chair, looked up at the ceiling, and closed his eyes. The look on his face was the look of a troubled man. He kept his eyes closed a long time.

Forget the funeral. Send a card.

• • •

Two blocks from the little red-brick apartment building where Eunice Barnacle lives, there is a park with swings and sliding boards and a jungle gym. Even in winter, on a sunny day, the park fills with children. With all the young voices squealing and shouting, and young feet running and jumping, it is as happy a place as you can find in Booth's Landing. This park is where Eunice Barnacle went, with her three-year-old daughter, on the day after Mary McDonald had died.

It was a Saturday, bright and cold, with a sky completely white. Eunice pushed her daughter on a swing, then sat on a green wooden bench, apart from the other mothers, while her daughter played in the sandbox. After a while, another woman sat down near Eunice. The women talked for a time, and then they sat without talking for nearly half an hour. Then Eunice said:

"You know what we need, Carrie?"

"What?"

"A union."

"Union? What do we need with a union?"

"You think you're paid what you're worth?"

"Eunice, what's got into you?"

"Nothing."

"That woman brainwashed you."

"Nobody brainwashed me."

"You could get us in trouble, Eunice."

"We're already in trouble."

"Not me. I'm not in trouble."

"That's what you think."

To a little girl in a bulky red jacket, in the sandbox, Eunice yelled, "Coretta, sweetie, five more minutes."

"Mommy, *no!*"

"Five minutes, Coretta."

The woman on the bench next to Eunice folded her arms across her chest. She was wearing an orange scarf over a silver-gray coat. Eunice was wearing a white scarf over a crimson coat.

"I've never been a troublemaker," the woman said. "One thing I've learned in life, Eunice. You go looking for trouble, you'll find it."

Eunice did not answer. The sun had gone behind a cloud. A chill came into the air.

A month ago, Eunice recalled, she had asked Mary McDonald if the union had really helped her. The old woman had thought a long time before she said, "To tell the truth, it had its good points and its bad points. Like most things." Eunice had asked her to explain the good points and the bad points. "Some other time," the old woman had said. "I'm tired now."

But the subject had never come up again, so now Eunice did not know what Mary McDonald would have said.

"Coretta! Sweetie!" Eunice called.

"But *Mommy!*"

"Time to go, honey."

The child opened her mouth as if to wail, paused, closed her mouth, stood, held out her arms, and began to toddle toward Eunice.

"Let's go home, sweetie. Mommy's tired."

• • •

At Santino's Funeral Home, Nick Santino and Harry Orbit were preparing the body of Mary McDonald for its final resting place.

"Here's one I'm sorry to see," Nick Santino said.

"Oh?"

"Mary McDonald."

"You knew her?"

"A nurse. Took care of my mother, back when she was dying."

Mary's body lay on a porcelain embalming table, under a sheet. Nick paused, looking at the face of the dead woman. The eyes were closed, the skin was wrinkled and pale, the lips were crooked. A white thread, half an inch long, lay on the face below the left eye. Nick lifted off the thread.

Nick and Harry washed Mary's body with warm water and a soapy solution. They cleaned Mary's fingernails. Through a needle that Nick placed in the jugular vein, they drained the blood from Mary's body.

Harry inserted cotton in both nostrils, to hold the nose straight. Nick sewed Mary's lips shut.

A machine pumped embalming fluid into Mary's body. After the fluid had entered Mary's hands, Nick crossed them over her chest. He applied adhesive glue to hold her fingers together.

Nick paused, looking at Mary's face. A refrigerator hummed in a corner of the room.

"This woman took care of my mother," Nick said, looking down at her. "She took care of my mother like she was taking care of her own mother."

Nick shooed away a fly that was buzzing near Mary's cheek. He touched Mary's hair with a gloved hand. He looked at Harry.

"This woman washed my mother's feet," Nick said, with

sudden intensity. "This woman cleaned my mother's toes with a toothbrush."

• • •

Mary McDonald, late in the last day of her life, fell into a sleep as deep as a child's sleep after an overactive day. Her eyes were closed, her head was tilted back, her lips were open, her breathing was steady, though not strong.

At one point a middle-aged woman in a nun's outfit came into the room, closing the door behind her. With a mild expression on her face and her hands crossed at her waist, the visitor stood looking down at the sleeping woman. Mary's eyes opened.

"Sister Rosa. How nice of you to visit."

"Don't mention it, dear. How are you?"

"Not long for this world, I'm afraid."

"Don't be afraid."

"No. I'm not."

"Have they given you something for pain, Mary?"

"Oh, yes. Thank God for morphine."

"I'll do that."

Mary thought for a moment, with a slightly puzzled expression on her face. Then she let the thought go.

"Sister Rosa?"

"Yes."

"When you died, *after* you died, was it—what you expected?"

"I'm not allowed to talk about that, dear."

"No. I guess not."

Mary closed her eyes again. She kept them closed for a long time. When she opened them again, the light in the room seemed different.

"Sister Rosa?"

"Yes, dear."

"Would you mind holding my hand?"

"Of course not, dear."

Sister Rosa put her hand on Mary's hand. The nun's hand was warm—warmer than Mary's, perhaps. Mary closed her eyes again, but opened them almost at once.

"There's something on my mind, Sister Rosa."

"What's that, dear?"

"The strike—you remember the strike?"

"Of course, dear."

"I hope you didn't take it the wrong way?"

"The wrong way, dear?"

"It wasn't about *you*, Sister Rosa. I hope you understand that."

"I do, dear."

"But the nurses—we couldn't let things go, the way they were going."

"I understand, dear."

"We couldn't roll over and die."

"Of course, dear. I understand."

"You do?"

"Mary, I'm *glad* you fought."

"You are?"

"Workers have to fight."

"You really think so?"

"The whole system depends on it."

"I'm not sure about that, Sister Rosa."

"Well, I am."

A sound came from the door, but no one was there. Sister Rosa looked at the door, then back at Mary.

"Would you like to see George?" Sister Rosa said.

"Is he here?"

"He's right outside."

"Could I see him?"

"Of course."

Mary closed her eyes. When she opened them, the light

in the room was different. Sister Rosa had gone, but George had not come in. A woman in a white uniform was standing at the bedside, taking Mary's pulse. Mary felt the pressure of her fingers on her wrist.

"I'd like to see George," Mary said.

"George?"

From the foot of the bed, someone said, "That's her husband. My father."

"Jane?"

"I'm right here, Mom."

How nice. I'm so glad you've come, Jane.

"Me, too."

Brad?

Mary felt confused. The nurse let go of her wrist.

Mary looked on the other side of her bed. Brad was there, in a navy sweater, and George, Jr., in a rumpled suit, with his hand reaching into a bag of pretzels.

"You had a good sleep," Brad said.

George said, "I'm right here, Mom. We're all here with you."

Mary looked at him. His belly bulged over his belt.

"You need to lose weight, George."

"Yes, Mom. I know."

"Promise."

George withdrew his hand from the bag without a pretzel.

"I promise, Mom."

I can't help myself, George. A mother's a mother till her dying breath.

But where was *her* George? Sister Rosa had said he was here.

Out loud Mary said, "I don't want a sundae. Let's go walk by the river."

The woman in the white uniform went out of the room. Mary's children talked softly to one another. Mary listened for a while with her eyes closed. She could hear the voices, but the words escaped her. When she opened her eyes, her husband was standing by her bed. The smile on his face made Mary want to get up and throw her arms around his neck. He was young and tall, his hair was the color of fresh corn, his fingers were as thick as cigars, and he had his clarinet with him.

The Rodent

"Dad, do you know anything about medieval scholasticism?"

"Get *off* me, doodoohead."

"How do I look, hon?"

Harold Winter, adjusting his green-and-gold tie in the mirror, said to Lisa, his sixteen-year-old: "Saint Thomas Aquinas." He ignored Anne, his nine-year-old, who had just called Robby, his twelve-year-old, a doodoohead. To his wife in her crimson dress, which he saw as a blur of color out of the corner of one eye, he said, without quite looking at her: "You look great, hon." From the stereo speakers in a wall unit, Louis Armstrong rasped out the words to "Ain't Misbehavin'."

"Don't call me doodoohead, squirt!"

"Doodoohead! Doodoohead!"

"Who was Thomas Aquinas?"

"Squirt! Squirt!"

"Ouch!"

"Robby, Anne, knock it off this second!"

In the mirror, at the same time that he heard his wife's voice, Harold saw a crimson shape advancing toward his children.

"He called me squirt," Anne complained.

"She called me doodoohead," Robby complained.

"Knock—it—off—right—now!" Peggy said in her "Mom means business" voice. Robby stuck out his tongue at Anne, who wrinkled her nose in response. The telephone rang. "I've got it," Peggy said, heading toward the den.

Harold turned from the mirror and walked toward Lisa, who was sitting on the piano bench in the living room, with her back to the piano. "What makes you ask about medieval scholasticism?" Harold asked. At the same time, with a swift motion, he threw a mock combination of punches toward Robby's midsection. Robby responded with a shriek of pleasure and a fierce karate kick. Anne scowled.

"Term paper," Lisa said with an unhappy expression on her face. "Mr. Winkle says he thinks medieval scholasticism would be a good subject for a term paper."

"Honey, it's for you," Peggy said, walking back into the room with her arms lifted and her hands fussing behind her neck. She was putting on a strand of white pearls to go with the dress.

The year was 1972. Harold Winter was forty-five years old; Peggy was forty-two. They had tickets to see a road company in a revival of *Kiss Me Kate* at the Ridgeville Playhouse that night. Later, Harold would recall this scene—the children squabbling, Satchmo singing, his wife walking back and forth in the crimson dress, himself getting ready for an evening out—with wry regret. If he had known the turn that his life was about to take—well, better not to think what he might have done if he had known.

Ridgeville is located in northern New Jersey, twenty miles northwest of Manhattan, in an area favored by affluent professionals. The Winter family had lived in Ridgeville, on Starlight Court, since the summer of 1963. The houses on Starlight Court reflected the tastes of interior decorators who rarely were required to worry about costs. The grass on Starlight Court shone like the grass in the photographs in real-estate brochures. The trees that shaded the well-kept lawns were as robust as the growth-stock portfolios that paid the gardeners' salaries.

Harold Winter picked up the telephone in his den and heard the voice of Richard Olson, a research analyst at Brice Pharmaceuticals. Harold had risen swiftly at Brice since he joined the company, nearly twenty years ago, after earning a Ph.D. in molecular biology at Cornell.

"I'm afraid I have some bad news, Hal."

"Not too bad, I hope."

"You might want to sit down."

Harold sat.

"Anything wrong?" Peggy asked when Harold came out of the den, ten minutes later.

"Work," he said calmly. "Just a problem at work."

"It couldn't wait till tomorrow?"

Harold shrugged, fastening his cufflinks. "I guess it might have waited."

"Daddy, Anne farted."

"Don't use that language, Robby."

"But she *did.*"

"I don't care. Watch your tongue."

"But Daddy!"

"No *but*!"

Harold turned to look into the mirror. Robby stuck out his tongue at him, not remembering that Harold could see him in the mirror as well as he would have if he'd been looking straight at him. Anne giggled into the chest of a small stuffed panda bear.

In the car ten minutes later, as they descended the long curve toward the intersection of Starlight Court and Chestnut Lane, Peggy said, "I've been thinking about Venice. I've never been to Venice."

Harold stared through the windshield without answering. Straight ahead, only a few inches above the horizon, the moon was big and beautiful. Their car, a silver Cadillac that Harold had purchased only three months ago, still was fragrant with the odor of new leather. Harold braked as the car approached the bottom of the hill. Then he said, "I think I'd better tell you about that telephone call."

At the Trevor Academy, everyone agreed that the fall semester had been difficult. Mr. Tropp, the chairman of the history department, suffered a mild nervous breakdown. Mrs. Ofek, the librarian, left at mid-semester to work in the alumni affairs department at her alma mater. Mr. Kromayer, the basketball coach, departed to pursue an entrepreneurial opportunity with a manufacturer of popcorn equipment. Mr. Chapman, the assistant headmaster, was fired after an auditor discovered that he'd supplemented his salary with kickbacks from a supplier of office goods.

"The Rodent's the one they ought to get rid of," Craig Wickham said, referring to Mr. Winter, the chemistry teacher, by his nickname. "What a specimen."

"They'll never fire the Rodent," Sam Hargrove said. "He's been here nearly as long as McCabe."

"Where do you suppose they *found* him?" Harry Zappacosta said. "I mean, what hole did he crawl out of?"

"A specimen," Frank Mitchell said. "That's the right word for him."

The boys were sitting or sprawling in various late-adolescent postures on the beat-up old furniture in the seniors' lounge. Sam Hargrove took the last sip of his soft drink and tossed the empty can into the center of a trash can six feet away. "Nothing but net," he whispered.

"How'd you do on the Rodent's last chemistry test?" Harry Zappacosta asked Craig Wickham. In reply, Wickham made a sound with his teeth and tongue that indicated he had not done well. The tip of his tongue pushed out between his pink lips as the sound emerged.

"That guy's a joke," Frank Mitchell said. He was lying flat on his back on the floor, with his hands clasped behind his head and his legs crossed at the ankles, which were propped on the edge of a chair. "There was stuff on that test we never talked about in class."

"Fletcher got an 89," Harry Zappacosta said.

"When Fletcher only gets an 89, you *know* a test is unfair," Craig Wickham said.

"I wonder what he does for fun?" Frank Mitchell said. "I mean, can you imagine any woman getting it on with the Rodent?"

"Minnie Mouse," Harry Zappacosta said. "The only woman I can imagine in bed with the Rodent is Minnie Mouse."

• • •

At the Christmas party later that same day, Miss Ulrich, the new librarian, found herself sitting next to Mr. Winter. "How is your year going, Harold?" she asked.

"Well enough," Mr. Winter said. He took a sip of his drink and added, in a matter-of-fact tone, "You know, I've been here seven years, and I've hated every minute."

"I'm sorry to hear that."

"I really shouldn't be a teacher."

"What should you be instead?"

Mr. Winter ignored the question. He seemed a bit drunk. "The boys hate me," he said. "They call me the Rodent."

"Yes. I know."

Miss Ulrich glanced at Mr. Winter out of the corner of one eye. He was a man in his early fifties with neatly trimmed salt-and-pepper hair, a sagging mouth, and a mournful expression in his eyes. Though he wasn't heavy, he gave the impression that, physically, he had let himself get out of shape.

"Boys can be so unfair," Miss Ulrich said.

"It's a cruel name, but it's not unfair," Mr. Winter said. "I don't like adolescent boys. I don't like teaching, and I don't like Trevor Academy. The boys sense it. That's why they dislike me."

"I wouldn't say they dislike you."

"Oh, yes. They do."

"Why do you stay, if you dislike teaching?"

"It's a job. I need some income, even if it's a paltry one."
Mr. Winter cleared his throat. "May I get you a drink?"

Miss Ulrich watched him walk toward the bar. Everything
he had said was true, she knew. The boys did dislike him, and
he seemed to dislike the boys. What's more, he seemed to
have no friends among the faculty.

"That's a very pretty dress," Mr. Winter said, handing her
a glass of white wine.

Miss Ulrich was wearing white stockings and a simple dress
with horizontal red and white stripes. She was a single woman
in her early forties, who looked closer to fifty. Her lips were
pale, her hips sturdy, her teeth were not quite even. A needy
and respectable old maid—that was what she was. She knew
it perfectly well, and she knew perfectly well that that was
what men saw when they looked at her.

As she neared the end of her drink, Mr. Winter asked Miss
Ulrich if she had plans for dinner. She did not. An excep-
tionally good Cantonese restaurant had recently opened in
town, Mr. Winter said. Would she like to join him? Yes, Miss
Ulrich said. She would be delighted to join him.

"The boys know they can get under my skin," Mr. Winter
said as they shared hot-and-sour soup for two. "That puts me
at a disadvantage. There've been boys that I wanted to strangle."

"A thought-murder a day keeps the doctor away," Miss
Ulrich said. "They can't arrest anyone for fantasies."

"I think I'd like another drink," Mr. Winter said. "Would
you like more wine?"

"I really had enough at the party," Miss Ulrich said.

"Let yourself go, Miss Ulrich."

"All right. Get me a gin and tonic."

"That's the spirit!"

"Never mix, never worry," Miss Ulrich said, with a giggle.

The last time she had been intimate with a man had been Labor Day weekend. She had gone to the beach for the day and allowed herself to be picked up by a man who owned an antiques shop in Wilmington. The man, Keith something-or-other, had taken her to dinner at a quiet Vietnamese restaurant. Later, when they kissed, his mouth had tasted of fried sea bass seasoned with coriander and hers had tasted of squid with lemongrass and chili. She liked making love after she had eaten an unusual meal. Tonight she had ordered braised oysters with black pepper sauce.

"It's snowing," Mr. Winter said.

He was facing the front of the restaurant, so he could see the front window. Miss Ulrich twisted her head and looked. The large, soft flakes were lovely in the square of the window. Below, next to a coat rack, green-and-orange fish swam in an aquarium.

The last time Mr. Winter had been intimate with a woman had been six months ago. Her name was Ricky, she wore intricate black lingerie, and her breath smelled of tuna salad. Mr. Winter had met her in the bar at a shabby hotel on Calloway Street, near the bus terminal. In a hotel room with pink-and-white-striped wallpaper, Mr. Winter had listened politely while she told him that she hoped to move to Los Angeles and make a career as a talent agent. He had paid her one hundred dollars for her services, which she provided without fuss or feigned emotion.

"Did you read in the paper about those high-class shoplifters?" Miss Ulrich said.

"No, what about them?"

"A couple in Hoppersville, a dentist and his wife. They hired a personal shoplifter."

"That's a new one. How are those oysters?"

"Delicious. Have a taste?"

Mr. Winter took a taste. "That's quite good. Have some of mine?"

Miss Ulrich took a taste of Mr. Winter's clams with black bean sauce. "Yum," she said, licking her lips.

"What did their personal shoplifter lift for them?" Mr. Winter asked.

"Whatever their hearts desired."

"What did their hearts desire?"

"Armani suits, a white fox fur coat, a Baccarat crystal eagle."

Mr. Winter sighed, as if he regretted that he could not afford a personal shoplifter on a teacher's salary.

"Some people will do *anything*," Miss Ulrich said. "Have you noticed?"

"Have another drink?" Mr. Winter asked.

"Harold, you'll have to carry me out to the car."

"That's fine with me."

"Will you have another?" Miss Ulrich asked.

"No, I have to drive."

"Well, then—" Miss Ulrich paused. Then she said, "Would you mind? I'd really like another, though I'm floating already."

"Please have one. We're not in any hurry."

The gin and tonic was Miss Ulrich's second, and she'd also had a glass of white wine at the Christmas party. When she stood to go, she felt giddy. Mr. Winter took her arm and guided her past the aquarium toward the door. They took a last look at the green-and-orange fish.

Outside, the snow was falling harder, though still in large, soft flakes. Two or three inches of snow had fallen in less than two hours. The wetness felt good on Miss Ulrich's cheeks. The cold made her feel more alert.

"Careful," Mr. Winter said, tightening his grip on her arm. "It's slippery."

Miss Ulrich said nothing. Mr. Winter began to drive, slowly, down Percy Street, right onto Willoughby, then up Washington toward Highgate. Miss Ulrich was thinking that she would invite Mr. Winter into her apartment for a hot drink. He would say yes, of course. She would fix both of them hot cocoa. The taste of the cocoa would overpower the taste of the Chinese seafood they had eaten, and the rich sauces. When they kissed, their tongues would taste of cocoa.

Mr. Winter was thinking that he should have dined alone. He liked the idea of sleeping with Miss Ulrich, but he did not like the idea of sleeping with Miss Ulrich and then seeing her every day in the school library or cafeteria. He did not like the idea of hurting Miss Ulrich or being the object of Miss Ulrich's reproachful gazes, or being involved in unpleasant scenes with Miss Ulrich.

Mr. Winter approached the end of Washington Street. He could still wish her good night at her door. He could kiss her on the cheek and drive home and fix himself a nightcap and watch a few minutes of Johnny Carson or some old movie. He could wake tomorrow in his own bed, look out the window to see how much snow had accumulated, fix himself a cup of strong coffee, and contemplate a future in which Miss Ulrich would never look at him with pain or bitterness or recrimination in her eyes. All that was necessary was to wish her good night at her door and kiss her on the cheek. It was not too late.

Mr. Winter turned slowly onto Highgate. Perhaps they would skip the cocoa, Miss Ulrich thought. In the darkness, through the icy mess on the windshield, Miss Ulrich saw a pair of headlights coming toward them, in a car that was moving a little faster than it should have been. Yes, Miss Ulrich thought, she would like to have the taste of oysters in her mouth when she kissed him. And she would kiss him, she would kiss him quite soon. At that moment the car coming toward them went into a skid, Mr. Winter jerked the wheel, and their car began to spin. Everything happened fast, on the dark street, in the soft snow, with wheels and cars and headlights spinning. The snow fell gently onto the spinning cars. Miss Ulrich died with a shriek that Mr. Winter remembered for the rest of his life. The taste of braised oysters, a rich and wonderful taste, was in her mouth as she died. Her eyes were wide open.

• • •

"I think your father was a hero," Henry Rider said.

Anne Winter looked at Henry Rider with a puzzled expression on her face.

"My father?" she said.

She was twenty-four years old, with a narrow, attractive face, a straight nose, pale lips, and black hair parted in the middle. She was not wearing any makeup.

"Yes. Your father," Henry said, staring at her. He was in his early thirties—a dark-haired man with a long face and sharply cut features. "I think he's a hero."

"Why?"

Henry hesitated. They were sitting opposite one another in a booth at a coffee shop he had chosen because he knew it was quiet. Anne Winter had ordered a turkey sandwich on rye bread. Henry had ordered a Caesar salad with grilled chicken.

"He blew the whistle," Henry said. "He stopped something bad from happening."

"My father?"

"You don't know?"

"Mr. Rider, I don't have the faintest idea what you're talking about. I haven't seen my father since 1980. That was seven years ago."

"Miss Winter, you know, don't you, that in 1972 your father worked at Brice Pharmaceuticals?"

"Yes."

"You know that he was fired?"

"Yes."

"Do you know why he was fired?"

"He was working on some big project that failed."

"Yes. That's one way of putting it."

"What are you getting at, Mr. Rider?"

"There's a certain kind of viral infection called G-27. It affects the kidneys. At Brice Pharmaceuticals in 1972, your father was in charge of a project seeking to develop an agent to combat that virus."

"All right."

"A lot of money was at stake. The company projected five-year sales of half a billion dollars, if they developed an effective antiviral agent."

Henry paused. Miss Winter nodded—a signal that he should continue. "Have you ever heard of a man named Richard Olson?" Henry asked.

"No."

"Richard Olson was a supervisor who worked for your father, evaluating this experimental drug. At a late stage in the evaluation process, he discovered that this drug produced some unsuspected side effects. Very serious side effects. He reported the discovery to your father."

Henry Rider lowered his eyes to take a long sip of coffee. When he lifted them again, he said, "You've never heard any of this, Miss Winter?"

"Never."

"Your father reported the problem to his boss, who happened to be my father."

That sentence startled her. Henry could see it in her face.

"Your father, Mr. Rider?"

"Yes."

Miss Winter waited for Henry to go on. He said, "Your father thought that these side effects were so troubling that, in effect, the company should go back to square one in its efforts to develop an antiviral agent. My father disagreed."

"What did your father want to do, Mr. Rider?"

"My father wanted to manufacture the agent and market it overseas, where safety standards are not as strict as they are in the U.S."

"I see."

"But my father lost the argument, Miss Winter. Would you like to know why?"

"Of course."

"Because your father held his feet to the fire. Your father said that if Brice tried to market this product overseas, he'd take the story public. He had all the data, you see, from Richard Olson. And he'd taken the precaution of copying everything—all the laboratory results—and putting the copy in a safe deposit box. So he was in a position to go public, if the company resisted."

"My father did that?"

"That's why he lost his job, Miss Winter. It wasn't simply that he led a big project that failed. From the company's point of view, the project didn't have to fail. They'd have sold the damned stuff overseas."

"That's what your father would have done?"

"Yes, Miss Winter. That's what my father would have done."

Anne said nothing for a long time. Henry Rider watched her with an expression of intense curiosity.

"I'll tell you something else that might interest you," Henry said.

"What's that?"

"Your father stopped my father in 1972, but he wasn't there to stop him in 1981."

"What happened in 1981?"

"Different drug, same story. Brice sold it in Africa."

"A bad drug?"

"Sixteen people died."

"What happened to your father?"

Henry Rider smiled, but his eyes looked angry. "Not a damned thing," he said.

"Nothing?"

"I told you, Miss Winter. Brice sold the drug in *Africa.*"

• • •

Roosevelt Towers, on West 116th Street in New York City, is a grimy, twelve-story, red-brick apartment building, built shortly after World War II, that attracts graduate students and young faculty members associated with Columbia University.

"You mean she had no idea?" Janet Rider said, preparing a salad in the old-fashioned kitchen.

"No idea," Henry Rider said, peeling the skin off a red onion. "The family fell apart, after her father lost his job."

"What happened?"

"One day he was a fast-track executive, and the next he was a nobody—a chemistry teacher at a third-rate private school. The wife couldn't deal with it."

"She left him?"

"She left him. The kids hardly ever saw him, growing up."

"What happened to the wife?"

"Made a nice career for herself, on the advertising side in TV. Plus she married a millionaire lawyer. Lives in Chicago now."

"And Winter? Does the daughter know where he lives now?"

"Baltimore." Henry brushed a strand of black hair back off his forehead. "Carrot?" he asked.

"Sure."

Henry started scraping a carrot.

"Has she seen him lately?"

"Seven years ago."

"Jesus. Cut up some cucumber, too, hon."

"Okay."

"What's she like?"

"Who?"

"The daughter."

"Young. Pretty. Intelligent." Henry paused to pop a slice of carrot into his mouth. "I think I gave her a good shock."

"I'll bet you did."

"She didn't have a clue."

"Didn't you write to her?" Janet was tossing the salad, in a big wooden bowl.

"Sure. I'd written and told her that I was an assistant professor, blah blah blah, writing a book about corporate ethics, and that I wanted to interview her about her father. And she said yes, she'd give me an interview. But when I talked with her, I could tell everything was new to her."

"Did you tell her about your father?"

"Yes."

"What did she say?"

"Nothing."

"Nothing?"

"I told you. All of this seemed to be new to her." Henry paused, with a bottle of red wine in one hand and a corkscrew in the other. "You know, when I told her I was writing about corporate ethics, I think that she thought I was going to tell her about something terrible her father had done."

"Really?"

"I don't think she's ever been close to her father. I don't think she's ever known him, or liked him, or thought of him as anything but a loser."

• • •

Anne Winter sat for a long time before picking up the phone. At last she picked it up, listened for the dial tone, hit three buttons, and abruptly hung up. She sat for another minute. Then she picked up the phone again. But instead of calling her mother, she called her friend Isabel.

Anne told Isabel about her conversation with Henry Rider. What bothered her, Anne said, was that, somehow, no one had ever told the whole story. Maybe she'd heard—there must have been dinner table conversations—but, since she was only nine years old, she hadn't understood what was being said. *Daddy lost his job*—that was all she remembered. Then it was: *We can't afford this big house.* Then: *Daddy has a new job. Daddy's going to be a teacher.* Then came the new school she hated, in the new town she hated. Then: *Mommy and Daddy can't live together anymore. But we still love you, Anne. We'll always love you.*

In any case, Daddy disappeared. And Mommy made a new life for herself. Mommy took the children to Philadelphia, got a job in the marketing department with the local CBS affiliate, did well, moved up, moved to Chicago, met George, married George, moved up some more. Daddy was left behind—far, far behind. Daddy was rarely seen or mentioned. Daddy was the man who had failed. Daddy was the man who sent presents that disappointed the children and, later, Daddy was the man who did not attend their high school or college graduations. Daddy was the man who lived far away and rarely wrote to them. Daddy was the man who drank. Daddy was the man who lost his teaching job after some poor woman was killed in a terrible car accident that happened while Daddy was drunk.

Isabel listened, as a good friend should.

"I spoke with my brother and sister," Anne told Isabel. "They're older, and I thought that maybe they would know more than I had. But they said no. All they remembered was that Daddy lost his job at the pharmaceutical company, and everything changed."

After her talk with Isabel, Anne felt refreshed. She rested for a few minutes, then took a deep breath and called her mother. "Mother," she said after they had chatted awhile, "I wanted to ask you about Father. Harold, I mean. Not George."

"Yes, dear. What about him?"

Anne's mother had a wonderful voice. When Anne read that famous line in F. Scott Fitzgerald, the one about the woman whose voice was full of money, Anne knew exactly how that woman sounded.

"A man came to see me about Father, a teacher in the sociology department at Columbia," Anne said. "He's writing a book about business ethics. He thinks Father is a hero."

"Does he?"

"Yes. He says that Daddy didn't simply lose his job. He says that Daddy was fired because he wouldn't go along with a scheme to market a bad drug."

"Yes, dear. That's true. Though I'm not sure that the drug was bad, and I'm not sure that it's fair to call it a scheme."

"You think the drug might not have been bad?"

"With any new drug, there's data to interpret."

"So Daddy might have misinterpreted the data?"

"There's a saying you might have heard, Anne: *To get along, go along.* Do you know what it means?"

"I suppose."

"Your father killed a project that mattered a good deal to his company. He didn't go along, and after that, he didn't get along."

"This fellow at Columbia thinks that Father was right."

"He might have been, Anne. I'd like to think he was."

"Why wasn't I ever told, Mother?"

"You were only nine. I guess we thought it was enough to say that Daddy had lost his job. Then, if I remember correctly, we didn't talk much about your father, after the divorce. Am I wrong about that?"

"No, Mother. I can't remember *ever* talking about him."

"I doubt it was that bad, dear. In any case, it was my fault. I was angry."

In Chicago, the former Peggy Winter, now Peggy Merriman, was sitting in bed with her legs stretched out and her back supported by the bed's headboard. She was a woman in her middle fifties, with a look and style she seemed to have modeled on the look and style of Lauren Bacall at the same age—sophisticated, sadder but wiser, wary yet basically good-hearted. Her hair was a golden blonde. Her legs were long. The phone call from her daughter came on a Saturday, just after a leisurely, late-afternoon bath. She was wearing a gold silk robe, a gift from her husband, who liked to buy the best for her.

The call from her daughter made Peggy Merriman think about a time in her life she would rather not have recalled. She had loved her first husband and enjoyed her life as the wife of a rising executive. After he'd lost his job, she'd wanted Harold to fight back, but he'd lost heart when it became clear that his reputation as a whistleblower had made him persona non grata in the pharmaceutical industry. He'd gone into a tailspin, become moody and uncommunicative, started drinking, and seemed unable to envision any future for himself except in a job he disliked at a school few people respected.

Anne said, "But, Mother, if he'd lost his job for a good reason . . ."

"Yes, Anne. You're right. But I was—oh, I was just angry."

"Because he lost his job?"

"Because he wrecked his career! You see, Anne, he was a star at Brice. He was making a lot of money, he had every reason to think he'd make a lot more, and I had certain expectations. I admit it. We needed a lot of money, Anne, to live the life I wanted to live."

"So you left him because he stopped making money?"

"Yes!" Anne heard her mother's voice rising into dangerous territory—a region where exasperation mingled with self-pity and self-justification. "I left him because he stopped making money, and, even more, I left him because I couldn't see myself living the rest of my life as the happy little wife of a chemistry teacher at a third-rate private school, in a third-rate town in the middle of nowhere. You only live *once*, Anne. That wasn't a life I was willing to settle for."

"I'm sorry I made you angry, Mother."

"You didn't make me angry, Anne. You just brought up a lot of old feelings. I was angry for a long time, but I fought my way through it."

"You know, Mother, I love you."

"Thank you, Anne. I love you, too."

Anne pictured her mother—the broad face, the strong nose and chin, the hair like the hair of Lauren Bacall—and said, "You went to the big city with three kids and no special skills, and you got a job and worked your tail off and you became—well, you became *you*."

Anne's mother laughed—a hearty, full-throated sound.

"All of us admire you, Mother. All the kids, I mean. The thing that has put us in a tizzy is that, now, for the first time, it looks as if we might have a reason to admire our father, too."

• • •

"Anne?"

"Hello, Father."

On a bright, cold Saturday in October 1987, Anne Winter had taken a train from New York City to Baltimore. Outside Penn Station in Baltimore, she had found a taxi line. She had given the taxi driver the address that had appeared on her father's most recent Christmas card. The driver had taken her to a city street of dreary-looking, two-story brick row houses.

"Come in. It's been a long time."

Anne stepped in.

"This is Rhonda," her father said.

Anne looked at Rhonda—a stout, smiling, rosy-faced woman with untidy silvery hair. Rhonda was wearing a plain housedress, green and pink flowers on a white background, and carrying a glass with an orange liquid in it. Her smile revealed a gold tooth.

"Pleased to meet you," Anne said, holding out her hand.

Rhonda switched the glass from her right hand to her left.

"My pleasure," she said, shaking hands. "Could I get you something to drink?"

"Coffee," Anne said.

"Coming up," Rhonda said, and walked from the room with a stiff gait.

The living room was drab but clean, with a sofa, two armchairs, a coffee table, and a TV. None of the furniture looked close to new, and none looked expensive, but the room felt comfortable.

Anne's father was wearing light-gray slacks and a dark-brown sweater, unbuttoned, over a yellow polo shirt. His hair was gray, sparse, and neatly combed. Anne was surprised at how small he looked. He was five-foot-seven, maybe five-six.

"Well," he said. "It's been a long time."

The last time Anne had seen her father, seven years ago, she had been seventeen years old, and he had been fifty-three. That had been in 1980, one year after the auto accident that killed Miss Ulrich and eight years after Harold Winter had lost his job at Brice Pharmaceuticals. Anne had traveled to Baltimore to see him during Christmas vacation in her senior year in high school—a time when she had been experiencing a high level of adolescent turmoil. Anne had gone to find her lost father, and she had found a man so far out of control that he'd arrived nearly an hour late to pick her up at the train station. The smell of liquor on his breath had made her turn her face away.

Now she had taken another train ride to see him, but with different expectations. Her thought now was that her father was a defeated man who needed to be rescued. In a difficult situation, he had done the right thing, many years ago, and he had paid a high price for his act of conscience. All the way down to Baltimore, gazing out the train window at the landscape rushing by, from the depressing grime of industrial New Jersey to the white stoops that fronted the row houses on the streets leading into Baltimore, Anne had been dreaming that she would connect with her father for the first time, that she would *have* a father for the first time, that she would console and comfort him, and he would console and comfort her, and a new life would begin for both of them.

Anne said, "I was hoping we could get to know one another, better than we've known one another in the past."

"I've stopped drinking," her father said. "That's the main thing you need to know."

"When did you stop?"

"Three years ago. Rhonda helped me."

Rhonda, who had returned from the kitchen with coffee for Anne, looked affectionately at Anne's father, but said nothing.

"Rhonda saved my life," Anne's father said. "We're both alcoholics. I met her at Alcoholics Anonymous. She turned my life around."

"That's wonderful," Anne said.

There was a pause, while everyone beamed at everyone else.

"If it hadn't been for Rhonda, I'd've been dead by now," Harold said.

On the train that morning, remembering the last time she had seen her father, Anne had prepared herself for the worst. She had imagined herself lifting him out of the gutter, or leading him out of the saloon and, patiently, nursing him back to health and happiness. A lovely thought but also, she realized now, childish and grandiose. She would not rescue her father because, apparently, her father did not need to be rescued. He sat there in his armchair, sipping orange juice, and Rhonda sat in the other armchair, also sipping orange juice, and Anne sat on the sofa, taking an occasional sip of her coffee.

"Are you working now?" Anne asked.

"I've got a job in a hardware store," Harold said. He added with a grimace, as if tasting something sour, "A man with a Ph.D. from Cornell, working in a goddamned hardware store."

Rhonda said, "You're lucky they took you, as far as you'd sunk."

"That's the truth," Harold said. "It's still a waste. A man with a Ph.D."

"Wasn't there something else you could have done, after what happened?" Anne asked.

"After I got fired, you mean?"

"Yes."

Harold shook his head. "I could get interviews," he said. "But whenever I got an interview, they'd ask why I'd left Brice, when I'd been doing so well there. So I'd tell them why, and that was that. Nobody looks to hire a troublemaker."

The afternoon drifted on, quite pleasantly. Harold asked Anne about her brother and sister and her mother. Rhonda told Anne about her job in the customer relations department at Baltimore Gas & Electric. A great deal of orange juice was consumed.

"I spoke with that professor," Anne's father said. "The one you gave my address to."

"Yes. He told me."

"I knew his father."

"Yes." Anne remembered the look in Henry Rider's eyes when he had told her how his father had sold bad drugs in Africa. "He hates his father," she said.

"No," Harold said. "He *loves* his father. But this book he's writing, this thing about whistleblowers, it's all because he can't stand thinking about some of the things his father did."

"I know," Anne said.

"I remember his father very well. Warren Rider."

"What was he like?" Anne asked.

"Good scientist," Harold said.

"Was he?" Anne looked at him, waiting for more.

Harold said, "Damned good scientist. Lousy human being."

•   •   •

Six years later, in his private room in a hospital in Baltimore, Harold Winter lay asleep. His eyes were closed, his face pale, his lips dry, his hair untidy. At one point, a tall, silver-haired man in a business suit came into the room, closing the door behind him. With a sad expression on his face and his hands crossed before him, the visitor stood looking down at Harold while Harold slept. At last Harold's eyes opened.

"Warren? Is that you?"

"Yes, Harold."

"I thought you were dead."

"I am."

Harold blinked, trying to clear his vision. The tall man with the silver hair was still there.

"Dead as a doornail," Warren Rider said. "Did you expect clanking chains?"

Harold blinked again. The visitor peered down at him.

"You're looking good, Warren."

"Thanks. I wish I could say the same for you, Harold."

"My liver gave out."

"Ah."

"Serves me right. I drank like a fish."

Warren Rider looked down at Harold without any particular expression on his face. Harold squinted up at him.

"I met your son," Harold said. "A long time ago."

"Yes. I know."

"He sent me his book. You know the book?"

"Yes. Did you read it, Harold?"

"I did. Smart kid."

"He hates my guts," Warren Rider said.

Harold began to answer, but Warren stopped him. "He hates my guts, Harold. He called me a murderer."

"You're his father."

"We weren't talking, the last few years of my life."

"I'm sorry, Warren."

"You see. I paid a price, too."

"Don't give me any sob story, Warren."

"That's not what I intended."

Harold closed his eyes and rested for a few minutes.

"Warren?"

"Yes, Harold."

"I killed a woman."

"Miss Ulrich?"

"Yes."

"Accidents happen, Harold."

"I was drinking."

"So was the guy in the other car."

"What difference does that make?"

"Two cars skidded in the snow, Harold. Same thing might have happened if you'd both been sober."

"Might or might not. Nobody knows for sure."

"Let God worry about it."

Harold closed his eyes. When he opened them, the light in the room seemed different. Warren was still standing there, looking down at him.

"You want something from me, Warren?"

"I just wanted to chat. I always respected you, Harold."

"Thanks." Harold looked away, but Warren waited until he looked back.

Warren said, "I did what I had to do, Harold."

"That's one way of looking at it."

"I was tough."

"No doubt."

"You have to be tough in business."

"And I was soft. Is that what you're saying, Warren?"

"If the shoe fits."

"Go away, Warren."

"I thought I might put your mind at ease."

"Oh. How do you plan to do that, Warren?"

"By showing you how things turned out for me."

"You made a mint, didn't you?"

"I made a lot of money, Harold. I can't deny it."

"Was it worth it?"

"I told you, Harold. My son hates my guts."

"He said so?"

"He called me a murderer."

"You still made the big bucks."

"No doubt about it, Harold. I made the big bucks."

"Left it to your kids?"

"Left it to my kids."

"That's all that matters, isn't it?"

"Tell my son."

Harold closed his eyes. The argument had tired him. Gold was the color he found himself looking at, with his eyes closed. He thought about Warren Rider and his son. He thought about his own children. A great weariness descended upon him. He slept.

• • •

"There's no telling," the nurse said. She had blue eyes and pale red hair. "There's no telling how long it will last, or whether he'll ever come out of it."

Anne and Rhonda nodded in unison.

"You might want to go home and rest," the nurse said. "I'll call you if there's any change."

"Oh, I wouldn't want to do that," Rhonda said.

"I'll stay, too," Anne said.

"That's fine," the nurse said. "Let me know if you need anything."

"We'll do that," Anne said.

The nurse left. Anne and Rhonda sat side by side in sturdy and uncomfortable armchairs—the kind all hospitals seem to buy. The walls in the room were a pale green. The dying man lay on his back in bed, breathing feebly, with his eyes closed and his mouth slightly open. A clear liquid dripped soundlessly from a plastic bag hanging on a pole through an IV line into his right arm.

"You want a section of the paper?" Rhonda asked.

"Not now, thanks."

Six years had passed since Anne traveled to Baltimore to make a new connection with her father. Harold was sixty-six now, Rhonda was sixty-two, and Anne was thirty, married, with two young children. The children were with her husband in New York. Anne had come to Baltimore three days ago, when Rhonda called to say that the end seemed near.

Anne had gained a few pounds since Rhonda first met her, and she'd lost the last trace of girlishness in both her looks and her manner. She had grown more confident in the way she dressed and carried herself. On happy occasions, she often dressed stylishly in black, but today she was wearing white slacks and a yellow sweater—bright and comfortable clothes for a death watch. If her father woke, his daughter would shine for him.

Rhonda was still a rosy-faced woman with a stiff gait and a big smile, though she had not smiled much in the past three days. She was stouter than she had been when Anne first met her, and her unruly hair had more white in it, less silver. She respected hospitals in an old-fashioned way, she feared doctors, and she dressed up for the daily visit as if she were dressing for some formal occasion. Today she was wearing a bulky beige suit over a pink blouse, with a scarf around her neck and a silver pin that Harold had bought for her on her lapel.

"The nurse is right," Rhonda said. "One of us ought to go home."

"Yes," Anne said. "Why don't you go get some rest?"

"I thought maybe you would."

Anne smiled without opening her lips and looked again at her father in bed. Rhonda's eyes, following Anne's, grew misty when they came to rest on Harold. She sighed. At the sound Anne held out her hand, and Rhonda reached out to allow her hand to be held.

"Harold loves jazz," Rhonda said. "Did you know that?"

"There's a lot I don't know about him."

"He chose a jazz song to play at the funeral service."

"Really?"

"Louie Armstrong."

"Dad likes Louie Armstrong?"

"Harold loves Louie Armstrong."

"What song?"

"I don't remember. I have it written down at home."

Anne remembered her father singing her to sleep in her bedroom on Starlight Court, where the family lived so long ago: *Hush, little baby, don't say a word, Papa's gonna buy you a mockingbird, and if that mockingbird don't sing, Papa's gonna buy you a diamond ring . . .*

"At least I'm here," Anne said. "Thank God for that."

"Yes, you're here."

And if that diamond ring is brass, Papa's gonna buy you a looking glass, and if that looking glass gets broke . . .

"One of us should get some rest," Rhonda said.

"Yes."

"We need our strength."

"Yes."

They sat there, hand in hand, while the last light of

evening faded outside. The hospital grew quiet. There were no patients walking up and down the corridors, no visitors coming and going, no doctors asking questions or giving orders, no nurses rushing, no orderlies running errands, no wheelchairs rolling or stretchers rattling in the halls.

The nurse who worked the night shift found the two women fast asleep, their hands lightly touching, when she came to check Harold's vital signs. The look that lingered on the face of the dead man was serene, as if he had answered some nagging question or redressed some final grievance.

No Place to Hide

At the age of forty-five, I find that I rarely have bad dreams. Indeed, I rarely have any dreams that I can remember. I live alone, in New York City, in an immense, gray-brick apartment building named Vanderbilt Towers, on the corner of 86th Street and Second Avenue. I work in a small advertising agency that specializes in business-to-business marketing. My daughter, Elizabeth, twenty-one, is a senior studying art history at Princeton. The wife who left me nine years ago now lives in New Mexico, trying to be the next Georgia O'Keeffe. The second marriage I once wanted has not come to pass.

On weekends, I like to walk east on 86th Street, over to Carl Schurz Park. I can stroll around Gracie Mansion, where the mayor lives. I can watch the toddlers playing on the swings or running through the sprinkler in the playground. From the promenade that stretches alongside the East River, I can gaze north to the Triborough Bridge, east to Roosevelt Island, or south to the Queensboro Bridge. I can watch the boats that come by—tugboats and speedboats and an occasional barge. Turning from the river, I can look at the women bouncing by in their jogging outfits or tanning themselves on the grass.

This afternoon—a sunny afternoon a couple of weeks after Labor Day—I was sitting on a bench on the promenade when a man I did not know sat down a few feet away. I gave the man a quick look and saw that he was black, thirty to thirty-five years old, and neatly dressed in cheap clothes.

"You don't recognize me, do you?" the man asked after a few minutes.

"Pardon?"

"I'm Millie's son. Millie Jones."

"Millie?" I searched my mind. "Millie who used to work for my mother? That Millie?"

"That's right. Millie Jones. I'm her son."

He asked politely about my parents, I asked about his, and then we sat in silence, looking toward the river. A breeze blew pleasantly over my face. I could feel the sun on the back of my neck as it slid down the sky behind me.

I remembered Millie, but I could not remember her son, so at last I said, "Listen, it's embarrassing for me to say this, but I don't recall your name."

"Sweetness," the man said, apparently not offended. "As in sweetness and light. I know it sounds like a nickname, but that's the honest-to-goodness name my mama gave me."

"Have we met before, Sweetness?" I asked. "Because if we have, I have to admit I don't remember it."

Sweetness said that that comment was very interesting, because he himself wasn't sure of the answer. As long as his mother had worked for my mother, he didn't know if we'd ever met. He couldn't remember.

"Then how did you recognize me?" I asked.

"What makes you think I recognized you?"

"Because you knew me," I said. "I mean, you knew who I was. And you asked if I recognized you. That was the first thing you said, wasn't it?"

"Not exactly."

Something slippery in his reply made me impatient. "Well," I said, "what exactly did you say? Remind me."

"I'm not sure I remember myself," Sweetness said. "But I didn't ask if you recognized me. Because it was obvious: I could see you didn't recognize me. So I said something like, 'You don't recognize me, do you?' . . . I think that's what I said. Something like that, anyway."

"OK," I said. "But the point is: you recognized me. How did you recognize me?"

"Oh, it was easy. I followed you."

"You *followed* me?"

"From that big apartment building where you live. Vanderbilt Towers, isn't it?"

"Yes, that's it."

He had asked his mother, he said, and she remembered that I used to live in this area. So he looked me up in the phone book, and even though there are dozens of men named Richard Green in New York City, it turns out that I'm the only one who lives in the part of the city called Yorkville.

"So why didn't you phone me?" I asked.

"Why should I have phoned you?"

"Well—if you wanted to talk to me . . ."

Sweetness smiled. "To tell the truth, Richard, I wasn't sure I wanted to talk to you. At first I just wanted to see you—see what you looked like. I followed you for a couple of weeks."

"A couple of weeks!"

"Yes."

"And today? What happened today?"

"I wanted to see if you would recognize me. So I came over and sat down. And even when I sat down, I didn't know whether I would talk to you. I thought I would see if you recognized me, and that would be enough."

"Enough?"

To satisfy him, he said. To satisfy his curiosity.

"You see," he added, "I may never have met you, but somehow I always felt a connection with you. My mother used to talk about you. You and your whole family—she talked about all of you. Your family meant a lot to her. After all, she worked for your mother for thirty years."

I sat there nodding, in the cool air of late afternoon on

the promenade by the river, but I said nothing. The stranger—I still thought of him as a stranger, even though it turned out that family history connected us—stared at me.

"Interesting," I said finally. "It's very interesting, but I'm still not sure what you want from me."

"Did I say I wanted anything?"

"No. But it seems as if that's where you're leading. It seems as if you must want—something."

"Maybe I do. It's quite possible," Sweetness said thoughtfully. "I hadn't thought about wanting anything, but now that you mention it, I can see how it would look that way to you."

"Well"—I slapped my hands on my thighs—"at least you've seen me!"

"I have! I've seen you and I've talked to you!" Sweetness looked at me with sudden excitement. "Let me tell you, this is a big day for me. This is a day I've thought about for a long time."

I did not reply, and Sweetness glanced at his watch: "Oh, how time flies! Listen, Richard, we *must* talk again. We've really just touched the surface. Don't you agree?"

"I guess so," I said helplessly.

"You guess so?"

"I mean . . . I'm sure there's a lot to say . . ."

"*Of course* there's a lot to say," Sweetness said. "After all, my mother worked for your mother all those years, and neither one of us can even remember whether we ever met."

"That's true," I said. "That's very true."

"Listen," Sweetness said, "we definitely have to get together again. No need to set up a time now. I'll find you."

I gazed at him as he got up and walked briskly away on the promenade, heading north toward the Triborough Bridge, until he vanished among the people jogging or strolling in the mild air of mid-September, on a day when New York City seemed as peaceful as Peoria.

2

"Yo! Richard!"

A month has passed. Yet even before I turned, as I strolled on the promenade alongside the East River, I knew who was calling.

"How's my man today?" Sweetness asked.

He was wearing scruffy white sneakers, crimson pants, and a zipped-up, olive-green, army-surplus jacket.

"I've been thinking about our talk," he said, trotting a few steps to catch up with me. "I'm so glad we finally started talking."

I looked at him, but said nothing. Ahead, the Triborough Bridge spanned the river in a tremendous gray arch—silver where the sun touched it.

"So much to say," Sweetness said. "If you know what I mean."

"I'm not sure I do."

"What I mean is, my life has been lacking in conversation with white people. *Serious* conversation."

"I see."

It was a brisk October afternoon. We walked north, toward the bridge. The sun brightened the river and bounced orange reflections off the buildings on Roosevelt Island. Birds swooped and dove over the water. On the promenade, people sped by on giant Rollerblades.

Sweetness said, "To tell the truth, that talk with you—that was the first time it ever happened that I can remember. I'm thirty-three years old, and that was the first time in my life I ever had a serious conversation with any white man. It's amazing, when you think of it."

"Not so amazing," I said.

"How about you?" Sweetness asked. "Tell me the truth. When was the last time you had a real conversation, a *serious* conversation, with a black man."

"Oh, I don't know," I said.

"Think!"

"It's hard to remember."

"I'll bet it is! Let me help . . . Five years ago? . . . Ten years? . . . Twenty?"

"Maybe never," I admitted.

"Never!"

I shrugged.

"Well," Sweetness said, "we surely are a couple of sad specimens. Here my mother worked for your mother thirty years, and neither one of us ever talked to one another, and neither one of us talked to anybody else, except black to black or white to white." He shook his head with a disapproving expression on his face: "A couple of sad specimens."

We passed Gracie Mansion, then turned around and headed south.

"How's that girlfriend of yours?" Sweetness asked.

I stopped walking and stared at him.

"She some kind of secret?" Sweetness asked.

"How do you know about her?"

"I have *eyes*, man. I pay attention."

"You spy—is that what you're saying?"

"I'm not sure I would put it that way. But OK, if you like— I spy."

"Look," I said. "I'd like to know what you're up to. I mean, what exactly do you want?"

"What makes you think I want anything?"

"You've been *following* me, for God's sake."

"Yes," Sweetness said. "I can't deny that."

I sighed. We began to stroll again.

"To tell the truth," Sweetness said, "I'm not sure what I want. This is new territory for me. Don't you feel that way? As if we've wandered together into someplace—new?"

"More as if you've dragged me," I said.

"OK, I've dragged you. I can see that. And I've dragged

myself. Don't forget that part of it. Every step I've dragged you, I've also dragged myself."

Joggers and Rollerblade-riders passed us as we strolled. From the playground came the shouts of kids playing basketball and the thump of the bouncing ball. The sound of traffic drifted over the park from York Avenue.

"Your name," I said. "Tell me about your name."

"Not much to tell."

"Come on, Sweetness."

"I thought you knew," Sweetness said. "My mama was so *proud*—so proud of the names she gave her children. I always figured she told your mother."

"She may have," I said. "That doesn't mean my mother told me."

"No. I guess not."

We were walking slowly now, our heads close together.

"My mama was crazy about names," Sweetness said. "She had seven children, and she wanted to give us good names— names that wouldn't be common. So what you have, in my family—you have Faith, Hope, and Charity. You have Justice and Mercy. And last of all—her babies—can you guess what she named her babies?"

I shook my head.

"Sweetness and Light."

"Ah! That's nice."

"Nice?"

"I mean"—I paused, searching for the right word—"it's sweet."

"Sweet!" Sweetness cried. "Indeed, it *is* sweet! Only my sister and me, we didn't think it was sweet, growing up. And when we got to be twenty-one, we changed our names."

"Oh?"

"My sister changed her name to Victory, and I changed my name to Vengeance. Sweet Vengeance."

"I see."

"Do you?"

"I think so."

"Mama *hated* those names, but we wanted them. So what we had at that time, in the Jones family, we had Faith Jones, Hope Jones, and Charity Jones. We had Justice Jones and Mercy Jones. We had Victory Jones. And we had me—Sweet Vengeance."

"But that was then?"

"Right. I got a little older—a little more mature, you might say—and I changed back to Sweetness."

"I guess that made your mother happy."

"It *did*. It did, indeed."

We walked on, heading north up the promenade. Three pigeons waddled a few feet ahead of us. The sun had gone behind a cloud. The bridge was a big gray arch that did not glitter.

"How do you live?" I asked.

"Hand to mouth," Sweetness said with a smile. "Hand to mouth. Pillar to post. You know how it goes."

"No job?"

"Oh, I've had lots of jobs . . . Odd jobs—you know. Little of this, little of that."

"I see."

"I get by," Sweetness said. "That nine to five shit—that's not for me."

"You live near here?"

"Near enough."

I felt myself getting impatient.

"Where?" I asked.

"Here and there. You know."

"I don't know. Where is here and there?"

"Around. I move around. Place to place."

"Sweetness, you're impossible."

"I hope so!" the black man cried. "I certainly hope I'm impossible!"

In his white sneakers, crimson pants, and olive jacket, he trotted away, into the crowd on the promenade. The sun lit him for a moment before he swerved off the path, out of sight, into the greenery of the park. Overhead, a cherry-red balloon with a string trailing behind it rose haltingly, with many twists and turns, leaving the city forever.

3

If Sweetness has been spying on my love life, he'll have to find a new occupation. Last week Angela dropped me. Yesterday, with eyes blazing, she came to pick up a few things she'd left in my apartment.

"You're not a bad guy," she said. "As men go, you're pretty normal."

I thanked her.

"I mean—you're a bastard, but you're a normal bastard."

I thanked her again.

"I guess you can't help yourself, Richard. You're just so—so *arrogant*! . . .So *pathetic*!" She took a deep breath: "So *male*."

What could I say? What did she expect me to say?

• • •

A week before Christmas, and Sweetness has returned. It happened two days ago, with a buzz on the intercom:

"Gentleman here says he knows you," the doorman said.

A gentleman?

"Sweetness," the doorman said. "Says his name is Sweetness."

"Richard, thank you!" Sweetness cried as I motioned him into the apartment. "Thank you! Thank you! Thank you! . . . You're a lifesaver. You're a saint! . . . Thank you!"

"I'm not a saint," I said. "What's up?"

"Got thrown out of the place where I've been staying. Little fight. Lived on the street three days."

I gestured for him to take a seat in the living room, but

Sweetness continued to stand. He was not quite dressed in rags, but his clothes were rumpled and dirt-stained.

"Cold out there," he said, briskly rubbing his palms.

I put water up to boil for coffee. When I got back to the living room, Sweetness was sitting in a chair, hunched forward, with a nervous expression on his face.

"Richard, I'm sorry to do this. I really am. I never wanted to bother anybody."

"Oh?"

"I stayed in a shelter two nights," Sweetness said. "What a zoo! Last night I stayed on the street." He shook his head with an expression of profound distaste. Then he looked at me. "I know it's a nuisance, Richard, but I need a place to sleep."

"Here?" I asked.

"Why not?"

"Sweetness, you told me you have a big family, all those brothers and sisters. Why not with one of them?"

"Let's just say I don't want to burden them."

"And you're willing to burden me?"

"Richard, it's late. I'm here. You're my friend."

"Your friend? Since when?"

"Richard, *please*," Sweetness said. "Just for one night."

• • •

"What I *need*," Sweetness said as we drank more coffee later that evening, "is a *job*. I need a *real* job. Not just sweeping up at Burger King. You know what I mean?"

I nodded.

"You think you could get me some kind of job like that?"

"Like what?"

"You know, a job that's not just shit. Where you work, maybe. I'd like to work where you work."

"Doing what? I'm in marketing. You know anything about marketing?"

"I can market."

I looked at him skeptically.

"If you teach me, I can do it," Sweetness said. "Would you teach me?"

I didn't say anything, but, looking at him, I felt as if my face had turned into a stone.

"Why?" he said. "What's so hard I couldn't do it?"

"Sweetness, you need *skills*."

"I've got skills."

"Writing? Do you have some advertising copy you could show me?"

Sweetness stared at me.

I went on: "Statistics? Finance? Computers? Any direct mail experience? Any business-to-business?"

We stared at one another, until at last a tear slipped out of the corner of one eye and slid, glistening, one full inch down the side of his black cheek.

• • •

"Where do you want me to sleep?" Sweetness asked.

"Out here. Sofa opens up."

"You know, Richard, one thing I gotta say for you. You have guts."

"Oh?"

"Most white people, they wouldn't let a black man they hardly know sleep in their apartment."

"We know one another," I said.

"Do we?"

"It's what you keep saying. Your mother worked for my mother for thirty years."

"And you figure we know one another?"

I shrugged.

"What I say, Richard, is you've got guts. How you know I'm not gonna come in your bedroom tonight and cut your throat?"

"Why should you?"

"Why shouldn't I?"

"What would you get out of it?"

"Wallet. Credit cards."

"Doesn't seem like much."

"It's *something*, Richard. It's more than the nothing I came here with."

"I guess it is."

"Maybe you should ask me to leave right now," Sweetness said.

"Look, Sweetness. I already asked you to stay . . . You want to stay, you can stay. You want to leave, you can leave. You want to cut my throat, I suppose you can cut my throat."

At the exact moment that I uttered this preposterous challenge, my courage fled. In the hours that followed, I did not sleep a wink. I could hear the low rumble of traffic on 86th Street, the cries of people still outside at two, three, four o'clock in the morning. *Idiot!* I kept saying to myself. *Idiot!* Every creak in the night plucked at my nerves. I lay tensely on my side, gazing toward the door, prepared to spring out of bed and fight for my life.

4

Sweetness promised he would find another place, but the next night at eleven o'clock, the intercom buzzed.

"Richard, I'm sorry!" he said as I faced him at the door. "I'm really sorry!"

"Me, too," I said, stepping aside to let him in.

"I couldn't find *anyplace*. I tried. Believe me, I tried."

"What about the shelters?"

"They scare me, Richard."

"What about your family?"

"That's no solution."

"*I'm* a solution?"

He asked me if he could stay a few days. Scowling, I felt my jaw tighten. But what could I do? It's Christmas, and I'm not Scrooge. I told him he could stay a few days.

"But that's it, Sweetness," I said. "You have to find some other place, and soon! I'm not a saint. I'm not my brother's keeper. And you're not my brother."

• • •

Robbery?

All day at the office, I worried. As I lifted my key when I got home from work, I half-suspected I would open the door and find nothing. No furniture, no clothes, not a book or a record on my shelves, not a knickknack, not a picture on the walls, not a stick of butter in the refrigerator, not a toothbrush in the bathroom.

"Hello!" I called as I stepped into the hall that led to the living room.

"Hello!" Sweetness called from the kitchen.

In the living room, it hit me. Nothing was gone, but a transformation had taken place. The carpet had been vacuumed; furniture had been dusted and polished; books had been straightened on the shelves; magazines had been gathered and placed in neat piles on the table where they belonged. The room looked as if a photographer from *Better Homes and Gardens* were scheduled to arrive any minute.

In the kitchen, I found Sweetness in an apron, holding a carrot in one hand and a slicing knife in the other.

"Thought we'd have a little salad," Sweetness said, looking sideways at me. "Found this stuff in the frig. Hope you don't mind?"

"No, that's fine," I said, then added, with a gesture toward the living room, "Sweetness, thank you. The place looks great."

"Don't mention it," Sweetness said. "Just wanted to show my appreciation. Earn my keep, you might say." He paused with half a carrot in his hand. "Richard, why don't you change out of your suit. Relax. Take a shower . . . Everything's under control here. Just you leave things to me."

5

Five days, and no end in sight. How long can this go on? This morning—Sunday—Sweetness seemed depressed. He stood at the window in the living room with his hands in his pockets, looking south at the jagged midtown skyline, while I lingered over the newspaper. Outside, the sky was the vivid blue of a sunny day in late December.

"How about a walk?" he said at last.

"Us?"

"Who else?"

We walked north, past a dry cleaners, past a bicycle shop, past a pizza parlor, past the famous restaurant where celebrities eat, past the little park between 89th and 90th where mothers take their toddlers as a change of pace from Carl Schurz Park by the river.

Above 90th Street, Second Avenue changed. The shops were dingier, restaurants cheaper. More black faces passed on the street. At 92nd Street, on the south side, I hesitated, but Sweetness urged me on.

Above 92nd Street, the buildings themselves seemed more rickety. Some stores were boarded shut, with graffiti scrawled on the boards. There was broken glass, mostly broken beer bottles, on the sidewalks and in the gutter. Awnings were ripped. Black kids in ragged clothes ran by. Black men looked at me with sullen faces. At 96th Street, on the south side, I stopped again.

"Enough," I said.

"Let's go just a few blocks more," Sweetness said.

"No. This is far enough."

"You're safe, Richard. Nothing's gonna happen."

"No, Sweetness. I'm not safe."

Seeing that I had the "walk" sign, I headed across Second Avenue, intending to walk back on the other side of the street. Sweetness did not follow. At the corner, I stopped, looking back. Sweetness was staring at me from the opposite curb. Other people, near and far, also seemed to be watching.

"Sweetness, damn it!" I cried.

Sweetness stared at me, while cars and trucks rumbled between us. I stood on the corner staring back, the most visible person at the big, bustling intersection of Second Avenue and 96th Street in Manhattan. When the light changed, Sweetness trotted across the street and rejoined me.

On a boarded-up storefront a few yards from the corner, someone had scrawled the message "GOD IS IN THE DETAILS" and above it, in larger letters, "BUY SHOES, NOT DRUGS." A few feet away, in orange crayon, someone had added: "YOUR DICK—DON'T LEAVE HOME WITHOUT IT."

6

On an ice-cold, ghost-gray, drizzly morning in Queens, one week after my walk with Sweetness, I take the subway to have brunch with my parents.

These visits of mine are a Sunday ritual. There they are, Sadie and Lou Green, in their tiny brick house, on their row of tiny brick houses. Row after row of tiny houses, with postage-stamp lawns. Just like the credits at the end of *All in the Family*.

The smell of my mother's cranberry-red sweater takes me back forty years. My grandparents were named Greenberg, but my father changed the name to Green. Even in America, he thought, it was better to be Green than Greenberg.

"Now Hank Greenberg, he had guts," he was saying about

the Hall of Fame baseball player who happened to be Jewish. "But DiMaggio—*he* was the greatest."

In fact, though I'm too young to have seen DiMaggio, I have a baseball glove that he signed, in 1949, after a midsummer game with the Red Sox at Yankee Stadium. My father, knowing that a child—perhaps a son—would arrive early in 1950, waited outside the Yankee locker room to catch the aging Clipper as he left. Now the glove with the autograph, a gift from my father on my twelfth birthday, sits on top of the TV in my bedroom. If you think it strange that a man in his mid-forties would live with a baseball glove on permanent display in his bedroom, I can only say that you don't know much about divorce.

"You know," he says, as we drain our coffee cups and the conversation drifts in and out of the past, "I remember my parents, your grandparents, may they rest in peace. They ran a tiny little grocery store in Jackson Heights. A mom-and-pop store, literally, but a business—their own business. And then an A&P opened across the street. And my parents, I still remember the look in their eyes the year that A&P was built. Like animals—like cattle—stunned by a blow. They were going to be slaughtered, and they knew it, and there wasn't anything they could do."

"Like cattle," Mom said.

"And they never got over it," Dad said. "They sold the store for nothing, and my father went to work selling shoes in some crumby little shoe store, and that was it—he made crumbs."

"Free enterprise," Mom said. "Free to be slaughtered."

My father is haunted by his father's disappointments, as I am haunted by my father's. Is this what people mean when they talk about the American dream? I'm sharing my apartment with a man I barely know, the son of a woman I dimly remember. Night after night, the suspicion grows that I've missed the boat, missed many boats, maybe even missed the last boat . . . America, is there something you forgot to tell me?

7

"Sweetness, you'll have to go soon."

"You don't like my cooking?"

"I can't afford a full-time servant."

"You can afford me."

"Sweetness, I don't *need* a full-time servant. I don't *want* a full-time servant."

We were in my living room, three weeks after Sweetness had begun his stay there. Outside, the January sky was a wispy white. Later, a soft snow would fall.

"You don't want *me*?" Sweetness asked.

"I don't want anybody. I'm a forty-five-year-old unmarried man. I don't want a roommate, especially a male roommate. I don't want anybody sleeping full-time in my living room."

"Ah!" Sweetness's face brightened. "You don't want me here when you've got a date. No problem . . . You have a date, just tell me. I'll sleep somewhere else."

I shook my head. "I'm not talking about a night now and then. I'm talking about the whole situation. I don't want—how can I put it?—I don't want to share my life with you. Is that clear? It's *my* life. It's *my* apartment."

Sweetness looked unhappy. "You want me to leave right now?"

"I want you to leave soon."

"Today?"

"By the end of the weekend. How's that? That gives you three more days."

• • •

"You ever been out with a black woman?" Sweetness asked.

"No."

"You want to?"

I made a noncommittal gesture.

"Don't like black women?"

"Sweetness, it's not a question of liking."

"What then?"

"It's a question of—opportunity."

"I'll handle that."

I shook my head.

"Sweetness, I don't like being fixed up," I said.

"How about being fixed up with a white woman?"

"I don't like it, period."

Sweetness stared at me. "I've been here a long time. Don't you ever get—you know?"

"Now and then . . . To tell you the truth, Sweetness, it's none of your damned business."

"I thought white boys had a thing about black women."

"Not this white boy."

• • •

"I don't get it," Sweetness said later.

"Get what?"

"Richard, what do you want from me?"

"I don't want anything."

"Why'd you let me stay here?"

"You asked me."

"You let anybody stay who asks?"

"No. I let *you* stay."

"Why?"

"You said you needed help. I thought maybe I could help."

"You want to help? I need a job."

"Sweetness, we went over that. A job means skills."

"I can cook. I can clean."

"What are you saying, Sweetness? You want to be my maid?"

"Why not?"

"I thought you didn't want a dead-end job."

"Beats the street."

"Sweetness, look. I hire a woman once a week to clean up the apartment. You want to put her out of work?"

"I clean up better."

"OK, you clean up better. But she only comes in one afternoon a week. She doesn't live here. She's—you know—she's a woman like your mother. She has a lot of jobs like this one."

"I need a job, Richard."

"That's your problem."

"You think I should steal?"

"I think you should find a real job, even if it is dead-end."

"Maybe I'd rather steal."

"That's up to you."

"Richard, do you listen to yourself?"

"What's that supposed to mean?"

"It means you talk in circles."

"Do I?"

"You say you want to help. But you don't have much to offer."

"That's right. I don't."

"Here's how it sounds to me," Sweetness said. "Sounds like I can look for a job at Burger King, or I can steal, or I can look for a job as a security guard. That's where I see this country heading. Half the black men in America gonna deal dope, and the other half gonna be security guards."

• • •

"You want me to beg?" Sweetness asked.

"No."

"Oh, yes, you do. You want me to creep up to you with my hat in my hand, like some old Uncle Tom, all bent and cringing, and say, *Please, sir, Mr. White Man, please can you spare me a crumb to feed my family.* That's what you want. That's the only black man you're not afraid of—some old, bent, shuffling geezer that had the shit kicked out of him so long ago he can't even remember what it means to stand up straight."

• • •

Sweetness said, "What I think is, you folks spend so much time worrying about *your* fear, you can't even see *our* fear. You see a black kid walking down the street with his radio blasting, and you think you've got a slave insurrection on your hands."

• • •

This afternoon, in a coffee shop on York Avenue, my daughter attacked her blueberry pancakes as if Princeton had not fed her for three months. In blue jeans and a white shirt, with her fresh face and her lively brown eyes, she looked like a college girl having breakfast with her middle-aged lover. In fact, her middle-aged lover is a Vietnamese photographer, exactly my age, whom she met last year at a gallery in Soho.

Later, back at the apartment, I introduced her to my guest.

"Pleased to meet you," Sweetness said.

"Sweetness's mother used to work for Grandma," I explained. "Did you ever meet Millie?"

"I don't think so," Elizabeth said.

"Anyway," I said, "Sweetness has been staying here for a few days, till he finds his own place."

"I'm really your daddy's secret lover," Sweetness said. "I'm surprised he never told you about me."

• • •

"What if I don't want to leave?" Sweetness asked later that day.

"I guess I'd have to call the police."

"You'd do that?"

"If I had to."

An hour later, he was gone. For the first time in more than a week, I cooked my own dinner.

8

"Richard, I don't want you to take this personally . . ."

That was the way, after sixteen years, I learned I had lost my job. It happened two weeks after Sweetness left. "Downsizing" was the word my boss used. Murray Hall, a man I used to like, is now a man I want to strangle. I sit alone in my apartment, raging and fuming, brooding and mourning, plotting revenge. I write contemptuous letters that I do not send. I imagine myself making wild love with Murray Hall's wife on the sofa in Murray Hall's office. I imagine myself making loud love with Murray Hall's daughter on the deck of Murray Hall's yacht. I imagine myself spitting in Murray Hall's face. In the middle of March, six weeks after being fired, I still feel as broken and defeated as I have ever felt in my life.

• • •

"You know what they say in Russia? 'If a Russian steals, he's a thief. But if a Jew steals, he's a Jew.'"

One or two nights a week, since I lost my job, I've treated myself to dinner at a cheap Russian restaurant named Perestroika, on 86th Street between First and Second avenues. In this way I got to know the hostess well enough that, a couple of weeks ago, after the other customers had left, she sat down at my table and began to talk to me about being a Jew in Russia.

"Jews always to blame," Olga said. "If dog piss in street, Jew made dog piss. If cookie disappear from cookie jar, Jew stole cookie."

"I never stole anything," I said, "but I still was tossed out with the trash."

"Business is business," Olga said, sounding very American.

I said, "The guys who were caught in the insider trading scandals, they get paid to give lectures about business ethics. And people like me"—the anger surged up in my throat—

"people like me turn bitter and mean, worrying about money."

"Is better not to steal," Olga said.

I shrugged. "You know what's best of all?" I said. "Inheritance. That's what Malcolm Forbes always said: 'I owe my success to ability—spelled i-n-h-e-r-i-t-a-n-c-e.'"

"Who is Malcolm Fords?"

"A rich American. He's dead now."

At the window, a homeless man with bloodshot eyes and a reddish beard peered in at us.

"More tea?" Olga asked.

I looked at her. She is in her early thirties, blonde and stocky, with a peasant's build—broad shoulders, heavy breasts, heavy below the waist.

"Only if you'll join me," I said.

"I still have work."

"I'll wait."

On the walls in Perestroika, there are vivid paintings in the style of Russian folk art—villages with peasants fiddling or dancing, forests with ghostly owls in the trees, villages with geese and ducks in the street and foxes lurking in the shadows.

"You like my paintings?" Olga asked when she joined me.

She had brought us tea in glasses, Russian-style, with a cube of sugar and a little dish of red berry preserves.

"You painted these?" I asked.

"Who else?"

I suppose I stared—first at the paintings, then at Olga. Then I said, "They're wonderful. How'd you wind up here?"

"My uncle is cook."

"But you shouldn't be working in a restaurant."

"No?"

"You can paint."

"I have to eat," Olga said.

• • •

"Russia was disaster," Olga said. "Here we can breathe. We can live. We can work."

Almost every afternoon between three and four, as April brightens the city, I have tea with Olga at Perestroika. We sit at a little table for two beside the front window. If a customer comes in, usually a lone man or woman, Olga gets up to discharge her duties as hostess. Another émigré, a gloomy young man who looks like photos of Franz Kafka in his youth, serves the food.

"In old days," Olga said, "hard life in Russia make people mean and angry and always pushing. Push! Push! Push! . . . To buy bread, you stand in line three, four hours. To get telephone, you wait ten years. To get chicken, you need one American dollar on black market, and dollar costs thirty rubles.

"Here in America is different," Olga said. "Here if you do your best, everything OK. In Russia, you do your best, but maybe not OK.

"In Russia, Jews suffer more. In Russia, Jews always—how you say?—looking over shoulder. Here I not looking over shoulder. I know I am immigrant, but I no feel like immigrant. I feel like citizen."

In Russia she had a lover, Mischa, an astrophysicist whose political activities got him into trouble when Brezhnev was in charge. The government sent him to Tiksi in Siberia, on the arctic coast, to clean latrines at an army outpost. "Cleaning latrines—an astrophysicist!" Olga said. "Only in Russia!" Now Mischa was in Israel, married, with two little girls. But Olga wanted nothing to do with Israel.

"Too many Jews!" she said, laughing. "And all those Arabs! They'll be fighting five thousand years . . . Maybe ten thousand! . . . Give me U.S.A. I'm American now."

• • •

"Let's go out this weekend," I said to Olga. "Where do you want to go?"

"I love New York. I go anywhere."

"The Statue of Liberty?"

She'd seen it.

"Empire State Building?"

She'd seen it.

"Radio City?"

Olga shook her head.

"What haven't you seen that you want to see?"

"The Knicks."

I took her to see a Knicks game. Afterward, in the shadows near the Papaya King at Third Avenue and East 86th Street, we kissed for the first time. I asked her to come back to my apartment.

"Not yet," Olga said.

"All right."

"Maybe next time."

"Whatever you say."

"Let's have tea," Olga said. "Have you ever tasted Kissel Romanoff?"

• • •

This afternoon, as I sat with Olga at our table in Perestroika, a tap on the windowpane made me turn. Sweetness waved to me. I waved back, then motioned for him to come in.

He pulled over a chair and sat—the third person at a table for two.

"Richard, long time no see."

"How've you been?" I asked.

Olga motioned toward the waiter who looked like young Kafka.

"I get by," Sweetness said. "You?"

"Lost my job."

"No shit. What happened?"

"My boss decided to downsize."

The waiter brought each of us tea in a glass, a cube of sugar, a dish of berry preserves, and a plateful of honey-ginger cookies. Sweetness dipped his spoon into the red preserves and brought it toward his tea.

"No!" Olga cried. "*Never* stir berries into tea. First eat berries. Then drink tea . . . For contrast."

"My mistake," Sweetness said, grinning. "I didn't mean any offense."

He took a bite of berries, then a sip of tea.

"Delicious!"

Olga beamed at him.

"When did it happen?" Sweetness asked me.

"January."

"And you're still out of work?"

"Bad job market."

"Tell me about it."

"You?" I asked.

"I get by."

"No job yet?"

"This and that."

"Sweetness," I said, with the old irritation breaking into my voice. "What do you mean, *this and that*?"

"A little of this, a little of that . . . What do you think I mean?"

"You're too mysterious, Sweetness."

"You want the truth?" Sweetness said fiercely. "I do *shit*! A little of this shit, a little of that shit. Washing cars, washing dishes, hauling furniture, picking up trash—any shit the white man doesn't want to do, that's what I do, Richard."

"OK, OK," I said. "I'm sorry."

We looked grudgingly at one another.

"Sweetness," Olga said suddenly, "can I paint you?"

• • •

We met at Perestroika at seven this morning—the second Sunday in May. Olga sat Sweetness alone at the little table by the window, with a mild light coming in on him. She set up her easel a few yards away. She did a few quick sketches in pencil, asking Sweetness to sit in various positions.

For the painting, Olga chose a position with Sweetness sitting sideways at the table, leaning comfortably back in his chair, his legs extended, the fingertips of his left hand resting lightly on his left thigh. She sketched his figure on the canvas in a few quick strokes. Then she began to add color.

"Can I look?" Sweetness asked.

"No," Olga said.

"When?"

"Maybe when is finished. Maybe never."

I stood behind Olga, watching. The painting was done in a style that differed greatly from the style of the Russian folk art she'd painted for the restaurant. It was austere, like the paintings of mournful clowns Picasso had done in his blue period. Only instead of being a study in blue, the painting was a study in brown. The brown figure stretched out in his brown chair beside a brown table, with his brown fingertips resting on his brown trousers, and a brown wall behind him, and brown light coming in through the window.

"Right. Maybe never," Sweetness said quietly. After a moment he added, "Have you ever thought about 1619?"

Olga, concentrating on the tip of her paintbrush, said nothing.

"Sixteen nineteen?" I asked.

"Sixteen nineteen," Sweetness said, "was the year they brought the first shipload of slaves to Virginia. Think of that first slave ship, cutting through the water, coming closer and closer to Virginia with its cargo. And don't you just want to scream—*No! Stop! Go back!* But the ship doesn't go back, and here we are—"

Suddenly Olga stepped back from the canvas. "Finished!" she piped up. "Now you can look."

Sweetness looked.

"What do you call it?" he asked.

"American Rainbow," Olga said.

9

"I don't understand," Sweetness said, "how a white man could be out of work for four months."

"It's easy," I said.

"Don't you have connections?"

"My connections haven't connected."

We were walking on the promenade alongside the East River, north toward the Triborough Bridge, in the middle of the afternoon on a bright day early in June, shortly after Olga had painted Sweetness's portrait. Olga was working in the restaurant. The promenade was crowded with joggers in their outfits—silver and orange, silver and blue, silver and black. From the basketball courts behind them came the cries of the players, the thud of the bouncing ball.

"You think you'll marry her?" Sweetness asked.

"We've only known one another a couple of months."

"I like her," Sweetness said.

"Me, too."

"So? You expect someone better to come along?"

I looked at the bridge glittering in the distance.

"You think she'd say yes?" I asked.

"Why shouldn't she?"

"Why should she?"

"You're a decent guy, Richard."

"A decent guy without a job. Why should she?"

"So get a job."

"Sweetness, I'm trying!"

"White folks," Sweetness muttered.

"What's that supposed to mean?"

"You white folks," Sweetness said, "you don't know what it means to try."

"That's *bullshit*, Sweetness."

"Is it?"

"I think so."

We walked on.

"Sweetness," I said, "I don't see *you* trying so hard. You ever had a job you stayed on more than two months? Tell me that."

"Go fuck yourself, Richard. I never had a job I could *stand* more than two months."

"You think only black people hate their jobs?"

"I never said that."

"So? What do you think, Sweetness?"

"What I think, Richard, is that in this country, black people thank their lucky stars if they get a job eating shit. *Oh, thank you, Lord! Thank you! Thank you! . . . Thank you for giving me this wonderful job eating shit!*"

I laughed.

"You think that's funny?" Sweetness asked.

"Yes."

"Ho, ho, ho! Maybe I'll go to work writing comedy."

"Sweetness," I said, "why don't you just go find yourself an ordinary, lousy job . . . Join the world. Isn't it time?"

"Oh, yes, it's time. It surely must be time."

"So? Why don't you?"

"Why don't *you*, Richard. Why don't you go find yourself an ordinary, lousy job?"

We turned and headed south, toward the 59th Street Bridge. Gulls swooped over the water sparkling in the sun. A big ferry crowded with people, circling Manhattan, came toward us up the river.

"Richard," Sweetness said, "I've got a proposition for you."

"Oh?"

"A business proposition."

"I can't wait."

"You want to listen?"

"I'm listening."

"We could go into business together."

"What business?"

"All you have to do is lend me your apartment."

"And then? What's the business?"

"Richard, you give me your apartment during the day, I put a girl in there, and then—that's the business."

"Are you crazy, Sweetness?"

"Do I sound crazy?"

"You want me to turn my apartment into a brothel?"

"A place of adult entertainment, Richard."

"That's not my trade."

"Turning a trick isn't rocket science, Richard. Anyway, I'll run the business. You just furnish the facility."

"Sweetness, this is crazy. I'm a Jewish guy with a mother named Sadie. I can't do something like this."

"Richard, you're a Jewish guy who's been out of work nearly four months. You're a Jewish guy with a kid in college. You know how much *money* we could make?"

"We'd wind up in jail."

"We could make a *fortune*, Richard."

I did not reply. The wind raised whitecaps on the water. A car honked in the driveway near the mayor's mansion.

"We're talking Upper East Side, Richard. You know what kind of clientele we could have? In that location, with that apartment? It's a gold mine."

"Sweetness, I'm no saint, but . . ."

"But what, Richard?"

"I've always made an honest living."

"Selling your brains?"

"What else do I have to sell, Sweetness? Tell me that. What else do you imagine a man like me could possibly sell?"

10

"I think I'll have more of that cake," Mom said, sitting opposite me at the table near the window where I usually sit with Olga. "What's it called?"

"St. Basil chocolate cake," I said. "After a famous cathedral in Red Square. Or what used to be Red Square."

The smell of tea hung in the air. Olga was puttering around behind the service counter with its Russian cakes and big shiny samovars.

"Olga," Mom called, "could I have more St. Basil?"

"You'll get fat," Olga said.

"I'm already fat," Mom said.

Olga brought Mom more cake.

"No more for you," Olga said to me.

"It's very good," Mom said to Olga.

"Thank you," Olga said. "You see on my hips I eat too much St. Basil."

"Your hips are perfect," I said, patting her.

Olga blushed. "American men awful liars," she said to Mom. "Just like Russian men. I have terrible big hips from Russian peasant heritage and too much cake." She tapped me gently on my bald spot. "He tells beautiful lies but I see through him."

• • •

"Richard, I shouldn't have asked you. It was crazy."

"You shocked me, Sweetness. I'll give you that."

"I shocked myself. God knows what I'd've done if you'd said yes."

On a bright afternoon late in June, we were strolling west on East 86th Street, toward Central Park. We crossed Park Avenue. Down the green middle, beneath the grand apartment buildings, flowers made vivid splashes of color—red and pink, violet and gold—shimmering in the sun.

"It really would've been a gold mine," Sweetness said.

"Sweetness, let's drop it."

"Just dreaming."

"There's something I want to tell you, Sweetness."

"What's that?"

"Olga and I might leave New York."

"Oh? Where to?"

"Florida. We're thinking of opening a restaurant."

"Why Florida?"

"It's a place where New York Jews retire."

"So you'll run a restaurant for the old folks?"

"That's the idea. A Russian restaurant might do pretty well. We thought we'd call it The Old Country."

"What about your mom and dad?"

"They already have friends down there, they're ready to move, and I'll be nearby if they need me."

"Sounds like you've got it all figured out," Sweetness said.

I said, "We're not exactly thriving in New York. You know that."

"Neither am I."

"So leave. You're not a slave."

"I'll come with you, Richard. You need a dishwasher?"

"Is that what you really want, Sweetness?"

He ignored my question. We crossed 86th Street and headed back, toward the East River.

I said, "People like me are leaving New York, Sweetness. That's no secret. We've been running away for years."

"I thought you were different."

"I'm not different."

"You think you can hide?"

"We can try."

"Where am I supposed to hide, Richard?"

"That's your problem."

At the corner of Lexington and 86th Street, we paused. A huge advertisement—EAT PERUVIAN STYLE BARBECUE CHICKEN—was painted in red letters on a building across the street.

"Richard, I've got a confession to make."

"What's that?"

"I've been meaning to ask you for money."

"Why me?"

"I figured you might say yes."

"Why should I? You're not my son. You're not my brother."

"I still figured you might say yes."

"So ask."

"Richard, could you give me some money?"

"For what?"

Sweetness hesitated, looking up at the advertisement. "Here's where I was figuring I'd lie to you, Richard."

"Oh?"

"I was figuring I'd tell you I needed money because my mama was sick, and couldn't pay her medical bills. You'd have believed that, wouldn't you?"

"Probably."

"Or I thought maybe I'd tell you I needed money because my sister had got herself pregnant, and didn't have money for an abortion. Would you have believed that, Richard?"

"Probably."

"How about if I'd said that my brother had got himself messed up with drugs, was just now getting out of jail, and needed help till he found a job? . . . Would you have believed that, Richard?"

"I suppose so."

"So here's my problem. Is there *anything* I could have said that you wouldn't have believed?"

"Don't play games with me, Sweetness."

"Don't you see, Richard? It seems like I can make up any kind of crap about my family, and you'd believe it. Doesn't that bother you?"

"No, Sweetness, it doesn't."

"Well, it bothers me."

"It's what I see all the time in the newspapers. It's what I see all the time on TV. What do you want me to do, Sweetness? Walk through life with my eyes closed?"

"That's not *my* family you're seeing."

"It could be, couldn't it? How am I supposed to know it's not your family? How many kids did your mom have?"

"Seven."

"Seven. So you tell me, Sweetness: How am I supposed to know it's not your family?"

"Because you know *me*. You know my mother."

"That doesn't mean I figure that nothing terrible could ever happen in your family. Give me a break, Sweetness."

"Richard, will you give me some money?"

"For what, Sweetness?"

"My mom's sick. She needs help with her bills."

"What about Medicaid?"

"It's not the bills she needs help with."

"So what is it?"

"Her TV broke. She needs a new TV."

"You're asking me for money to buy your mom a TV?"

"She's *old*, Richard. All she does is watch TV."

We had stopped on the corner of Third Avenue. Both of us were breathing heavily. We glared at one another.

"How much do you need, Sweetness?"

"The kids want to get her a really good TV."

"How much?"

"We've all pitched in. But we still need a hundred dollars more."

"I'll lend it to you."

"You will?"

"I'll lend it to you right now so you can buy your mom a new TV. But you've got to pay it back to me. You and your brothers and sisters."

"Oh, Richard, you're great!"

"I'm not great."

"You'll have that money back within a month. I swear!"

• • •

Sitting in Perestroika with his shoulders hunched and a gloomy expression on his face, Sweetness looked uncomfortable. He told me that he had a confession to make. Then he told me that the hundred dollars he'd borrowed wasn't really for his mom.

"Sweetness, I believed you!"

"You really thought that seven of us couldn't come up with an extra hundred dollars?" Sweetness asked.

"I guess I'm gullible."

"It's for me, Richard."

I looked at him.

"I've been thinking about what you said. About New York not working for you anymore."

"Yes?"

"I'm saving up, Richard. I'm saving up to move out of New York."

• • •

I didn't invite Sweetness to the wedding. Olga and I had a fight about it.

"He's your friend, isn't he?" she said.

"No," I said, "he's *not* my friend."

"So what is he?"

"He's"—I hated to say it, but I took a deep breath and went on—"he's just a guy whose mother worked for my mother."

• • •

On the first Sunday in August, forty people jammed into

my apartment for the wedding ceremony. Afterward, everyone stood around talking, drinking, and eating the Russian hors d'oeuvres that Olga's uncle had prepared. There was herring with onions and potatoes, smoked salmon, stuffed eggs with red and black caviar. My mother and father joined us, sitting side by side near the door to the tiny terrace, eating eggplant dip on pumpernickel, smiling at friends they knew and nodding at those they didn't.

When the doorbell rang, I wondered who had come late.

Sweetness, in white sneakers, yellow pants, and a black T-shirt. We faced one another at the door.

"Sorry to interrupt," he said. "Could I see you, just for a minute?"

"You're seeing me," I said.

"I mean, could I see you *alone*?" he said.

We went into the bedroom. Coats were heaped on the double bed.

"Richard," Sweetness said, "I feel bad that you didn't invite me."

"Yes, well—we couldn't invite everyone."

"I thought I was special."

"Sweetness, it's a small apartment."

Sweetness said, "I guess I should have known." He waited for me to say something, but I just looked at him. At last he said, with an unhappy expression on his face, "Richard, I didn't come here to fight. I came to clear the air. What I want to say is, this past year, I've been out of line."

"How so?"

"You see, Richard, I thought—I convinced myself—that there was some kind of special connection between us. But there wasn't. There *isn't*. I see that now."

He paused again, but I still didn't have anything to say.

"Everything we went through together, Richard, I'm not sure either one of us really understood it. It was as if I thought you owed me something, some way. And you don't. You really don't. I see that now."

"But you didn't see it before?"

"Richard, you have to realize it was a strange year for me. I went crazy—in a quiet way. It's as if I had a fever. But it's over now."

"Sweetness," I said, "this past year, it's as if you just kept *pushing* me. Just kept pushing and pushing, to see how far I would bend, or whether I would break."

"That's exactly right."

"But I couldn't figure out what you were pushing *for*, Sweetness."

"Neither could I, Richard. It was like two blind people in some stumbling dance, or two deaf people trying to sing a duet. Anyway, it's over now. It's *over.*"

Suddenly, out of nowhere, I saw something change in his face, and before I could make a move to stop him, he pushed me, hard, and then pushed me twice more, pushed me backwards across the bedroom floor, saying, "It's over, it's over, it's over!"

I finally lifted my arms to defend myself, but he stopped. We stood a foot apart, glaring at one another, breathing out loud.

"It's *over*, Richard," Sweetness said with great finality, and he turned away from me, opened the door to my closet, and began examining my suits.

"For my new life, I need a new suit," he said, taking out a charcoal-gray pinstripe, $795 from Brooks Brothers, and folding it over his forearm.

"And this—this looks like it might have some resale value." He picked up my videotape camera, examined it with mock admiration, and, like a bank robber making his exit in a movie, began to back away from me, toward the bedroom door.

"I hope you won't make a fuss, Richard. Of course, you

have all those guests outside. I suppose they'll stop me if you holler. Or the doorman—he might stop me if you call down. But I'm going to take a chance—"

In mid-sentence his attention was diverted; he had seen the glove autographed by Joe DiMaggio, on top of the TV in my bedroom.

"Now this"—he picked up the glove, examined the autograph, and nodded—"this is something I just can't leave behind." With my best suit folded over his left arm, my videotape camera in his left hand, and the glove autographed by Joe DiMaggio in his right hand, he bowed gravely in my direction. "As I was saying, Richard, I'm going to take a chance that, instead of spoiling your wedding party, you're going to let me walk right out of here."

He was right: I let him walk out of my apartment. But as soon as he was gone, I buzzed the doorman, told him that a man who had stolen a suit, a videocamera, and a baseball glove was on his way down, and asked the doorman to stop him.

"Stop him?" the doorman said. "How?"

11

And so we moved to Florida: Mom and Dad, Olga, Olga's uncle, and me. In Delray we opened our restaurant, The Old Country. After four expensive years studying art history, Elizabeth has decided to go to law school. And Sweetness? Sweetness has disappeared. God knows if any of us will ever see him again.

• • •

In bed one night, Olga asked me why I'm so angry.

"Angry?" I said. "Who's angry?"

• • •

A terrible scream woke me.

"Richard, Richard, wake up!" Olga said, shaking me by the shoulders. "What's wrong?"

I shook my head, trying to clear it. The dream came back to me.

"I dreamed that I was running . . . running on a beach somewhere, in the evening. And somebody was running after me, with a sword, and gaining ground. And then—" I shook my head, but the dream stayed with me.

". . . and then the beach disappeared and I was in New York, at the Plaza Hotel, getting my shoes shined. And after I got my shoes shined, I went to the barber's shop, to get a shave. And Sweetness was the barber at the Plaza Hotel. He smiled at me while he sharpened the razor."

I fell asleep again. This time I dreamed that I woke up at dawn in New York. All alone, I went for a walk. I was the last white man in New York. The streets were empty. I turned a corner and stood facing the Statue of Liberty, across the water. Suspended from the torch a man was hanging with a rope around his neck and his arms tied behind his back. His feet also were tied. The man twisted in the wind. A sheet was wrapped tightly around him, from head to toe.

I woke up with a scream.

"Oh, Richard, Richard!"

On her knees, Olga shook me.

"Olga?"

"Richard, wake up!"

"Oh, Olga, I had another dream! I saw a man hanging!"

"Who?"

"I couldn't tell. It might have been anyone."

"Anyone?"

"He was wrapped in a sheet. He was hanging from the Statue of Liberty."

"The Statue of Liberty?"

"His hands were tied behind his back. His feet were bound."

"Oh, Richard!"

"He was twisting."

"Richard!"

"He could have been anyone."

"Oh, Richard! Richard! Richard!" Olga sobbed. "America is wonderful country. Why you have bad dreams?"

Points of Light

I. Sick of New York

"I'm sick of New York," Dora Weiss said, plucking a thread off the sleeve of the mud-brown sweater she was wearing even though it was only the first week of October. Lately she'd been chilly all the time. She also lost her balance, she forgot where she was going, she got headaches, she couldn't read for more than five minutes, her ankles were swollen, and her knees ached. "It's just too much for me," she said. "I want to sit in the sun."

"You're not sick of New York, Dora. You're sick of life," Sidney Pollokoff said.

"You wouldn't move, would you?" Ruth Cohn asked. "What about Ben?"

"Ben doesn't care where he dies," Dora said. "They have nursing homes in Florida. Where's the law that says a Jew has to die in Queens?"

"That's right," Lucille Rosenberg said. "You can die in Arizona. You can die in California."

"I wouldn't want to be buried there," Ruth Cohn said.

"What difference would it make?" Sam Dyer said.

"How would the children visit my grave?" Ruth said.

"You want your children to visit a pile of dirt?" Dora said. "Grow up, Ruth."

"For myself," Sam Dyer said, "I can do without any company, thank you. Let the kids visit one another, and leave me to rest in peace."

Even before she took their order, their waitress had brought them a bowl of pickles and a big bowl of creamy coleslaw. Then she brought their drinks—seltzer, ginger ale, Dr. Brown's famous celery soda, called Cel-Ray.

"There's nothing like Cel-Ray," Sam Dyer said. "I'd give up sex before I gave up Cel-Ray."

"Sam!" Ruth Dyer said.

"New York can sink into the ocean, as far as the rest of the country cares," Dora said. "It's the city Americans love to hate."

"Not just Americans," Sam Dyer said. "It's the city New Yorkers love to hate. But we wouldn't live anywhere else."

"Speak for yourself, Sam," Lucille Rosenberg said. "I'd get out in a second, except my children live here. That's all that holds me."

The year was 1995, and most of Dora's friends had been growing more cynical about the city for the past thirty years. Not Dora, however. Dora had never turned against New York.

"It's a cesspool," Ruth Cohn said.

"A giant rotting in its own waste," Sam Dyer said.

"It's still a great city," Dora said.

"Dora, open your eyes," Sidney Pollokoff said. "Take a walk. Look around. *Look.*"

"Calcutta," Ruth Cohn said. "They say it's just like Calcutta."

"A Third World city."

"A disaster."

Once a week, Dora and Ben Weiss met old friends for lunch at the Lucky Star Delicatessen on Jewel Avenue in Queens. Eating foods their doctors had forbidden, drinking seltzer and Dr. Brown's Cel-Ray, savoring the odors of pastrami and corned beef, consuming huge quantities of pickles and coleslaw, they filled the room with laughter. It was all an endgame, Dora thought, Jewish endgame. They complained about their children, *kvelled* about their grandchildren, compared their latest ailments, and reviewed the state of local, national, and world affairs.

"A fabulous invalid," Ruth Cohn said.

"That's Broadway," Dora said. "They call Broadway 'the fabulous invalid.'"

"Really? I thought it was New York. 'New York—the fabulous invalid.' I thought I heard that somewhere."

"It may be an invalid," Sidney Pollokoff said, "but it's not so fabulous. Not these days."

The waitress brought their sandwiches—salami, pastrami, corned beef, turkey, all on fresh rye bread. The meaty aroma stopped the conversation for a moment. Spicy mustard in a glass jar, with a tiny spoon sticking out, was passed from hand to hand.

"Did you read about Laurence Olivier and Danny Kaye?" Fred Kleiman said. "Now tell me—was that the odd couple?"

"Did Dan Rather get a hairpiece, or what?" Ruth Cohn asked.

"I like Tom Brokaw's hair," Betsy Abramowicz said. "And that dimple on his chin. He's adorable!"

"And those twinkly blue eyes!" Dora said mockingly. "Betsy, really! Who cares if he's adorable?"

"Make fun of me if you want, but I like to look at a man who's nice to look at," Betsy Abramowicz said. "Tom Brokaw is definitely a cutie-pie."

"Dora, how's Alan?" Ruth Cohn asked in a low voice, leaning across the table toward Dora and looking at her with a mournful expression.

Dora shrugged with a weary expression on her face. Alan's son, her fourteen-year-old grandson Carl, had died of leukemia the year before.

"Alan?" Dora said. "He lost his son. You don't get over that so fast."

"You *never* get over it," said Lucille Rosenberg, whose son had jumped off a roof at Harvard in 1967. "Life goes on, but you never get over it."

"Life is wreckage in the end," Sidney Pollokoff said. "Don't let anybody tell you different."

Dora said, "What I'd really like is to creep into a corner, curl up, and disappear. That's what God would have arranged if She'd had any sense."

"You know what my mother told me before she died?" Ruth Cohn said. "She had a cancer that had spread everywhere—her bones, her colon, her liver. This was in 1957. She was thin like a sparrow. And one day we were talking, and the one thing she regretted, she told me, was that she hadn't eaten more ice cream. Strawberry ice cream—that was her favorite." Tears welled out of Ruth Cohn's eyes: "Oh, how silly! I made myself cry."

"Just curl up in a corner," Ethel Pollokoff said softly. "Yes, that's what everyone wants."

"Alan hasn't found a new job?" Betsy Abramowicz asked.

Dora sighed. "Who wants a music teacher these days? We told him to learn something practical, but no! He knew better."

"It's not his fault," Lou Cohn said. "Times are tough."

"I don't think times are tough," Sam Dyer said. "It's not 1932."

"What bothers me is the ambitions these young people saddle themselves with," Ethel Pollokoff said. "They aim too high."

"What's too high?" Dora asked. "Alan just wants to teach music in some high school without knives. Is that too much to ask?"

Ruth Cohn held up a fork with a french fry on one end of it. "My cousin's son Herman, he looked for a job for nine months, and when he found one, you know where it was? . . . Oklahoma!"

"Oklahoma!" the New Yorkers exclaimed simultaneously.

"Oklahoma!" Ruth Cohn repeated. "Not even in Tulsa . . . *Near* Tulsa, that's what he told me . . . A little town near Tulsa."

"What does he do?" Dora asked.

"He's a—whattaya call it?—a communications specialist." Ruth looked at her husband. "Isn't that it, Lou?"

"He communicates," Lou Cohn said.

"He had to go to Oklahoma to communicate?" Sidney Pollokoff asked.

"A little town near Tulsa," Sam Dyer said, shaking his head. "And his grandfather died in Auschwitz . . . Can you believe it?"

"My mother liked strawberry ice cream," Ethel Pollokoff said, "but what she really loved were those raspberry-cream chocolates. Remember those? I haven't had one in twenty years."

"You can't tell me Tom Brokaw isn't cute," Betsy Abramowicz said.

"As soon as I can work out the details, I'm moving," Dora said. "What's wrong with Delray? They have nursing homes. They have sunshine. They have cemeteries. What else do you need at our age?"

"A new bladder," Sam Dyer said, and everyone laughed.

"Did you hear the latest New York horror story?" Sidney Pollokoff asked.

"Which one?" Dora said wearily, dipping her head to take a sip of Cel-Ray.

"The one about the fourteen-year-old mother who killed her six-day-old son, and then chopped up the body and fed the pieces to the dog."

"Give me a break, Sidney," Dora said. "I told you I'm sick of New York."

"There's no way Tom Brokaw's dumb," Ruth Cohn said. "He might not be another Eric Sevareid, but there's no way he's dumb."

Fred Kleiman said, "I read that they've found a gene, a single gene, that's involved in half of all human cancers."

"Amazing," Lucille Rosenberg said.

"Near Tulsa?" Sam Dyer said, looking at Dora with a baffled expression on his face. "How can anybody live near Tulsa?"

II. New York Party

Irma, sometimes I hate this city. I think of you back there in Tulsa, eating ribs at Syzmanski's or mud pie at McDermott's, or driving over to Muskogee for the air show, or hanging around with the gang at the Blue Oyster, and I'm jealous. I really am. I think maybe my kid sister is having more fun than her brother in the big city.

You don't believe me? Let me tell you about this party I went to last Saturday night. It was a typical New York party, which means the first person I meet is a man from California. He spends about ten minutes telling me how New York freaks him out, with his wife standing there nodding beside him.

"I'm scared to death," the wife says. "These people on the streets—they scare me."

A man in a scarlet turtleneck eases into our group. People do that in New York the same way they do it in Tulsa. "I'm bicoastal myself," the man in the scarlet turtleneck says, "but I'll be out in L. A. starting next month. They're shooting my screenplay about Fanny Fisher. Remember her?"

"Not really," the man from California says.

"Oh, Larry, you remember!" the man's wife says, jabbing him in the side with her elbow. "The shower curtain heiress who murdered her tennis pro in some sleazy motel room the night before the Super Bowl . . . Cut off his tongue and his prick."

"No wonder I forgot," the man from California says.

"New York is still the place that scares me most," the

woman from California says. "Why, in the paper just this morning, there was a story about a man who hacked his wife to death with a butcher's knife because she burned the lasagna, and a story about a homeless woman who set herself on fire at the bus terminal, and a story about a retarded man who suffocated to death in a locked closet while his sister partied in the next room, and a story"—she turns toward her husband—"Larry, what was that really awful story?"

"The baby," Larry says.

"Right!" the woman says. "A woman pretended to be asleep while her boyfriend beat their two-year-old daughter to death, because the kid urinated on him."

"Good old New York," the man from California says. "That's just business as usual in New York."

"Stuff like that happens all the time," the man in the scarlet turtleneck says.

"It doesn't happen in Tulsa," I say.

Somewhere in the middle of all this, a woman in black had come into the group, and also an elderly couple. "Tulsa!" the old woman says. "Did you say Tulsa?"

"You have something against Tulsa?" I ask.

"Oh, no!" the woman says. She has white hair and bright eyes, and her hands fly every which way when she talks. "It's just that we were having lunch yesterday with a friend who knows somebody who lives in Tulsa."

"Near Tulsa," the old man says.

"Near Tulsa," the woman says. "He's a communications specialist living near Tulsa. Herman Cohn. Would you happen to know a young man named Herman Cohn?"

Honest to God, Irma, she asked me if I would happen to know a young man named Herman Cohn.

"No, ma'am," I say. "Till I came to New York, I never knew anyone of the Hebrew persuasion."

She didn't say anything to that, but her face turned red, and I thought maybe I'd said something wrong. So I stuck out my hand and said, "My name's Hoover. Hoover Smith."

She shakes my hand and says, "Dora Weiss. And this is my husband, Ben."

I shake hands with the old guy, and then he leans toward me with his left hand cupped to his ear and says, "Homer? Did you say Homer?"

"Hoover," I say. "H, double O, V, E, R. My daddy named me after his hero."

"Who would that be?" the old lady says.

Well, Irma, you should have seen their faces when I told them! You can bet they never met anyone named after J. Edgar Hoover.

Meanwhile, the group around us was still telling their New York horror stories.

"What really bothers me," the woman in black says, "is that they're cutting back on services right and left, but they spend a fortune on those AIDS babies."

"They ought to rename the city's government," the man from California says. "Call it 'Thieves R Us.'"

"At least we've got an honest mayor now," the woman in black says.

"The mayor's a little Napoleon," the woman named Dora says.

"I think the blacks are the worst," the woman from California says.

"Oh, pooh," her husband says. "The blacks haven't stolen any more than the Irish or the Italians stole, when they ran the city."

"Welcome to the Big Apple," Dora says, smiling at me.

"White or black," the man from California says, "it's plunder, plunder, plunder!"

The woman in black says, "What bugs me is the money we spend on those AIDS babies. And it's all wasted! I mean—they die anyway."

The old man with the woman named Dora was humming softly: "'New York, New York, it's a wonderful town!'"

"We ought to pay those black mothers to kill those AIDS babies," the woman in black says. "That's what a sane country would do. Just pay them to kill those babies."

Nobody said a word, but the old lady looked so red I thought she'd have a stroke. Finally she says, "Congratulations! You've just reinvented the Nazi extermination program for defective children."

"It's something to think about," the woman in black says.

Honest to God, Irma, that's what the woman said, and that's what New York is like. One thing's for sure—I've never heard talk like the talk I hear in this city. Someday I'll put it all in a book. I hear America singing—ha! You should hear New York talking. Give my regards to the gang at the Blue Oyster. And watch out for the sun at the air show. I know how hot it gets.

III. At the Deli

"The man could have made an effort," Dora said, holding a bite of coleslaw on a fork an inch from her lips. "He could have pretended to believe he could run the city, instead of whining about all the problems he inherited."

"It's the truth," Ethel Pollokoff said. "He did inherit problems."

"You have to stand up to the unions," Sidney Pollokoff said. "The only way to govern the city is to stand up to the unions. At least our current mayor understands that."

"Oh, Sidney!" Dora said. "Do you really think it's so simple? What am I, the last liberal in America, surrounded by my conservative friends who think the world would be a better place if all the liberals were dead?"

"The unions have bled this city dry," Sidney said, "and our mayors just keep caving in. And why not? They know the tune, and they know that a mayor's job is to dance to it."

Like the chorus in a Greek tragedy, Dora and her friends watched the action in their afflicted city, debated guilt and innocence, lamented lost glories, pitied the victims, raged against malefactors, deplored injustices, condemned indiscretions, regretted follies, mocked absurdities, quivered with rage, trembled with fear, wept and wailed, gnashed their teeth, tore their garments, pulled at their hair, and shook their tiny fists at the indifferent sky.

"The city's always been a cesspool," Ethel Pollokoff said. "What's new about that?"

"Look at Tammany Hall," Sidney Pollokoff said.

"Tammany got things done," Ben Weiss said. "It wasn't all bad."

"What good did Tammany do?" Betsy Abramowicz asked. "I never heard anybody say anything good about Tammany."

"You never read any history," Dora said with a cutting look that everyone pretended not to see. Betsy Abramowicz, whose son the world-class cardiologist made five hundred thousand dollars a year at Mount Sinai, was rumored not to have read a book since 1945.

"Pickles, please," Fred Kleiman said, and Ethel Pollokoff passed him the pickles.

"Tammany did plenty," Dora said. "When immigrants needed help finding a job or a place to live, or finding food, or filling out citizenship papers, it was Tammany that helped."

"All it asked in exchange was your vote," Sidney Pollokoff said. "Forever."

"That's true," Dora admitted.

"The trouble with Tammany," Sam Dyer said, "was that it wanted poor people to stay poor. It handed out Christmas turkey, but it wanted people to need those turkeys every year. The grateful poor—that's what Tammany depended on."

"Plus all the contracts it could hand out," Sidney Pollokoff said. "Christmas turkeys for the poor, jobs for the party hacks, contracts for business, and payoffs for the politicians."

"It's still that way," Fred Kleiman said mournfully.

"In the old days this stuff outraged you," Dora said to Sidney, teasing him. "That was before you discovered how much you admire rich people."

"That was before I discovered how little I admire reformers," Sidney replied. "The good-government types never accomplished anything—Jimmy Walker was right about that . . . 'A reformer,' Jimmy Walker said, 'is a guy who rides through a sewer in a glass-bottomed boat.'"

"I remember Walker," Sam Dyer said. "What a character! With his spats, and his derbies, and his fancy jackets! And his mistress—what was her name?—Betty something."

"A showgirl," Ben Weiss said. "The mayor's mistress was a showgirl."

"Remember the Central Park Casino?" Sam Dyer said. "Walker spent more time in the Central Park Casino than he did in city hall. Judge Seabury nailed him."

"I remember that," Dora said. "I was just a little girl, but I remember Seabury's hearings."

"They called it the Tin Box Parade," Sam Dyer said. "One of those Tammany hacks was trying to explain to Seabury how he'd managed to save so much money on such a small salary. And he said he'd saved the money in a box at home, a little tin box."

"And they had a parade of witnesses," Dora said, "each one more crooked than the last, and they called it the Tin Box Parade."

"And Walker resigned," Ben Weiss said. "Sailed off to Europe with his mistress."

"That's when we got La Guardia," Ethel Pollokoff said. "After Walker." She looked at her husband. "Now, Sidney, you may hate reformers, but you can't tell us you hated La Guardia."

"La Guardia was a special case," Fred Kleiman said. "With La Guardia, we really did have good government. More or less."

"But he wasn't a Goo-Goo," Sidney Pollokoff said. "La Guardia was *not* a Goo-Goo."

"What's a Goo-Goo?" Ruth Cohn asked.

"It's what professional politicians call the good-government types," Sam Dyer said. "Goo-Goos."

"I'm a Goo-Goo and proud of it," Dora said. "What's wrong with good government?"

"Nothing, but where do you find it?" Sidney Pollokoff said. "Where's the market where you can go and buy good government? Who do you pay, and how much? . . . The best you can do is buy less government. That way at least there's less of your money going down the drain."

"You need voters who care," Dora said.

"Bull!" Sidney Pollokoff said. "Voters who care wouldn't make a bit of difference."

"You know what voters want?" Fred Kleiman said. "Something for nothing—that's all. They want efficient government, they want honest government, they want services, they want benefits, but they don't want to pay a penny for any of it. That's what voters want—something for nothing. It's human nature."

"That's true," Dora said. "The voters and the politicians are just two sides of a coin. Lazy voters and lousy politicians."

"I miss Ed Koch," Betsy Abramowicz said.

Ben Weiss made a sound as if he were choking.

"He shot off his mouth," Dora said. "I don't think he deserves any medal for that."

"He told the truth," Sidney Pollokoff said.

"This city can't stand too much truth," Sam Dyer said. "What New Yorkers want is a mayor who tells soothing lies."

"Ed Koch helped tear the city apart," Dora said. "We need a mayor who can heal wounds. Not one who pours in salt."

"The hell with healing wounds!" Sidney Pollokoff said. "What we need is a mayor who gets tough."

"Oh, Sidney!" Dora said.

"It's true," Sidney said. "What we need is a mayor who gets tough with the unions, tough with the West Side liberals, and tough with the punks running loose in the streets. Crack down on the punks and the beggars and the welfare cheats— that's what I say. Give us streets we can walk on. Then the wounds will heal themselves!"

"Oh, Sidney!" Dora said, shaking her head. "You sound like the people you used to hate. When did you get so angry?"

• • •

"Sidney has moved to the right of Mussolini," Dora said that night, lying in bed with a book on her lap and her head propped on three pillows. "I almost threw my sandwich at him."

Ben Weiss was sitting on the edge of his bed, clipping his toenails.

"I remember when he was a liberal," Ben said.

"I remember when he was a *Marxist*," Dora said. "In 1936 he lived in a basement apartment on East 4th Street, and every two minutes he'd jump up, run over to his rickety bookcase, and read you a paragraph of Marx, or Engels, or Trotsky, or Emma Goldman, or Henry George, or Rosa Luxemburg."

Clip! Clip! "That was a long time ago," Ben said.

"You should have seen him!" Dora said. "He had a chin

with a dimple like Kirk Douglas, a full head of curly black hair, and eyes that *blazed*—they just blazed. And smart! Oh, Lord, was he smart!"

"So how did he wind up to the right of Mussolini?"

Dora sighed. "My crowd argued about everything, but there's one thing we all agreed on: In a smart group, Sidney was the smartest. So when I hear him now—it shakes me." Dora looked at her husband, who was still sitting on the edge of his bed, with his back to her, in white-and-blue striped pajamas. "As smart as Sidney is," she said, "I can imagine that I'm wrong about everything, and he's right about everything. Isn't that amazing?"

Clip! . . . Clip! . . . Clip!

"You remember that kid we met at the party?" Ben Weiss said. "From Tulsa."

"What about him?"

"He told me he doesn't understand New York," Ben said. "He told me he doesn't understand the way people talk here."

"What about the way people talk here?"

"That woman from Brooklyn—the one who wants to kill the AIDS babies. She shocked him."

"She shocked *me*," Dora said.

"It's just talk."

"It's not just talk. She meant it."

"It's just talk. You know how people talk in New York."

"I'm sick of it, Ben. It scares me."

IV. The Galaxy

"Suspended?" Ruth Cohn said.

"He's lucky they didn't expel him," Dora said. "The brat!"

"Poor Dora!" Sidney Pollokoff said. "It's as if Eleanor Roosevelt discovered that her grandson voted for Ronald Reagan."

"Sidney," Dora said, "you can say what you want about

George McGovern, but I'll give you a smack you'll never forget if you start making cracks about Eleanor Roosevelt."

"Saint Eleanor!" Sidney said. "What's the catechism? 'Better to light a candle than to curse the darkness.'"

Dora took a pickle out of the bowl in the middle of the table and flung it at Sidney. It hit him on the shoulder. "Dora!" Sidney cried. "Resorting to violence?"

"Why don't we change the subject?" Lucille Rosenberg said.

"If Dora hadn't jumped all over me, I was going to congratulate her," Sidney Pollokoff said. "I think her grandson has acted admirably. What I especially like is his sense of humor. Did you see that line the *Times* quoted? . . . 'We just picked up some trash off the green to restore pride and sparkle to the college we love so much.'"

"Sidney, don't torture me," Dora said.

"If the college administration had any guts," Sidney said, "it would have torn down those shacks itself. Taught those black kids a lesson."

"What lesson?"

"That the world has rules that apply to them, too. Those officials shouldn't buckle under to the spoiled-brat mentality that minorities on campus have these days."

"Oh, Sidney!"

"It's true, Dora. Your grandson and his friends performed a service. They did for the administration what the administration didn't have the guts to do for itself."

"I don't see it that way, Sidney."

"Back up for a second," Ruth Cohn said. "What shacks? What are you talking about?"

"The Black Students Alliance built three shacks on the college green," Dora explained, "as reminders of the way American slaves had lived. The administration wouldn't take down the shacks, so a group of conservative students—my grandson Ethan's group—tore them down in the middle of the night."

"It was all in the papers," Sidney Pollokoff said. "The disgraceful part isn't the attack on the shacks. It's what happened next."

"What happened?" Lucille Rosenberg asked.

"The black kids went crazy, occupied the dean's office, rifled his files, and instead of calling the cops, the administration rewarded the hoodlums by calling off classes for a day to have a teach-in about racism."

"Dora," Sam Dyer said, "do you remember when we used to visit Sidney at that tiny place he had near Washington Square, and he'd spend the whole afternoon playing Paul Robeson records?"

"I certainly do," Dora said.

"If Ethan was my grandson," Fred Kleiman said, shaking his corned beef sandwich for emphasis, "I'd tell him to stop crapping around and start cracking the books."

"That's what Alan's been telling him, " Dora said, "but it doesn't do any good. You know how kids are. He's fighting a holy war. Just like the kids in the sixties, only his hero's Ollie North."

"Better than Che Guevara," Sidney Pollokoff said.

"What a voice Robeson had!" Ethel Pollokoff said. "I remember those records."

"Wasn't he a Communist?" Ruth Cohn asked.

"Of course he was a Communist," Sidney Pollokoff said. "You don't think that bothers Dora, do you?"

"It's an honor to be taunted by a man who admires Nancy Reagan more than Eleanor Roosevelt," Dora said.

"I never said that."

"Why not say it, Sidney? If you don't admire Nancy Reagan more, I'd like to know why. Your convictions are closer to hers. Face it, Sidney, she's your type."

"She's not my type," Sidney said. "I've always liked thoughtful women. That's why I like you, Dora, even though I think you're wrong about almost everything."

"I'm not wrong about my grandson," Dora said. "He's fighting a holy war and he's full of holy righteousness . . . You should hear him babble about Rush Limbaugh. Talk about stars in the eyes!"

"The way you used to babble about I. F. Stone?" Sidney asked.

"I *still* like I. F. Stone," Dora said. "Eleanor Roosevelt, Paul Robeson, I. F. Stone—I like all of them!"

"The whole pink pantheon," Sidney said.

"Hell, Sidney," Dora said, "how can you even mention Rush Limbaugh in the same sentence as I. F. Stone? You know better than that."

"You know what I remember about Eleanor Roosevelt?" Sam Dyer said. "They had some conference down south, and the local authorities insisted on segregated seating. And Eleanor picked up her chair and set it down so it straddled both sides of the aisle, and she sat down dead in the middle . . . It was just a little incident, but that's what I remember."

"And I remember how she took on the D.A.R.," Lou Cohn said.

"When was that?" Betsy Abramowicz asked.

"It must have been about 1939," Sidney Pollokoff said, with a faraway look in his eyes. For a moment he seemed to forget that he had given up being a liberal. "Marian Anderson wanted to sing at Constitution Hall in Washington, and the Daughters of the American Revolution refused to let a black woman sing."

"They owned the hall," Dora said. "The D.A.R. owned Constitution Hall."

"Right," Sidney said. "And Eleanor Roosevelt resigned from the D.A.R., and used her influence, and the next thing anybody knew, there was Marian Anderson singing at the Lincoln Memorial, with seventy-five thousand people listening."

"That was a great day," Dora said.

"That *was* a great day," Sidney said. Then he looked at Dora and added, "That was a time when liberals wanted equal opportunities for everybody. Now they want equal outcomes. That's where you and I disagree."

"I don't want equal outcomes," Dora said to Sidney Pollokoff. "I just want people that are born without a penny to have a fair shot."

"Dora, how's Ben?" Ruth Cohn asked.

"Worse and worse," Dora said. "I'm afraid that soon I won't be able to take care of him."

"Socialism is dead," Sidney Pollokoff said. "Dead! Dead! Dead!"

"Old age is a shipwreck," Fred Kleiman said. "Who was it who said that?"

"Churchill?" Lou Cohn said. "De Gaulle?"

"Who knows?" Dora said, shaking her head. "Who can remember?"

• • •

"There's nothing wrong with me," Ben Weiss said. "I know you think there is, but there isn't."

Dora looked at her husband, then at her son.

"Nobody said there's anything wrong with you, Dad," Alan said.

"I know what you think," Ben said. "I see the way you look at one another."

Dora pulled herself out of her chair. "More coffee?" she asked Alan, who was sitting on the sofa in her living room with an empty cup in his hands.

"Yes. Thanks."

"Ben?" She looked at her husband.

"I'll wait," he said. Dora went into the kitchen to get coffee for Alan. Ben leaned toward Alan and whispered, "So I made a mistake. OK, I made a mistake . . . I'm not allowed?"

"Dad, you sent them a check for ten thousand dollars!"

"They said they needed it," Ben Weiss said in a plaintive voice, like the voice of a child who knows he has misbehaved.

"Ten thousand dollars!" Dora said, responding to her husband's last remark as she came back from the kitchen. "Since when did you become such a hotshot philanthropist."

"I'm not a hotshot," Ben said. "They needed money, and it seemed like a good cause."

"Ben, for God's sake!" Dora's voice shook with exasperation. "It's *not* a good cause." She handed the cup of coffee to Alan and, not speaking out loud, mouthed the word "Alzheimer's."

"She thinks I have Alzheimer's," Ben said, looking at Alan. "Alzheimer's, Schmalzheimer's. You know what I have?"

"What?"

"Ben Weiss's Disease! That's what I have! I have a personal disease that God invented just for me."

Dora raised one eyebrow

"Alzheimer's!" Ben Weiss cried. "Any dope can get Alzheimer's. But only Ben Weiss gets Ben Weiss's Disease."

"Makes sense to me," Alan said.

"John D. Rockefeller," Dora said, shaking her head. "He gives away money like he's John D. Rockefeller."

"Frank Sinatra got fat like a pig," Ben said, either forgetting the subject or trying to change it. "I saw him last night on television."

"A hotshot philanthropist!" Dora said. "My husband the hotshot!"

"He used to be skinny," Ben said. "All skin and bones, with a skinny microphone." He looked at Alan. "You should have heard him in his prime."

"He was always a stinker," Dora said. "Remember when they called him the King of Swoon? . . . Swoonatra—the King of Swoon . . . He was skinny like a rail, and he wore those floppy bow ties."

"What I don't understand, Dad—" Alan began.

"That was a long time ago," Ben said. "Now he's fat."

"Ben, *we're* fat," Dora said.

"We're not," Ben said. "We may not be thin, but we're certainly not fat." He looked at Dora with a twinkle. "I'm not, anyway."

"Dad," Alan said, "what I don't understand is, how could you give all that money to the Republicans? Haven't you always been a Democrat?"

"Always!" Ben Weiss boomed.

"So how in the world—"

"Alan, what's all this about good cholesterol and bad cholesterol?" Dora asked. "Since when did they start having good cholesterol?"

"It's something new," Alan said to his mother. "But I was trying to ask Dad a question . . . Dad, how could you give all that money to junk mail from the Republicans? I just don't understand it."

"Junk mail! Who said anything about junk mail?" Ben Weiss said.

"Alan, I have Danish," Dora said. "Cheese, apple, or cinnamon-raisin."

"Apple, please."

"Let me show you, Alan," Ben said, getting up and starting toward the den.

"How about you, Ben?" Dora said. "Cheese, apple, or cin—"

"Cheese! Cheese!" Ben called as he left the room. "For fifty-two years I've been eating cheese. Can't you remember after fifty-two years?"

He came back carrying a large, glossy envelope. Handing it to Alan, he said, "Tell me what you think. Is this junk mail?"

Alan examined the package. It came from something

called the Republican Victory Task Force. An impressive logo—an eagle with wings spread in a design that looked like the presidential seal—appeared on the upper left corner of the envelope. On the back, a larger version of the logo was used as a seal. Alan's father had taken care to open the envelope without tearing the eagle. Inside, a letter asked Alan's father to make a gift to help the Republican Party save the country from the "outspoken, combative, extremist" Democrats who threatened to ruin it.

"That's Mom," Alan said, laughing. "They're asking you to do your part in the fight to save the country from Mom." He laughed so hard his stomach started to hurt.

"Ten thousand dollars!" Dora said. "Mr. Hotshot Philanthropist sent them ten thousand dollars." Dora and Alan laughed together—a loud, chortling sound.

"I hope the two of you choke," Ben Weiss said.

"Dad, it's not that we want to be mean. Only, really, it's so absurd. I still don't get it. It's a great letter, but what was it that got you to write a big check? You've always hated these guys."

Ben Weiss looked lost. "I got confused," he said.

"That's it?" Alan said. He looked earnestly at his father, and his own expression became somber. "You got confused?"

Tears glistened in Ben Weiss's eyes and began to roll down his cheeks. "I thought it would help. I thought—I thought the country needed help . . . I got confused."

Alan walked over to his father and patted him gently on the shoulder. "Dad, I'm sorry. I didn't mean to laugh."

"I wanted to help," Ben Weiss said. "I love this country."

Alan said, "I love you, Dad," and he bent over with his hand on his father's shoulder and kissed him on the top of the head. "Don't worry about it. We'll get the money back. I'll call them tomorrow and explain."

"Ten thousand dollars!" Dora said.

"Congratulations, Dad," Alan said. "Remember George

Bush—the thousand points of light? I think you've become a point of light."

Ben Weiss grunted. Dora said, "For ten thousand bucks, they ought to make him a galaxy."

• • •

"Grandpa, how are you," Ethan Weiss said.

In yellow slacks and an apple-green polo shirt, an old man's outfit, Ben Weiss gazed at his grandson. The boy was wearing neatly pressed gray slacks, a navy sport jacket, a white shirt with a button-down collar, and a crimson tie with silver dots on it. He looked like a contestant on *College Bowl* in 1962.

"Up crap's creek," the old man said. "You ever heard that expression?"

"I don't think so," Ethan said.

"Up crap's creek," Ben Weiss repeated. "I'm up crap's creek without a paddle."

The young man smiled.

"Don't get old," Ben Weiss said.

"Tell Grandpa about your new job," Dora said.

"What happened to his old job?" Ben asked.

"He didn't have an old job," Alan said. "I told you, Dad. Remember? The college suspended him. The shacks."

The old man looked at his grandson. "I remember."

"Tell him about the job," Dora said.

"Grandpa, you know Melville Hyde?"

"Melville Hyde from television?"

"Yes. He gave me a job to be a special assistant in his office, until the suspension is over."

"Melville Hyde the racist?" Ben Weiss asked Dora.

"He's not a racist," Ethan said. "The liberal media misrepresent his views."

Dora said, "Isn't he the man who said, on immigration policy, that the U.S. already has enough Zulus?"

"It might be better if we didn't discuss politics," Alan said.

"That's the way he talks," Ethan said, looking at his grandmother. "He doesn't pull his punches."

Dora said, her voice rising, "Isn't he the man who says that we ought to attack homelessness the same way we'd attack any other infestation of vermin—with rat poison?"

"If it weren't for the liberal media—" Ethan began, but Dora interrupted him: "Isn't he the man who says that blacks in Africa will be ready for self-rule when they stop eating one another?"

"If we talk politics," Alan said, "we'll wind up yelling. I don't want to sit here yelling."

• • •

After his son and grandson had left, Ben Weiss went upstairs for a nap. An hour later, he came downstairs carrying his checkbook. "Dora," he said, "what's the name of that bleeding-heart group you always give twenty-five dollars to? Love Thy Neighbor?"

"Thy Brother's Keeper," Dora said, looking up from her magazine. When she saw the checkbook, she added, "Don't do anything foolish, Ben."

Ben filled out a check and walked over to show it to her.

"Is that foolish?" he asked.

It was a check for five hundred dollars, made payable to Thy Brother's Keeper. A note told them to use the money for AIDS babies.

"Quite foolish, dear," Dora said.

"I'm sick of talking. It seems like all we do is talk."

"We're old, Ben."

"I don't give a damn. I can still write out a check."

With a faintly pleased look on his face, Ben Weiss went into the next room to get an envelope and stamp. "You remember that kid from Tulsa?" he said when he came back.

"Hoover?"

"Right. Hoover."

"What about him?"

"You think he'll ever understand us?"

"Us?"

"You know—the city."

"Ben, I don't understand us."

"The city scares me, Dora. It's full of hate."

"You think Tulsa isn't?"

"I don't know."

"We could move," Dora said.

"Where would we move?"

"Depends."

"On what?"

"Where do you want to die, Ben?"

"In bed."

Dora smiled. "In bed in Delray?"

Ben got up and went over to the table where he'd put the envelope with the check in it. "It's too much, isn't it?" he said.

"What?"

"Five hundred bucks."

"It's a gesture," Dora said.

"It's not as if we're rich," Ben said.

"No."

"Maybe I'll give fifty."

"OK."

"You think fifty's enough?"

"Fifty would be plenty."

"We're not made of money."

"No."

Ben wrote out a new check. "I'm giving twenty-five," he said.

"OK."

"Dora?"

"Yes?"

"Am I still a galaxy?"

Dora did not answer.

"A star?"

Dora shrugged.

"A candle?"

Family Ties

My father is dying. In a hospital room that smells of stale urine, stale sweat, and stale air, an IV line drips antibiotics into an arm that rarely moves. The arm is pale and sturdy, thickly covered with silver-gray hair. Once that arm struck my mother with so much force it knocked out two teeth and loosened three others.

My father is my mother's second husband. The first, Harry Copperfield, charmed my mother with his gift for good times. They went to see popular movies—Bogart and Bacall in *The Big Sleep*, Alan Ladd and Veronica Lake in *The Blue Dahlia*, Cary Grant and Ingrid Bergman in *Notorious*. This was in Baltimore in 1946. The war was over, and young people wanted to have fun. Harry took my mother out dancing, took her to nightclubs, took her to eat crabs at Obrycki's and bratwurst at Haussner's. At a Christmas party that year, my mother told me later, he did an imitation of Perry Como singing "Prisoner of Love" that made her laugh so hard she decided to marry him.

Harry never talked about the war, though it had taken three years out of his life. His goal, he told my mother, was to be as rich as Rockefeller—*any* Rockefeller. In pursuit of this unlikely objective, he had opened a window-repair business that he operated out of a garage he rented in Eastpoint, in southeast Baltimore, near the sewage disposal plant.

In 1949, the marriage fell victim to the laws of economics. Harry's window-repair business depended on a steady supply of windows in need of repair. When nature failed to break windows at a satisfactory pace, Harry recruited teenage boys from Dundalk High School to smash windows after dark.

Business boomed for six months. Then one of the boys was caught. Charming Harry, the lover of crab cakes and Boston cream pie, potential rival of the Rockefellers, and scourge of Perry Como, was sentenced to three years in the Baltimore city jail on Madison Street.

Now, in the hospital cafeteria at three o'clock on a Saturday afternoon, I sip coffee while my mother snacks on tea and rice pudding.

"You should forgive him," my mother says, speaking not of Harry Copperfield but of her second husband, my father.

Forgive him? Has she gone out of her mind?

"I forgave him years ago," I say.

"Don't lie to me, Susan."

"Don't make me lie."

She looks at me with a weariness that startles me. Her eyes are the color of weak bourbon, her lips the color of a stone. On her breath, I can smell the cinnamon from the rice pudding. She was born in 1924, during the presidency of Warren Harding. After graduating from high school, before she met Harry, she worked as a secretary at the McCormick Spice Company. She is seventy-one years old.

"I want you to tell him that you love him, Susan. He's an old man dying. Whether you've forgiven him or not, I want you to do this for me."

In the early 1950s, my mother divorced Harry Copperfield while he was still in jail. A new man had come into her life, a short, strong man, with thick eyebrows and a skeptical look in his eyes. John Hayes worked as a journalist for a newspaper called the Baltimore *Daily Observer*, now defunct, in the days when journalism attracted a certain type of raffish, slightly disreputable middle-class man.

I was born in 1954, the first of two daughters. Looking back, I try to remember when I first realized that something had gone wrong in my parents' marriage. From the years before 1960, all I seem to remember is Miss Fife, my pencil-thin teacher in kindergarten at Cross Country Elementary School, and Ronnie Hall, a gangly, freckled high-school boy who lived down the street from us and who was arrested, one morning in 1959, in the murder of a little girl he had lured into the back room of a pet supply store where he worked after school.

"He hasn't been a bad husband," my mother says.

"Mom! For God's sake!"

"It's true," my mother insists. "We had our problems, but he *changed*. After that terrible beating, he changed."

I sip my coffee. She doesn't mean a terrible beating my father inflicted upon her. She means a terrible beating he took.

"Did you know, Susan," my mother says, "that for the past twenty years, your father has sent me flowers every Friday? Did you know that? Did I ever mention it?"

"About a thousand times, Mom."

If my father ever hit my mother when we were growing up, he took care not to do it in the presence of witnesses. I can recall tremendous yelling and tense silences, but I cannot recall the sound of slapped flesh.

The shouting frightened me badly enough. What were they yelling about? Or, rather, what was *he* yelling about, for my mother responded in a whisper, if at all.

Ugly things happened in that house. Have you ever seen a woman cower? My mother stands nearly as tall as my father, but in my memories, he towers over her, shouting, while she cringes beneath him, pulling away physically, trembling and whimpering like a whipped dog.

I can remember a fight about a cup of tea. My mother liked to let her tea cool before she drank it, but on this night she miscalculated, the tea was too cool, and she threw it away. My sister and I were sprawled on the floor, drawing pictures.

In the armchair where he sat reading the evening paper, I could see my father seething.

"Is there a money tree out back?" my father asked.

"What?" my mother said.

"I said, 'Is there a money tree out back?' The way you threw away that tea, I thought there must be a money tree out back that I don't know about."

"For God's sake, John, it's only a cup of tea."

"You *would* say that."

My father stared at his newspaper, but he wasn't reading. I could see the anger raging and boiling inside him.

"It's the goddamned *principle*," he said suddenly, lurching out of his chair, throwing down the paper, and glaring at my mother. "It's waste—pure waste! You teach the children to waste!" Now he was roaring, while my sister and I gazed with wide eyes from the floor: "*Work!* What do you know about work? Have you ever worked a day in your life? Have you ever earned a dollar? Have you ever earned a dime?"

With sudden fury, he kicked the stool out from under my mother's feet. In her chair, in an orange dress that I still remember, my mother was pale, trembling. My father paced the room, ranting, with a wild glare in his eyes. "I don't know why I bother!" he concluded. "I don't know why I bother at all!" And he slammed the front door behind him as he stalked into the night.

"Hello, gang."

My sister, Kate, and her husband, Peter, have arrived at the hospital. Kate is three years younger than I am, and I have never greatly liked her, perhaps because she is friendly and open and warmhearted, whereas I am chilly and reserved. Remembering Kate as a child, I remember someone who pleased every grownup she ever met.

Beaming, looking as pert and peachy as a TV anchorwoman, Kate moves swiftly toward me down one aisle in the hospital cafeteria. I feel a surge of resentment. What a fool I've been! I teach music at a public elementary school in Baltimore, whereas smiling, sweet-tempered Kate has an M.B.A. in health care management from the Wharton School and a job working as a director of strategic planning for a notoriously ruthless chain of nursing homes written up recently in *Baltimore Business World.* Money, I've noticed, means more and more to me as I grow older, and less and less to her, since she has plenty of it.

On the elevator rising to my father's floor, we nod politely toward a volunteer, a silver-haired woman in a blue smock, pushing a cart full of floral arrangements. A technician with a mobile electrocardiograph machine has a copy of Magic Johnson's autobiography sticking out of his pocket.

A week ago Dr. Templeton, my father's cardiologist, explained the current situation to us. My father suffers from chronic congestive heart failure, caused by the slow deterioration of his heart muscle over a period of years. The weakened muscle cannot pump blood efficiently through the body, which is why my father runs out of breath when he climbs a short flight of stairs, and why he must pause to gulp air if he parks too far from the entrance to the shopping mall.

Because his heart does not pump the way it should, fluid backs up into my father's lungs: that's why he sleeps with his head and shoulders elevated on three pillows. Fluid also has built up in my father's kidney and liver, and in his feet, his ankles, his thighs, and his lower back. In effect, Dr. Templeton told us, my father is drowning, tissue by tissue, though, if he's lucky, his heart might fail before the fluid completely floods his lungs.

After this briefing, I made the mistake of asking the doctor to repeat some of what he'd said, to make sure I understood. Then I asked questions. The irritation that flared in the doctor's eyes as I wasted his time with this bumbling interrogation has left some tension between us.

Now Kate bends to kiss my father on the forehead. "How's it going, tiger?" she asks.

"It's not enough to die," my father says. "This goddamned hospital won't be satisfied till it takes every penny I ever made."

In 1974 my sister, at the age of seventeen, fell in love with the advanced-placement physics teacher at one of the city's private high schools. I was then a sophomore at the University of Maryland, with a double major in music and elementary education. When I came home Christmas week, Kate told me about Harvey. He was twenty-eight years old, married, with a one-year-old daughter named Hope and a three-year-old son named Howard. He had studied physics at Yale and liked to do mathematical puzzles.

"I'm sleeping with him," Kate told me.

I myself had never slept with anyone except Kevin Flanders, a junior majoring in business administration who took my virginity in a sour-smelling dormitory bedroom on a gray afternoon about half an hour after Evil Knievel failed in his nationally televised effort to fly across the Idaho Snake River on his Sky-Cycle X-2. You probably won't know what I'm talking about unless you were around in 1974, but that's all right. Kevin Flanders will not take it personally, I hope, if I confess that I remember more about the TV coverage of Evil Knievel's flight than I remember about the frantic huffing and puffing that followed.

"You'd better be careful," I said to my sister after she told me about Harvey.

"*He'd* better be careful," Kate said.

In the end, both of us were right. The physics teacher wound up on his knees, begging his wife to forgive him. Kate wound up pregnant. On a bright day in April, two weeks after the abortion, my father wound up in the hospital with his first heart attack.

Four months later, saying that his performance had slipped, the newspaper where my father had worked for twenty years let him go.

"Those bastards couldn't wait to get rid of me," my father said.

Like many fading journalists with mouths to feed, my father turned to public relations. Hunzinger's department store in Baltimore hired him to write its employee newsletter. He wrote about the triumphs of the company's softball team and paid homage to the employee of the month, Sally in home furnishings or Ernie in purchasing—always, my father noted in private, someone who labored cheerfully at an annual wage that could not have supported Clarence Hunzinger for a week.

One day in 1976, I was reading an article about the latest drop in SAT scores when the phone rang. It was Kate, now nineteen, calling from her dorm at Bryn Mawr.

"Susan," she said, "I think Dad's beating Mom."

"Are you kidding?"

"I saw them today. I drove into Baltimore and had brunch with them. We called you, but you weren't home."

At this time I had my first job, at an elementary school in Havre de Grace, about an hour by car from Baltimore. When my parents called to invite me to brunch, I figured out later, I must have been in bed with Carl Rivers, a twenty-four-year-old redhaired carpenter who reminded me of Steve McQueen at a time when most of the men I'd known in my life reminded me of Wally Cleaver's buddies in *Leave It to Beaver*.

"What makes you think he's beating her?" I asked.

"She has a black eye. She says she got hit by a Frisbee."

"How do you know she didn't?"

"Because later, in the kitchen, she started to cry."

In the kitchen, cleaning up, my mother had told Kate what was really happening. My father had changed since the newspaper fired him. Some poison seemed to be eating him up inside. He hated working for the department store. He hated the company song and the company slogans and the company picnic. He missed his friends at the newspaper, though his generation of tough-talking journalists had begun to give way to a generation that seemed soft and spoiled to him. He had always had a bad temper, but now, it seemed, some vital control had slipped. Now, my mother told Kate, he would hit as well as yell.

"What should we *do*, Susan?" my sister asked, in a voice on the verge of tears.

"How am I supposed to know?" I asked. "For God's sake, Kate, I'm just a teacher. I teach *music*, remember? I teach music to kids in *grade* school."

"We have to do something," Kate said.

"Let me think," I said.

• • •

As my father fades away, losing weight and force, the signs of diminished strength sadden me. I read him an article about health care reform that would have outraged him five years ago, but now he merely sighs. "Clinton was a *fool*," he says, his face chalk-blue against the white of the hospital's pillow. "Didn't he know *anything* about the people he was fighting? Didn't he know *anything*?"

Politely, my father tells the hospital's chaplain that he is not interested in receiving spiritual assistance. He asks me to read H. L. Mencken to him. For my father—perhaps for any journalist who started his career in Baltimore in the 1950s— Mencken is better than booze. Some sentences make my father laugh out loud. "It is only the savage, whether of the

African bush or the American gospel tent, who pretends to know the will and intent of God exactly and completely." And: "If we assume that man actually resembles God, then we are forced into the impossible theory that God is a coward, an idiot, and a blunderer." My father loved that.

How long can he last?

No way to predict, Dr. Templeton says.

"This hospital," my father says, "will not let me die until it takes every penny I ever made."

His pain is getting worse. American men don't like to admit pain, but sometimes my father groans, softly and evenly, for fifteen, twenty, thirty minutes at a time. The look that comes into his eyes is the look of a tortured animal. "Oh . . . oh . . . oh . . . oh . . . oh." My husband tells me it's hard for him to visit.

Hard for *him*!

"Have you had that talk yet?" my mother asks in the hospital cafeteria.

"What do you want me to say?"

"I want you to forgive him, Susan. He was a good father. He's been a good husband. I want you to help him die."

"Mom, you're driving me crazy."

In 1976, after Kate told me about my mother's black eye, I consulted my boyfriend the red-haired carpenter. Not realizing that I expected him to be Steve McQueen, he scratched his head and finally said something like, "Gee, Susan, I guess you ought to do *something*, but the thing is, what can you do? I mean, I guess you could report it to the police, but it's not as if you have any *proof*."

Thanks, big guy.

The bicentennial year wore on. Patty Hearst was convicted of bank robbery. Hanoi was named the capital of a reunified Vietnam. Saigon was renamed Ho Chi Minh City. The tall ships made their celebratory sail in New York harbor. On

Thanksgiving Day, my mother served the holiday meal with a black eye—actually, a pink and crimson and pale violet eye—that she attributed to a clumsy encounter with a closet door.

That was when I remembered Harry Copperfield. I had never met him, but I found his name in the telephone book and called and told him that I was Ellen Peary's daughter and that I had a problem that I didn't want to discuss over the phone, and he agreed to see me.

On the day after Christmas in 1976, we met at a bar in Timonium, north of Baltimore, where Harry now worked as a salesman in a sporting goods store. All my life, when I thought about Harry, I had thought about Perry Como, but it turned out that I should have thought about Boog Powell, the big first baseman on the great Baltimore Orioles teams with Brooks Robinson and Frank Robinson, because Harry weighed about two hundred fifty pounds, he was wearing a loose-fitting Hawaiian shirt and tight-fitting blue jeans, and he had blue eyes and blond hair that was cut in the closest of crew cuts.

"I think my father is beating up my mom," I told him after the waitress brought us our beers.

Harry looked at me a long time, and then he said, "What makes you think that?"

I told him what my mother had said to my sister the day she started crying in the kitchen, and I told him about the black eye on Thanksgiving Day.

"That bastard," Harry said. He took a sip of beer, and then he looked at me and said, "Susan, you know what a three-time loser is? You could get me locked up for a long time."

Harry's troubles with the law, it turned out, had not ended when he hired kids to break windows for his window-repair business. In 1957, he had been caught in a bribery ring involving supplies for the Baltimore city schools. The scheme took advantage of holes in the city's accounting, purchasing, and receiving systems. A school official would certify full delivery of supplies that hadn't been delivered. The school would pay the supplier, who would pay some amount to the official who had certified that the supplies had arrived. Caught by undercover agents in a sting operation, Harry wound up in jail again.

"So what I'm trying to tell you," Harry concluded, "is that I can't go and personally beat the shit out of this guy, because if I get caught, I might spend the rest of my life someplace where I'd rather not be."

"I'm not asking you to beat him up," I said. "What I'm asking is whether you know some way to make him stop."

"He's a bully," Harry said. "The way to make him stop is to beat the shit out of him."

I looked at him a long time, not saying anything.

"Listen, Susan," Harry said finally, "what you have to realize is, when you pay to have somebody beat up, there's always a chance that something might go wrong. This is your father we're talking about. If something goes wrong, your father might wind up in the morgue."

I thought about my mother carrying out the turkey with her black eye on Thanksgiving Day. I thought about my mother cringing and cowering, trembling and whimpering, while my father screamed and cursed at her after she threw away a cup of cold tea.

"Harry," I said, "you don't owe me anything. You don't owe my mother anything."

Harry sighed.

"Harry," I said, "I don't want to do anything that makes you uncomfortable."

Another sigh.

"Harry," I said, looking at him out of the big serious brown eyes that have gotten me into so much trouble in my life, "I'm just an elementary school music teacher who doesn't know how to handle these things."

That did it. Harry took a deep breath that puffed out his

chest beneath his Hawaiian shirt, and then he said he would help me. He couldn't do the job himself, but he would find somebody who would have a talk with my father, and if a talk didn't work, well—

"Anything else you want?" Harry asked in conclusion, in that bar in Timonium on the day after Christmas in 1976.

I thought for a while—really thought—and then I said, "I'd like my mother to get flowers. Every week for the rest of her life, I'd like my mother to get flowers."

• • •

"Dad," I say, standing next to my father's bed in the hospital room. "There's something I want you to know."

He looks at me with a sidelong glance, not turning his head. "What's that?" he says.

"I want you to know that I—well—you know we haven't always seen eye to eye."

"I forgave you a long time ago, if that's what's on your mind."

He forgave me!

I take a deep breath, getting a good whiff of the urine-scented air.

"Thanks, Dad. That means a lot to me."

Without lifting his head—he's too weak to lift his head—he turns to look at me. "You don't have to lie, Susan. I know you hate my guts."

Later that afternoon, in a corridor next to a cart with all kinds of emergency cardiac equipment on it, I tell my mother she doesn't have to worry. Dad and I had a good talk.

A light snow was falling from a fluffy gray sky on the last Sunday in February 1977, when I got the call from my mother. I can still remember the panic and astonishment in her voice. My father was in intensive care, she reported, with four broken ribs, a broken nose, and a punctured lung.

In the apartment where I lived at the time, there were

dirty dishes in the sink and a smell of waffles and maple syrup in the air, and on the radio that I could hear faintly from the living room, Paul Simon was singing "Fifty Ways to Leave Your Lover."

"Oh, God, Susan, he took an awful beating," my mother said.

"Any idea who did it?"

"Your father says he was wearing a mask."

"You know anybody with a grudge against Dad?"

"Not *that* bad a grudge. Oh, Susan, you should see him! There's blood all over."

"I'm coming right over, Mom. You just hold yourself together."

Three weeks later, I met Harry Copperfield at the bar in Timonium. He was wearing an orange shirt, blue jeans that would have looked awful on any big man, and white sneakers like the sneakers kids wore in the 1950s. He said he didn't think my father would cause much trouble anymore.

"You know," he said. "I didn't owe you anything. Your mother ditched me for this jerk that beat her up."

That was the last time I saw Harry. In 1988, he was killed in a single-car crash at one in the morning on the Jones Falls Expressway, on the badly lit stretch up near the Ruxton Road exit. A woman who was not his wife died with him in the crash. He left behind two grown children, Earl and Veronica, whom I met at the funeral, but haven't seen since.

Why should I see them? Harry wasn't my father.

Last night my father tore the IV line out of his arm, picked up the iron pole, and tried to break the window so he could jump out. Two orderlies dragged him away from the window—dragged him gently, a nurse told me, since his strength is gone.

When my mother, my sister, and I arrived at the hospital this morning, my father was lying in his own excrement, curled up in a fetal position, softly crying. Now a nurse's aide has cleaned him and given him fresh sheets, but he's still curled up and whimpering. Like my mother so many years ago, he sounds like a whipped dog.

My mother also is crying, soundlessly, in a cheap armchair near the bed. My sister asks me what we should do.

"How am I supposed to know? You're the hotshot executive."

"That's not fair," Kate says.

All day long in the hospital, while nature does its dirty work, I feel furious. Did I inherit from my father some capacity to seethe? Dr. Templeton arrives for his daily visit late in the afternoon. As he leaves, I follow him into the hall.

"Excuse me, doctor, if you have a minute."

His smile tells me that he never has a minute.

"Could we sit down somewhere in private?" I ask.

"I'm afraid I'm in rather a hurry."

Turd!

"Just for a minute," I say. "*If* you don't mind."

Dr. Templeton is not a man who sits, but eventually we are standing face to face in the visitors' waiting room. I tell him again that I'm distressed about the pain my father is experiencing.

"Yes," Dr. Templeton says. "We can control that."

"But you *haven't* controlled it. You said three days ago you could control it, and you haven't."

"Sometimes, with pain medication, it's difficult to determine the exact dosage."

"Doctor, this is my father we're talking about. Do you understand? This is my *father*."

"Miss Peary, I appreciate your feelings, but if you would be kind enough to leave medical matters to me. Now, if you'll excuse me—"

I want to excuse him, but there's no excuse for him. Anyway, something red is happening inside my head. I remember Harry Copperfield in his Hawaiian shirt and the beating my father took after I gave the OK, and I remember his two black eyes and his four broken ribs and his punctured lung. I remember my mother crying long ago about a cup of wasted tea and I remember her crying this morning when she saw my father lying in his own excrement.

"DOCTOR," I say, "PLEASE SIT DOWN."

Looking stunned, the doctor sits. I sit.

"Doctor," I say, "my mother is only a weak old woman and I'm only a grade school teacher, but that doesn't mean you can shit all over us."

This is a lie. He *can* shit all over us.

We're sitting on a sofa covered with uncomfortable plastic cushions manufactured, I think, especially for hospital waiting rooms. The cushions are of a color, roughly the color of pickle juice, that I associate with large institutions. The doctor looks angry. It's offensive to him that I've said that he can't shit all over us. And he's right, he's perfectly right. My heart pounds inside me. I'm still feeling furious, but I'm also feeling desperate. Where are you, Harry, when I need you?

"Doctor," I say in a cold tone, hiding my desperation, "I don't suppose the name Harry Copperfield means anything to you."

The doctor shakes his head.

"I didn't think so," I say. Then, as if the words were coming from someone else, as if some alien has seized control of my speech, I hear myself saying: "You don't have many patients with personal connections in the Vatican, do you?"

Another shake of the head. Did I really say that? I feel a surge of panic, but that other person plunges on: "And in the cement industry? Not many friends in cement?"

A third shake, with his eyes wide open.

"Dr. Templeton, I don't want to alarm you, but Harry Copperfield is a close personal friend of my father who will be extremely distressed if he hears that I am distressed about the care my father is receiving. Do you understand me?"

The doctor opens his mouth, but nothing comes out. What have I done? Have I made a threat? Yes, I've made a threat. I've threatened my father's physician. *My God*! I've threatened a doctor! Why didn't I just pluck out my eyes? Why didn't I just tear out my tongue?

"Doctor," I gasp, "please forgive me."

He stares at me with a look I have never seen before on the face of any physician.

"Doctor, my mother is only a weak old woman and I'm only a grade school teacher. We can't make you do anything. Forget about Harry Copperfield. He's dead. I'm sorry I mentioned him."

The doctor looks at me, his mouth hanging open, as if he's looking at a crazy lady with a gun pointed at his heart.

"Promise me you'll forget about him," I say. "Do you promise? *Please* promise."

"I promise."

"Thank you, doctor. Just take care of my father. That's all I want. That's all my family wants. Really. That's absolutely all we want. Forget about the Vatican. Forget about Harry Copperfield. I'm sorry I mentioned him. He's dead."

• • •

That night, after the rest of the family has gone home, I sit alone with my father. The doctor has given him enough medication to knock out a platoon. He drifts in and out of sleep. The smell of disinfectant from the recently cleaned bathroom blocks the other sickroom odors. My father's hands are crossed on his chest. The fist that knocked out two of mother's teeth will never strike again. The voice I remember from childhood, bullying and abusing, has shrunk to a whisper. I feel a faint smile inside me, too weak to get out.

After all these years, I cannot like or forgive him, but when my father wakes, he will find me sitting here, and the pain will not be so bad.

Class Warfare

My name is Vince Marino. I was born in East Harlem in 1936, in the days when East Harlem was still mostly Italian. My family lived over a liquor store on 115th Street, opposite Our Lady of Mount Carmel. The city was different then. I can remember big Italian flags hanging side by side outside the rectory, and sea urchins and olives and pomegranates on sale at the sidewalk markets on First Avenue, and fancy ironwork on the fire escapes, and streets swarming with kids. The neighborhood was full of kids without money.

In those days, the great event every summer was the festival honoring the Madonna, in July. A brass band led a huge procession through the streets. The heat hammered down from the sky and shimmered up from the pavements. Thousands of people marched barefoot, following the jewel-studded statue of the Virgin. Big banners stretched overhead. A priest recited the *Dispensorio*. Donations were tossed from tenement windows.

I was the last of six kids. In the thirties, before I was born, my father worked in one of the piano factories up on 133rd Street. Then he worked for the Knickerbocker Ice Company. Then, after the war, he got a job with the NMDU, the Newspaper and Mail Deliverers Union. At about the same time, the neighborhood changed, and when I was twelve, the family moved to Bensonhurst, in Brooklyn.

To picture me, you should picture a guy who played guard on the high school football team, but was too small to play in college. At seventeen, I was five foot eight, one hundred seventy pounds. Today, I'm five foot seven, two hundred ten pounds. That's partly fat, but mostly beef and muscle. My wife, nagging me to lay off the butter, tells me I'm the kind of guy who's never sick a day in his life until he keels over a week after he cashes his first Social Security check.

What else? . . . I drink, but not enough to hurt myself. I gave up smoking nine years ago, after an operation to take out colorectal polyps. I have back problems. I cheat on my taxes, but not on my wife. I've never taken a vacation outside the U.S. I play poker once a week with a bunch of guys who look and sound exactly like Archie Bunker's buddies, the guys from the loading dock, in *All in the Family.*

For the past fifteen years, I've driven a Cadillac—not to show off, just because I like it. Right now it's a burgundy Cadillac I bought two years ago, in 1990. My wife drives a silver '84 Dodge. We were married in 1959. For fifteen years, we lived in Bensonhurst in an ordinary two-story brick house on a street with small, neat lawns and shabby trees. Then we moved to Garden City, on Long Island, to a split-level house with a two-car garage on a street with big, neat lawns and no shade.

My wife, Mary, is one year younger than I am. She was sixteen when we met, in 1953, at a dance. That summer, you couldn't go anywhere without hearing Patti Page singing "Doggie in the Window." Mary was a great dancer who wasn't afraid of boys. In the days when nice girls didn't go all the way, I took her to see *From Here to Eternity,* with Burt Lancaster and Deborah Kerr writhing on the beach, and afterwards, in Central Park, we nearly killed ourselves not doing what we both wanted to do.

Like me, Mary only has a high school education. Bringing up the kids was her career. At night, now that we have some time to ourselves, we like to watch TV or rent movies for the VCR. We like movies with people like Burt Lancaster and Kirk Douglas, Paul Newman, Elizabeth Taylor, Robert Mitchum,

Richard Widmark—people who were big when we were growing up. The stars who came up later look small to us.

"Kids can break your heart," my mother told me, but it hasn't happened yet. We have three. Our youngest, Angela, is in her second year at Long Island Community College, studying to be a nurse. Matthew, the middle one, works for a funeral home in Paramus. He's a salesman, but they gave him a fancy title that makes him sound like something else. Bereavement counselor, something like that. The people who run those funeral homes are full of cute stuff.

Our oldest, Anthony, got a law degree from Fordham in 1986. He lives downtown in Manhattan and works for a firm with offices on 34th Street and Fifth Avenue, near the Empire State Building. You probably don't know it if you live outside New York, but the Empire State Building is a crappy office building in a rundown commercial area where nobody goes unless they're paid to go there.

Like my old man, I work for the NMDU, delivering newspapers to stores and newsstands before the sun comes up. It's not what you would call challenging work. If you know anything about newspapers, which probably you don't, you'll say, "Isn't that a mob-run union?" And I'll say, "Yeah, it's a mob-run union. You have any problem with that?"

And you'll say—what?

You'll say nothing. You'll say nothing at all.

2

Last night, at Freddy's, a bar near the Brooklyn plant where they print the *Chronicle*, the guys were drinking beer out of thirty-two-ounce mugs and shooting the breeze, the way they do, about the unions and the company.

"You hear the latest?" Harry Simms said. He's a man my age, in his fifties, with silver-gray crewcut hair, a big face, big neck, big shoulders, big chest, and a stomach like you might see on a heavyweight who keeps in shape even though he's nearing the end of his career. In a movie thirty years ago, Lee J. Cobb might have played him.

"What happened?" I asked.

"They've got themselves a gunslinger."

"Baines?"

"How'd you guess?"

That's Clifford Baines, of Baines & Ivory, the country's number one union-busting law firm. Where I work, everybody knows what it means when management hires Clifford Baines. It means that management wants to break the union.

The waitress brought over two bottles of Guinness and another basket of tortilla chips. "So what happens now?" Juan Ramirez asked. He's a young guy, a pressman, with skin as bright as a new penny, a trim black mustache, a tiny earring in his left ear, and long black hair that curls down over his collar. "A strike?" Juan said. "If they hire Baines, does that mean we strike?"

Harry Simms shook his head. "That's what Baines wants," he said. "If we strike, he can bring in permanent replacements."

"He can do that?"

"He can and has, other places. If we strike, he can bring in permanent replacements, run the paper without us, maybe decertify the union."

"So we don't strike?" Juan Ramirez said.

"Listen," Harry Simms said. "You remember Bible class?"

Ramirez nodded.

"You remember Jesus Christ?"

Another nod.

"You remember turn the other cheek?"

Ramirez remembered.

"No matter what that bastard does," Harry said, "we turn the other cheek."

Ramirez looked puzzled. He reminded me of a puppy dog, one that has taken a few knocks, trying to figure out how to make his way in the world without getting the shit kicked out of him.

"Because if we strike, management wins," Harry said. "Just remember that. Remember that if the day ever comes when Clifford Baines spits in your eye."

3

Harry Simms is the guy I go to when I want to understand what's really happening with the company and the unions. Harry is friends with Joe Gilder, whose daughter married Steve Cronin, whose father is head of the pressman's union.

It was August when the company hired Baines & Ivory. Then—nothing. Now it's December. All the wives are going crazy trying to get ready for the holidays. Secretaries look more harried than they look the other eleven months of the year. You see eggnog in the windows at liquor stores and, in the city, you smell real roasting chestnuts. On the streets, everyone has a buttoned-up, bundled-up, wintry look. In January, management will make its opening bid in the negotiations for a new contract.

So what has Baines done? I asked Harry. Basically, Harry said, Baines is getting ready to publish the paper without the unions.

For one thing, Baines flew three different teams of management employees down to Fort Lauderdale for "strike school." About ninety guys in all. Down to the old plant where they used to print some newspaper that doesn't exist anymore, to learn how to run the presses at the *Chronicle* if they have to.

Second, Baines put together a big strike-planning team, to hammer out procedures for publishing the paper during a strike. Every department has a complete written plan—how it will operate if the unions walk out.

Third, Baines flew top executives to London, to learn how

that Australian big shot—you know the one—broke the British unions.

"Then, of course, there's security," Harry told me. "They've beefed up security."

"How much?"

"From what I hear, they've gone from fifty men to about a hundred fifty."

"Nice little army."

"That's the standing army," Harry said. "Then they've got reserves—another thousand men, on contract, if they need them."

I made a face.

"And," Harry said, "there's also the 'executive protection service.' For Baines and all the other big shots." He smirked. Harry is a world-class smirker. "Just in case some union guy loses his head," he said. "Just in case some union guy gets tired of living with management's prick up his ass."

• • •

January, and it's *cold*. The city has put away its Christmas decorations, people have put away their Christmas faces, and the company has put its cards on the table. It's pretty much what we expected.

The company wants to cut the work force by one third.

The company wants to kill all union control of hiring.

The company wants to kill all the work rules we've fought for over the past fifty years.

The company wants to kill the manning tables—the tables that tell how many people will be used for a particular job.

The company wants to kill the seniority rules.

The company wants to kill the old labor-management pension boards and cut the unions out of pension management.

The company wants . . . The company wants . . . You get the picture.

4

My lawyer son, Tony, has a friend who works for Baines &
Ivory. The funny thing is, when you talk about unions, this
friend who works for Baines & Ivory isn't half as much of a
hard-ass as Tony is.

Tony is a big, smart kid who probably lies awake eating his
heart out about the deals that fall into the laps of Harvard
lawyers and not into the laps of Fordham lawyers. He's six
feet tall and solid as a tree, with a body that gets noticed on
the beach and shiny black hair that sometimes slips down
over his eyes, which look exactly like mine: coffee-black,
clear, hard, and suspicious.

It's strange how things work out. You want your kid to get
ahead, and when he gets ahead, you feel as if you've lost him.
Talking to Tony, sometimes I feel as if an enemy alien has
taken over my own kid's body.

"All Clifford Baines wants," Tony says, "is for the unions to
face reality."

"All Clifford Baines wants," I say, "is to cut off the unions'
balls."

"You've got it wrong, Pop," Tony says. "The reality is, with
modern technology, the paper doesn't need all those printers and pressmen. Those guys are dinosaurs."

What can I say to him? Anybody with half a brain knows
that the paper doesn't need all those printers and pressmen.
That's the whole point.

"The company," I say, "cares more about those damned
machines than it cares about its people."

"The company wants to survive," Tony says. "It can't survive using nineteenth-century technology in the twenty-first
century."

A smart kid, but not as smart as he thinks he is. The
cufflinks he flashes when he punches out a point probably
cost more than the diamond I bought his mother when we
got engaged.

"We're willing to compromise," I say. "It's the company that won't compromise. It wants to break us."

"What about the manning tables?" Tony says.

"What about them?"

"You've got twelve guys assigned to do a job that six can do. Six guys working, and six guys jerking off."

"Without those tables," I say, "the company would have three guys doing a job that needs six."

"All the company wants," Tony says, "is for the union to drop the work rules that *require* it to pay for all those guys jerking off."

And so it goes. He'd be a great corporate lawyer, my son. He has the mouth for it.

• • •

The talks drag on. At Freddy's, you can hear the same conversation every night. The Yankees and the Mets. The Knicks and the Rangers. Getting laid and getting high. Fuck this and fuck that. The company and the unions.

The company is the Manchester Company, based in Chicago. One thing to remember, Harry Simms says, when you're trying to figure out what's happening in the negotiations, is that our New York operation is pouring red ink all over this parent company in Chicago. If the company pulls the plug on the New York operation, corporate profits go up.

There are ten unions. There's one for the machinists, the electricians, the photoengravers, the stereotypers, the printers, the paper handlers, the mailers—you name it. Those are the production unions.

When push comes to shove, only three of the unions matter. The pressman's union, which is the largest union for production workers. The Newspaper Guild, which is the union for reporters and for some clerical and advertising workers. And my union, the NMDU, which you can think of as basically the drivers' union, though you might also think of it as Don Corleone's union, if you want to be a wiseass.

At Freddy's, eating truckloads of tortilla chips and downing rivers of beer, we try to figure out management's strategy. "To understand what the company's up to," Harry Simms says, "you have to understand the shutdown liabilities."

"What're they?" Juan Ramirez asks.

If the paper folds, Harry explains, the company has to pay shutdown liabilities, which include severance payments, unfunded pension liabilities, and the big one—payments to printers and stereotypers who got lifetime job guarantees in the 1974 automation agreement. If you don't remember, which probably you don't, that was the agreement that let the paper introduce electronic typesetting.

"The union let the company bring in the new technology," Harry says, "but we made the company take care of the guys who used to set print by hand. Otherwise, they'd all have been up crap's creek."

As a practical matter, Harry says, what the shutdown liabilities mean is that it will cost the company a bundle if it voluntarily shuts the paper.

A second option, for the company, is to demand additional concessions from the unions. But the last time we bargained, five years ago, the company promised to build a big new plant, which it never built, and now there's no way the union is going to give more concessions unless the company builds the new plant, and there's no way the company is going to spend $300 million on a new plant for a paper that's bleeding big bucks.

The third option is to sell, Harry says, but the company won't sell. Too much corporate ego. Remember what the song says about New York? If you can make it there, you'll make it anywhere. The company doesn't want to admit it can't make it in New York.

So what will the company do, if it rules out those three options?

"Strike," Harry says. "The company has to sucker the unions into a strike."

"What about the shutdown liabilities?" Ramirez asks.

"If a strike *forces* the company to close the paper, then the shutdown is involuntary, and the company's off the hook."

The guys grunt.

"That's why the company put that horseshit proposal on the table," Harry says. "It's not just that the company is willing to *risk* a strike. It's that the company wants to *force* a strike."

"Which is why we turn the other cheek," Ramirez says.

"When you think about it," Harry says, "the company probably doesn't just want a strike. It probably wants a strike it'll *lose*. The company can live with a strike it wins, because if it wins, it breaks the unions. But what those bastards would like best of all, the way I see it, is a strike they lose, because then they can shut down the whole damn thing, forever."

"Without any shutdown liabilities," Ramirez says.

"You've got it," Harry says. "Those bastards in the boardroom—I'll bet that's what they're angling for. Not to win a strike, but to lose it."

• • •

"Bullshit," Tony said when I told him Harry's theory.

"Why bullshit?"

"Because it doesn't account for the facts."

"What facts?"

"For one thing, it all depends on those shutdown liabilities. And I talked about those with my buddy at Baines & Ivory. You want to know the real facts about those liabilities?"

Tony looked at me with a challenging look that made me want to smack him. He's a swaggering kid with big shoulders who fills out a suit the way Robert Mitchum did thirty years ago, in *Night of the Hunter.*

"OK," I said. "Tell me about the liabilities."

"Those guys that got lifetime job guarantees in 1974, they're not immortal. A lot of them have died; a lot have retired. That liability might have been $300 million ten years ago, but it's down to maybe $75 million today."

I thought about that. A smart kid can be a real pain in the ass.

"That's still a lot of cash," I said finally.

"Yeah, but there's more. That scheme Harry believes in—it's clever, but it's also illegal."

"How so?"

"Because you're supposed to bargain in good faith. If a court finds that the company conspired to force a strike, the company not only pays those job guarantees from the '74 agreement, it also pays a huge penalty for labor-law violations."

"What if the company buys the judge?"

"There's *still* a problem with Harry's theory."

"What's that?"

"Think, Pop."

I thought, but I couldn't see a problem.

Tony said, "You told me the company is spending a fortune getting ready to publish through a strike. It's sending executives to strike school, it's putting together contingency plans, it's beefing up security."

"So?"

"So, Pop, if the company wants to lose the strike, why is it spending a fortune to win it?"

I asked Harry Simms, who didn't have an answer. Harry asked Joe Gilder, who asked Steve Cronin, who came back with an answer from the union leadership. The company is spending the fortune to make it look *as if* it wants to win a strike, the union said, so that nobody will be able to say that the company forced a strike it wanted to lose.

Is it true? Who knows? Not me—that's for sure.

5

Last night, all hell broke loose.

"The damned company suckered us into it," Harry Simms said this morning.

"The union started this strike," some company spokesman said on TV. "The union deliberately provoked this strike."

Here's what happened, as near as I can get a handle on it.

Pete Ferrara is a member of the drivers' union, but he doesn't drive a truck. He works at a tying machine that binds newspapers into bundles and puts them on a conveyor belt that feeds them down to the delivery truck. He also puts a top sheet on each bundle, which is the only thing he does that anyone could call work.

The way the company sees things, Pete ought to be a member of the mailers' union, because any work that has anything to do with bundling or counting newspapers or getting them onto the trucks is the responsibility of the mailers' union. Letting drivers bundle or count newspapers, the company says, is giving the drivers a license to steal.

The way the drivers see things—well, it doesn't matter how the drivers see things, because the company is right. Letting drivers bundle or count newspapers *is* giving them a license to steal. That's why the drivers' union has fought with the mailers' union for control of jobs in the packaging area. This is one of those fights that is like Mike Tyson fighting a white guy with a beer belly. You can guess who won. The mailers' union is the white guy and the drivers' union is Tyson, so Pete Ferrara, who doesn't drive a truck, is a member of the drivers' union, even though he works in the packaging area. You follow?

Actually, Pete used to drive a truck. But three or four months ago, he tripped over some baling wire and tore cartilage in his left knee, and the doctor gave him a note saying he should stay off his feet, so the union took him off his truck and put him on a job at the tying machine. So, last night, Pete Ferrara was at the conveyor belt, but instead of standing at the belt, he was sitting on some metal shelves a few feet away. Which is no big deal, because, as Harry Simms says, "That job can be done sitting down, standing on your head, standing on one foot, playing with yourself, or whatever."

So Pete is sitting on one of those shelves, and a mailroom supervisor named Tom House comes over and tells him he'll have to stand up.

What Tom House says, this morning, is that Pete was sitting with his back to the belt, reading a newspaper, and putting on the top sheets by reaching behind his back, without watching, so the sheets went on crooked and screwed up the tying machine.

Which is perfectly possible.

If the top sheets go on crooked and the tying machine gets jammed, the conveyor belt stops, and if the conveyor belt stops long enough, the presses shut down and the company loses money. Which is a good way to make the company notice you exist.

What the company says, this morning, is that unions have staged a series of deliberate slowdowns and stoppages, including conveyor jams, in order to make prolonged negotiations expensive for the company.

Which is perfectly possible, Harry Simms says.

What is more than possible, but an actual, known, undeniable fact, is that Tom House is a mailers' supervisor, not a drivers' supervisor. And Pete Ferrara is a driver.

Here is where Mark Boggs comes into the story. Boggs is a union business agent with a gimpy leg who handles day shifts at the Brooklyn plant. Boggs also is a hothead who takes no shit from anyone and who pokes around where he doesn't belong, which is the reason, I suppose, that he seems to pop up when something goes wrong on the night shift, even though he's not supposed to be there.

So there is Tom House, the supervisor, telling Pete
rara to stand up, and there is Pete Ferrara, refusing to stai.
on his bum knee, and over at Freddy's, there is Mark Boggs,
shooting the breeze with the guys, and Boggs gets a call saying could he please come over to the plant, there's a little
problem.

"What gets me," Boggs says this morning, "is that it's one
of those new supervisors, a *nonunion* supervisor, who calls me.
Which makes me think: why does management call over a
union hothead unless management wants something little to
turn into something big?"

Anyway, Mark Boggs hobbles over to the plant on his
gimpy leg and sees Tom House telling Pete Ferrara to stand
up, and Boggs says to Pete, "You sit right there! You just sit,
because this guy"—and Boggs points at Tom House—"this
guy is a mailers' supervisor, and he can't tell you what to do."

Then Phil Olson, the production manager for the plant,
shows up, and he says to Pete, "OK, you can sit, but you have
to sit facing the machine."

Everything might have ended there, except Olson is a
management guy, and he figures management has to teach
Mark Boggs a lesson.

"Mr. Boggs," Olson says, "did you tell this man to sit
down?"

"I certainly did," Mark Boggs says.

Olson says, "I assume that you realize, Mr. Boggs, that you
have no right to direct the work force?"

Boggs says, "I was not directing the work force. I was helping a fellow human being in pain."

Olson says, "You have a choice, Mr. Boggs. You can walk
out on your own steam, or security can carry you out. What'll
it be?"

Boggs says, "You just call security, Mr. Olson, because
there is no way in hell that I am walking out on a fellow
human being in pain."

, there wasn't much work going on, anyway.
atching Olson and Boggs, to see what would

ay or may not have figured, depending on
...gs, is that more was at stake here than just
Boggs to leave the work site. In fact, once security
arrived, it was easy to get Boggs to leave. The thing was, most
of the drivers from the packaging area went with him. And
nobody, from the mailers' union or the drivers' union, went
back to work.

So that's the story.

Did the unions start a strike, the way the company says?

Or did the company sucker the unions into a strike, the
way Harry Simms says.

You tell me. All I know is, the unions never wanted a strike,
but now we've got one.

• • •

The Battle of Wounded Knee—that's what the guys are
calling it this morning. It started when Tom House ordered
Pete Ferrara to stand up, it escalated when Mark Boggs told
Pete Ferrara to stay right where he was, and it spun out of
control when Phil Olson told security to take Mark Boggs out
of the plant.

But that wasn't the end of it. Oh, no. In the middle of the
night, with Boggs and a couple of hundred drivers milling
around out on the street, the battle had just begun.

The men had walked off the job, but they still had a legal
right to walk back. That's what Harry Simms says. They had a
legal right to come back until replacement workers had filled
their positions.

So how long did it take the company to bring in replacements? Take a guess. A week? A day? Half a day? . . . The
answer is, forty-three minutes. In the middle of the night,
while the city that never sleeps was sleeping, the first busload

of replacement workers pulled up at the Brooklyn plant less than an hour after the walkout—a bus with Pennsylvania plates on it, and a dozen replacement drivers inside, and three guards to protect them.

As it turned out, three guards weren't nearly enough. At the main entrance to the plant on Pacific Street, the bus driver took one look at the crowd of union drivers swarming around out there on the street, and he barely even slowed down. He went right around the block, heading for a back entrance.

Not that it did him any good.

Outside the back entrance, the union men had set up a trash-can barricade. When the bus stopped to avoid plowing into the barricade, the guys on the street threw rocks, bricks, and trash cans at the bus, smashing the windshield and the mirrors, until finally the bus driver took his bus, with the replacement workers still aboard, over to the parking lot of the McDonald's on Tillary Street.

A second bus with more replacement drivers in it arrived, but it didn't do any better than the first. Around the plant, from two in the morning till five, the union controlled the street.

Somewhere in this period, something funny happened inside a fenced parking lot full of *Chronicle* delivery trucks. Three of the trucks got firebombed, and about forty got their tires slashed and their radiators punctured.

By five in the morning, about one hundred cops had arrived, with riot gear. They sealed off the area around the plant, and at 8:45 A.M., six hours behind schedule, the first delivery trucks headed out, in convoys of three, with each truck carrying one replacement driver and one security guard, and each convoy protected by a police escort, front and rear.

The Battle of Wounded Knee had turned into a war.

6

"The company didn't want a strike," my son says. We're chomping on veal chops that probably don't weigh an ounce over ten pounds, at Robert DeNiro's restaurant in Soho.

"Then why'd it provoke a strike?" I say.

"It didn't provoke one," he says. "Why would the company provoke a strike on October 25?"

"What's so special about October 25?"

"Because the company makes a fortune on holiday advertising," Tony says. "If the company wanted to provoke a strike, it would do it *after* the holidays, not before."

Smart kid.

So what happened? I don't know. Maybe it was just a case of a bunch of guys, on both sides, getting pissed off. It wouldn't be the first time.

• • •

November. The holidays are coming, but the wives are still calm, the secretaries don't have the frazzled look they'll have in about three weeks, and the pushcarts that bring the smell of roasting chestnuts haven't yet hit the streets.

We're one week into the strike now. Mostly, it's been more of the same. Buses carrying replacement workers to the plants, and strikers throwing rocks, bottles, and bricks, smashing windshields and windows, punching scab drivers, sometimes setting buses on fire.

One thing the company has proved: it can print the paper without the pressman's union. The union can mouth off all it wants about the importance of a skilled and experienced labor force, but it's just hot air. For a week, the company has run the presses with a bunch of scab novices, just the way it said it could.

Besides the company proving it can run the presses, what really bothers the guys at Freddy's is the guild, which is the union for all those newspaper writers who like to imagine they're tough. After a lot of hand-wringing, and a lot of blah-blah-blah, and a lot of talk about honoring the picket lines "for now," the guild finally joined the strike. But lots of guild members crossed the line—not just people in advertising and circulation, and not just clerks and secretaries, but photographers, and sportswriters, and a bunch of feature writers.

What did you expect? Mary asks me.

Writers! They may talk tough, but if you ask the guys at Freddy's, they're not worth their weight in warm piss.

• • •

"It's not enough," Harry Simms says. "It's not enough to attack scab drivers at the plants."

So we're attacking trucks on the streets.

All over the city, in the early morning hours, we've got guys out with bricks, rocks, bottles, and baseball bats. All over the city, trucks keep getting their windows smashed and getting run off the road. All over the city, trucks keep getting their radiators punctured, their tires slashed, their windows broken. All over the city, trucks keep bursting into flames.

"It's a disaster," Harry Simms says. "The company has us right where it wants us."

Why?

"The company has guards in the trucks with video cameras."

"So what?"

"They're taping our guys breaking the law," Harry says. "They're taping union violence. The way things are going, they'll have half our guys in jail before the month is out."

So what do we do? We move into phase two.

• • •

Phase one: we attack the drivers.

Phase two: we attack the dealers.

Early November. We're not deep into winter, but the air's cold enough to sting.

"Hey, Muhammad!"

There are about twelve thousand newspaper dealers in the New York area, but as far as the NMDU is concerned, every one of them is named Muhammad.

"How you doing, Muhammad?"

"OK."

"What's that there?" I point to a pile of papers.

"*Chronicle*," Muhammad says.

The three guys with me start picking up the stacked papers, carrying them to our van.

"Hey!" Muhammad says.

"Listen, Muhammad. That newspaper is bad for your health. You understand me? You keep selling that paper, you'll need to buy extra medical insurance. You follow?"

We move on. Twelve thousand newspaper dealers in the New York area, but we don't have to frighten every one. Word gets around.

"Muhammad, wasn't I here yesterday?"

"Yesterday?"

The guys with me toss the bundled papers into the gutter. Then they come back. I give a little nod. They start taking magazines off the newsstand, crumpling them, throwing them into the gutter. They knock all the gum and candy bars onto the sidewalk. The sidewalk is a mess. The newsstand is a mess.

"Muhammad, you remember now? I came here yesterday?"

Muhammad nods, shaking.

"You've got a nice little newsstand here, Muhammad. Looks like it's made of wood." I rap my knuckles on the newsstand. "Is this the kind of wood that burns, Muhammad?"

You may think I like this, but I don't. I do what I have to do, but that doesn't mean I like it. Tough guys don't go around picking on little guys. You never see John Wayne riding into some little town to push around little guys.

"You got a problem, Muhammad?"

"Glue."

"Glue? Oh, geez, boys. Look at this. Somebody put Krazy-Glue in the locks on Muhammad's newsstand. Who'd do a thing like that? Tough luck, Muhammad. Krazy-Glue in the locks. You ever seen anything like it boys? Wiseguys. The world's full of goddamn wiseguys."

7

Mid-November, and the company's in trouble. At the start of the month, eight days into the strike, the company announced that it's giving away two hundred thousand copies a day. *Giving* them away. Why? Because the vendors won't sell them. By the company's own admission, the paper is being sold at only about two thousand of its twelve thousand retail outlets. And that's what the company admits *publicly*.

So what does the company do, if vendors are afraid to sell the paper? Naturally, it hires more street hawkers. And who does the company hire? Naturally, it hires the homeless.

Just what the average New Yorker wants! To walk up to some bearded, stinking wacko or wino or druggie to buy his morning newspaper.

One thing you can say in favor of these new employees. They don't have any windows to be broken, locks to be glued, or newsstands to be burned down. Aside from the fact that nobody wants to get near them, they're a perfect sales force.

How many papers are reaching readers? Not more than 50 percent, Harry Simms says. Maybe as little as 25 percent.

"The next thing that'll happen," Harry said last night, "is that the advertisers will crack. They pay for circulation, and when they see they're not getting it, they'll crack."

We've already started to see it happen. The union has a guy who keeps track of this stuff. Some advertisers have quit.

Hightop Travel. Roberts Menswear. Sammway Grocery Stores.

Sometimes you have to use a little muscle. One company, Fleisher Furniture, ran a TV commercial that said, "See our ads in Sunday's *Chronicle*." The next thing you know, somebody calls Fleisher Furniture, asks if they've got good fire insurance. No more ads for Fleisher.

Out! That's what we want. We want those ads out of the newspaper.

Del Genio Bedding—out.

Kisseloff Home Center—out.

Downes department stores—out.

Let's say you run a big department store where ladies like to shop. Would you want fifty union guys with pickets outside your store, handing out brochures, and maybe saying something crude to every lady that tries to go in?

Thompson's department stores—out.

Quality Menswear—out.

Poor Josephine Crockett. She runs that big furniture business—you know, Crockett Convertible. A tough lady, Josephine. She didn't pull her ads—not until yesterday.

Who would send a death threat to good old Josephine? Can you imagine? Those crazy union guys. Some of them don't know how to treat a lady.

• • •

A Molotov cocktail is not the subtlest weapon in the world. You get a bottle. You get gasoline. You get a wet rag. You pour gas into the bottle. You stuff the rag into the bottle. You light the rag. You throw the bottle.

"That one?"

November 20, three o'clock in the morning. We're in the South Bronx, near a bodega owned by a guy named Ramon, in a neighborhood that makes me feel about as safe as I'd feel in Beirut. We've got on gloves, woolen caps that pull down over our ears, and heavy coats, but, believe me, we'd rather be home in bed with our wives, even if our wives have seen better days.

"Yeah, that one."

The door is locked, but there's still some kid at the cash register. I knock on the window. The kid looks up. From behind me, a brick sails through the window. I light the rag, toss the bottle. I see the kid's mouth hanging open as he starts to scream.

Three days go by. Nothing in the newspapers.

That makes me feel better. If the kid had died, it would have made the papers.

8

"You hear about Duffy?"

Jack Duffy, a big-name columnist on the *Chronicle*, has been walking the picket lines with us since the strike started. Until yesterday. Yesterday, he signed a fat new contract with the *Post*, our main competitor.

"Asshole," Ramirez says.

"What do you expect?" I say.

"Hey," Mike Farrow says. "You think L. T. is losing a step?"

"I hate those guys," Ramirez says.

"Which guys?" I say.

"You see that play on Sunday?" Mike Farrow says. "In the fourth quarter, where L. T. was chasing Elway?"

"Those writers, some of them," Ramirez says. "Duffy's a guy I respected. I thought he was on our side."

"Duffy's on Duffy's side," Phil Winter says. "How much did Duffy get? Two hundred thousand? More?"

"In the old days," Mike Farrow says, "L. T. *kills* Elway on that play. In the old days, Elway's lucky if he wakes up before Christmas, after L. T. crunches him."

"It makes me mad," Ramirez says.

"Forget about Duffy," I say. "He's only human."

"Asshole," Ramirez says.

Solidarity. Forever.

• • •

"Hey, looky here!" Harry Simms says.

We're in Freddy's. Harry shows me the latest article in the *Times*.

"What of it?" I say.

"Look close," Harry says. "It's all about *allegations*. It's not about violence, it's about *allegations* of violence."

"Is that bad?" I say.

"Bad?" Harry says. "Are you kidding? It's great!"

"Great? Why's it great?"

"Because they're too lazy, those hotshot reporters, to find out if the allegations are true. So they just fall back on hearsay. They report what the company says, and they report what the union says."

"What does the union say?"

"The union says the company's allegations are just allegations. The union says there have been a few scattered incidents, but as for a *pattern* of violence, as for *coordinated* or *organized* violence, the union absolutely denies it."

"Absolutely?"

Harry flashes his world-class smirk: "Absolutely."

The next day, Harry shows me another article. The headline reads, "*Chronicle* and Police Vary on Degree of Violence." The article says that the company alleges there have been over 600 strike-related incidents, but that police records show only 157.

"Those turkeys," Harry says.

"Who?"

"The reporters. Those guys are a disgrace."

Juan Ramirez finishes reading the article. "I don't get it," he says, looking puzzled. "Why the big difference?"

"That's a good question," Harry says. "When one side talks about 600 incidents and one side talks about 157, you'd think maybe a reporter would ask that question." Harry lifts his beer and takes a long swallow. "You'd think maybe a reporter would *investigate*," Harry says, "instead of sitting on his ass. You'd think maybe a reporter would *earn* his goddamned paycheck, instead of just collecting it."

Harry looks at the guys sitting around the table. We look back at him over the mugs and bottles. "I called union headquarters," Harry says finally. "It took them all morning before they got back to me. You know what they said?"

What?

"They said that the count the police give, it's just for New York City. And the company's count, it's for New York City, Long Island, Westchester, Connecticut, and New Jersey."

The guys nod.

"You think some reporter might have figured that out?" Harry says. "You think some reporter might have *investigated* the goddamn numbers?"

A waitress with a figure like Twiggy's, twenty years ago, comes over with six mugs of beer, two bottles of Guinness, and a basket of tortilla chips.

"Now look at this." Harry picks up the newspaper and points to the caption of the photo that goes with the article. Juan Ramirez leans over and reads out loud: "Despite *Chronicle*'s claims, little harassment reported to police."

The guys laugh.

"Little harassment," I say. "I could show them a little harassment."

Harry stands up. "Those reporters!" he says. "You ever *talked* to them? You think they can find out what's going on in this city? You think they can find out what's going on in this strike? Some of those guys, it's a miracle if they can find their dick when they need to pee."

9

The paper's bleeding. Seven hundred fifty thousand dollars a day. That's how much it's bleeding. That's what it *admits*.

"Class warfare," Tony says.

"You're damned right," I say.

It's the middle of January. I take the whole family to Peter Luger. My treat. The best steakhouse in Brooklyn. A smell that makes you think you died and went to steak heaven. A smell that makes you think about a triple bypass. We all eat as if we'll never eat again.

"That's what you really believe in," Tony says. "Class warfare. Us against them."

"Damned right," I say.

"You know what your union is doing?" Tony says. "You're killing that paper. You're bleeding it dry."

"Let it bleed," I say.

"Can't we talk about something else?" Mary says, caught as usual between her bigmouth husband and her bigmouth son. Even though she's on the wrong side of fifty, she's still a good-looking woman, with carrot-colored hair and clear blue eyes. She's wearing an ivory suit over a pink jersey, a necklace of lettuce-green stones, and diamond earrings. I'm happy to be with her.

"It's not just us," I say, leaning toward Tony. "The company started this fight. We didn't want a strike. The company suckered us into it."

"Nobody knows that for sure," Tony says.

"OK," I say. "Nobody knows for sure. Not even you."

"You're right," Tony says. "You're always right."

"I'm not always right, but I'm right about this."

"Class warfare," Tony says in a tone that's tuned to get my goat. It's not quite a sneer, but not quite not a sneer.

"You've got it," I say. "Class warfare. No holds barred. Us against them."

Tony laughs. "Workers of the world, unite. You have nothing to lose but your rackets."

• • •

The last ditch. That's where we are now.

It's February. Snow on trees and on rooftops. Snow in the gutters and snow piled high where the snowplows have dumped it. Not one bird in the city. In the ten seconds it takes you to get on your gloves, your hands go numb.

On February 15, the company and the unions will make one final effort to negotiate. All the big shots, forty people or more, will sit down in some big room at the Waldorf-Astoria, with some "super mediator."

What's the union's strategy?

"We'll hold firm," Harry Simms tells me. "The way we figure it, the company will sell the paper in the end. That means we position ourselves to negotiate with the new owner. And that means we hold firm now."

What's the company's strategy?

"They'll hold firm," Tony tells me over the phone, after talking to his friend at Baines & Ivory. "The way their lawyers see it, the company has said over and over again that the offer on the table is its bottom-line offer."

"Is it?"

"I don't know, but if the company blinks now, the union can charge that the company didn't negotiate in good faith. That might expose the company to big liabilities for labor-law violations. So they won't budge."

Harry was right, and Tony was right. Neither side budged, and yesterday, February 28, the "super mediator" gave up. That means the company has to close the paper or find a buyer for it.

• • •

It's March 21, and yesterday we got our new owner—one of those bored billionaires who's desperate for something to do with his life. Harry Simms says that the paper's a toy that the billionaire has set his heart on, that he's willing to pay more than it's worth, and that he's willing to make some concessions to the unions.

Jackson Heights. A Chinese laundry, a Korean market, a Thai restaurant. A black kid, eight or nine, in Michael Jordan sneakers and a T-shirt with a picture of Malcolm X on it, moves snappily up the street bouncing a basketball. From the Papaya King on the corner come smells of papaya, banana, and strawberry juice. Overhead, on a sunny day that feels like May, the sky is blue and silver.

"How you doing, Muhammad?"

"No problem, boss."

I drop a bundle of papers on the sidewalk next to his newsstand. He looks at me.

"That's a great newspaper," I say. "The New York *Chronicle.* I hope you sell a million."

"Me too, boss."

• • •

"So what's the deal?" Mary asks when I get home.

In the basement, she's painting one of her watercolors. A yellow lighthouse, a gray sky, black water. We have her paintings all over the house. Oils and watercolors, mostly flowers and landscapes. Last year she did one I loved—a tall windmill on a meadow of brown grass beneath a big stormy sky.

"We'll probably lose about one third of our work force."

She stops painting. Holding the brush, she turns to look at me. She's wearing a smock over a white workshirt and faded blue jeans.

"And?" she says.

"He'll trim the manning tables, but he won't eliminate them."

"And?"

"We'll keep the seniority rules. We'll keep control of our pensions."

"And?"

"He'll fire the scabs."

"And?"

"He'll fire the nonunion plant supervisors."

"So you won?" All this time, Mary is looking at me. A smudge of gray paint makes a crescent on one cheek. I lean over and kiss the other one. "You won?" she says again.

"Yeah, we won," I say. "They tried to break the union, and we didn't break."

I remember all the guys who are going to lose their jobs, about one third of the work force, and I remember how some people think the company wanted to sell the paper all along, and other people think that the paper will die anyway, in two or three years, unless we make the cuts the company wants.

Then I remember how the old company had said it wanted to clean up the union. What would've happened to me if the company had cleaned up the union?

Mary is still looking at me, not smiling, with a worried look in her eyes.

"We won," I say again. "They couldn't break us."

10

A couple of months after the unions made their deal with the new owner, the kids took Mary and me to a fancy restaurant in Manhattan, four stars, for our thirty-third wedding anniversary.

"So you won," Tony said in the sarcastic way that Mary says he learned from me. "Another glorious chapter in the history of American labor."

"Could we please talk about something else," Mary said.

"Let the kid talk," I said.

"You know why you won?" Tony said.

"Why?"

"You won because might is right. You won because you scared the shit out of the dealers on the street."

I shrugged.

"It's true, isn't it?" Tony said.

"Might *is* right," I said. "Didn't they teach you anything in law school?"

"Muscle," Tony said. "That's why you won."

Angela, my daughter who wants to be a nurse, was listening with a bright look in her eyes. She's a great girl, full of fire and compassion. I worry about her.

"Tony," she said, "the unions had to *fight*. Can't you see that?"

"You think the company doesn't use muscle?" I said to Tony. "You think the company doesn't use fear?"

"It doesn't break the law," Tony said.

"It *buys* the law," I said. "It makes the law or buys the law. For God's sake, don't you know anything?"

Mary laughed—a big laugh that made me happy we'd been together all those years.

Angela said, "How can you be against the unions, Tony? What's wrong with you?"

"What's wrong with me? What's *wrong* with me?" Tony laughed. "Tell her, Dad. Tell her about your union."

"It's a good union," I said mildly. "Working people need unions."

"Oh, for God's sake," Tony said.

"It put you through law school," I said. "I didn't hear you complaining about my union when I wrote out the checks to pay your tuition bills."

"Could we *please* talk about something else," Mary said.

"Intimidation," Tony said. "That's what pays this family's bills. Violence, intimidation, and harassment."

"Intimidation!" I said to Tony. "Have you ever looked into the eyes of a fifty-five-year-old working man?"

"Tell her about the rackets," Tony said, looking at me and then at Angela. "Don't give her this crap about 'working people.' Tell her how the world works."

This put me in a difficult position. I took a sip of water. But he wouldn't let up. Not Tony. He can be a bulldog when he wants to be.

"Go ahead," he said. "Tell her what you were really fighting for."

I sat there holding that glass of water up against my mouth, taking tiny sips, buying time. Because he had me cornered, and both of us knew it. What were we really fighting for? We were fighting for *control*. The Newspaper Delivery Mob controls the union. Everybody knows that, or almost everybody.

"Go ahead," Tony said. "Tell her."

Tell her? I looked at my plate.

Tell her that members of the union steal thousands of newspapers every night and resell them to nonunion distribution companies? Tell her that the mob extorts bribes from wholesale distribution companies that want to operate as nonunion shops? Tell her that the mob sells NMDU union cards to people who shouldn't get them? Tell her that the mob steals seniority rights from nonmob union members and transfers them to mob members? Tell her that the mob extorts no-show jobs and phony overtime from company supervisors it bribes or intimidates? Tell her that the mob uses NMDU trucks to move and sell illegal goods? Tell her that the mob uses newspaper plants to operate loansharking, prostitution, and drug-dealing rings?

"Go ahead, Dad," Tony taunted. "Tell her what you were *really* fighting for."

I put down my glass of water on the table, took a deep breath, and looked Angela straight in her blue-gray eyes. "Your brother is full of shit," I said.

"Oh, brilliant," Tony said. "That's really brilliant."

"OK," I said, still looking at Angela. "The company fought to break the unions. We fought back, and we broke the law— I admit it. You satisfied?"

"I was never dissatisfied," Angela said.

"The trouble with your brother," I said, "is that he doesn't know any history. If he knew a little history, he'd know that working people have to fight."

"And the rackets?" Tony said.

I sighed. The rackets. What could I say about the rackets?

I looked at my family, my wife and my three handsome children, seated around the table on this happy occasion, my thirty-third wedding anniversary, at the four-star restaurant in Manhattan where doctors and lawyers and corporate executives celebrate their anniversaries and the food is so fancy that half the time I don't even know what I'm eating. Without the NMDU, would anyone in my family ever eat sweetbreads with black morel mushrooms or duck in a sauce dotted with black juniper berries?

"At least they're *our* rackets," I said.

• • •

So there you have it—as Tony said, another glorious chapter in the history of American labor.

Did the company want to break the unions? . . . You bet.

Did the unions win the war on the street with bombs, with bricks, with bottles, with threats of violence and acts of violence, with an organized campaign of terror, intimidation, and harassment? . . . You bet.

Did politicians wink at the violence? Did the police fail to pursue it? Did the press fail to investigate and report it? Did the church prefer to ignore it? . . . You bet.

Were the unions fighting to preserve obsolete privileges? . . . You better believe it.

Were the unions fighting to preserve work rules that protect incompetence, idleness, inefficiency, and petty theft? . . . Can anybody doubt it?

Was the NMDU fighting to preserve corrupt and illegal rackets? . . . What can I tell you?

A couple of weeks ago, I said to Mary, "You know, maybe

it won't be so bad, getting older." Mary looked at me and said, "Vince, don't piss on my head and tell me it's champagne."

A few days later, Mary and I rented a great movie from the fifties, *On the Waterfront*, to watch on the VCR. You might remember how, in the end, Marlon Brando beats the shit out of Lee J. Cobb, the crooked union boss, and then Cobb's thugs beat the shit out of Brando, and then Brando, all busted up, staggers up the dock to the hiring hall with Cobb cursing on the dock behind him, while all the honest union guys step back, like the Red Sea parting for Moses, so Brando can stagger all alone a hundred yards or more with the blood streaming down his face and Father what's-his-name who's really Karl Malden looking on like he's watching Christ dying on the cross, and the girl who loves Brando even though he set up her brother to be killed looking on like she's watching Christ risen from the grave, and in the audience, if you're in a movie theater, you hear the sound of women sniffling or sobbing and the sound of men blowing a week's worth of snot into their handkerchiefs.

Well—if you've ever seen it, you'll never forget it. So there I was, two or three weeks ago, a man in his mid-fifties in royal blue pajamas with tears running down his cheeks and half a dozen tissues crumpled around him on his bed, and his wife in pink pajamas crying in the next bed, and I said, "You know, hon, the thing that gets me is, I'd like to be Brando beating up Lee J. Cobb, but in real life, I'm not even a big shot like Cobb, I'm just one of Cobb's thugs beating the shit out of Brando."

Mary smiled—she has a beautiful smile—and wiped her eyes with a tissue she picked up off the bed, and looked at me with a sad, sweet smile like the smile on Eva Marie Saint's face while she watches Brando staggering toward the hiring hall with redemption getting surer and sweeter with every step he takes.

Mary looked at me, smiling, and the sad, calm look on her

face reminded me of the jewel-laden statue of the Virgin carried in the big procession through the big noisy crowd in the streets, with the brass band and the barefoot worshipers, at the festival of Our Lady of Mount Carmel when I was a kid in East Harlem. That was an awful long time ago.

"I'm just one of Cobb's thugs beating the shit out of Brando," I said, "only the guys I beat up are scared bastards who can't fight back."

Mary wiped her face again, but her eyes were still shiny with tears.

"Hell, Vince," she said. "It's a beautiful movie. Don't spoil it."

Mr. Moth and Mr. Davenport

Jefferson House is a twelve-story, middle-income, red-brick apartment building in a town named Flynn City, fifteen miles west of Detroit. The neighborhood is pleasant, with broad streets and plenty of shade. You rarely hear screeching brakes or raised voices. No one litters. No one feels menaced. People are unhurried and polite.

Marie Zimmerman and her husband, Oscar, a lithographer, moved into a one-bedroom apartment in Jefferson House after Oscar's first heart attack, in 1961. Oscar died in his sleep in 1967. In December 1978, six weeks after old Mr. Simmons went to live with his daughter in Ann Arbor, a new tenant moved into 4-J. Mrs. Zimmerman met him in the laundry room.

"I'm Marie Zimmerman," she said. "4-M."

"Harry Moth. 4-J."

After that, Marie did not speak to Harry for two months, except in passing. On a Tuesday early in February, at ten in the morning, they both happened to be on the elevator going downstairs when Harry made a sudden, gasping sound. His fist banged the side of the elevator, which shuddered in response.

"Are you all right, Mr. Moth?"

Looking at Marie, Harry fell against the rear wall of the elevator, opened his mouth, and slid to the floor. He was a big, blunt-featured man, well over sixty, with white, unruly hair. Marie herself had just turned seventy.

"Call a doctor," Harry said, on the floor in a corner of the elevator, in a voice Marie could barely hear.

Three weeks later, when Harry came home from the hospital, Marie paid a visit.

"You saved my life," Harry said.

Marie shrugged.

"Come in. Have some coffee."

"Okay."

"You live here alone?" Harry Moth asked, while he prepared coffee in his kitchen.

"I'm a widow," Marie said.

They sat down with their coffee mugs at the table in Harry's dining nook. Outside, the sky was a pale blue, without clouds.

"Well," Harry said, "tell me about yourself." He was not a subtle man.

"What do you want to know?" Marie asked.

"Everything."

Marie started talking. Harry leaned back in his chair. He looked at Marie across the table.

Her father had come to the United States from Hungary in 1911, Marie said. She was one of eleven children, but only six had survived to adulthood.

"I had a sister who died in the flu epidemic, and a brother who died in the war," Harry said. "World War I."

In St. Louis, in 1912, Marie said, her father helped dig the foundation for the new city hall. Then he worked laying railroad tracks in Minnesota. Then he worked mining coal in Iowa. By 1914, he had saved enough money to bring his wife and children to the United States. Marie was five. They came via steerage on a German steamship. Steerage was horrible, Marie said, but Harry noticed that the look on her face was serene. It had all happened a long time ago, the look on her face seemed to say.

Harry liked looking at her. She had frizzy white hair that

rose prettily from her head like a white woman's afro. Her eyes were sky-blue, lively, and clear. Her nose was straight. Her skin, full of tiny wrinkles, looked fragile.

Marie remembered urine dripping onto her face from the child sleeping in the bunk above her in steerage. She remembered people throwing up, their hands clutched to their bellies. The air stank.

Every morning, Marie said, stewards would herd the passengers in steerage up onto the deck. Then they burned buckets of sulphur in the hold. Fumes from the sulphur killed the stench.

• • •

Harry Moth was a good listener. Marie noticed that right away. It was nice talking with a man who knew how to listen.

"What about you?" Marie asked when she got tired of answering Harry's questions.

"I'm just an ordinary guy," Harry said.

Marie waited for him to say more.

"I worked lots of jobs," Harry said. "I drove a truck. I was a short-order cook. I worked in a sewage treatment plant."

With his heavy hands, his big arms and shoulders, and his heavy chest, he looked like a man who had done those jobs.

"What about now?" Marie asked.

"Now I'm retired."

"You ever been married, Harry?"

"Twice. I guess you could say I'm a two-time loser."

"Too bad."

"Yeah." Harry stared into his coffee mug.

"Kids?" Marie asked.

"Three. They don't have much to do with me."

"I'm sorry."

"That's life."

Mr. Communicative, Marie thought.

"How about you?" Harry asked.

"I also have three. A daughter in Philadelphia, a son in Tucson, and a son in New Orleans."

"They talk to you?"

"Sure. They talk."

"That's nice. Tell me about your husband."

"Some other time, Harry." Marie stood. "Thanks for the coffee."

•   •   •

At Ellis Island, Marie told Harry, she was stripped naked and forced to walk through a big pool of water with Lysol in it. Something was sprayed onto her hair to kill lice.

Marie was there with her mother, two brothers, and three sisters. They waited on wooden benches in huge rooms. They ate at long tables in dining halls that could have served an army.

"Terrible food," Marie told Harry. "I still remember how awful the food was."

A boat took Marie and her family from Ellis Island to lower Manhattan. A train took them from New York City to Iowa. Big tickets telling their destination were pinned on their coats. Flies buzzed in the warm weather. The seats in the train were made of braided cane.

In Iowa, they moved into a wooden shack built by the coal company. The house stood on a dirt street that ran alongside the railroad tracks. Across the street they could see the coal mine.

•   •   •

"You've got a real head on your shoulders."

That was what Oscar Zimmerman said to Marie, a long time ago. She was fifteen when she met him. At that age she already had a job, working for the American Can Company in Cleveland. Her parents and her younger brothers and sisters still lived in Iowa. Marie lived with her oldest brother and his wife.

She worked on the top floor in a five-story building. Every day, she walked up five flights of stairs to go to work. She was one of six women painting milk cans by hand. The lithographing department also was up on the fifth floor. Painted tin was dried in kilns. Men with leather gloves worked with pieces of hot tin. Marie would never forget the heat from the kilns.

That's something you can't describe, Marie thought, lying on her back in bed in her apartment more than forty years later: the heat from those kilns.

One day the men at the kilns stopped working. They wanted more money. The boss, a red-haired man with his sleeves rolled up, took the women who were painting milk cans and put them to work at the kilns. The men who stopped working had taken the gloves, so the women worked without them. A piece of hot tin slipped, slicing Marie's thumb to the bone. She still had the scar.

In bed, Marie put her finger on her spot. Yes, there it is.

When she went home with her thumb all bandaged and told her brother what had happened, his face turned an angry red.

"Scab!" he shouted, scowling at her. "Those men walked off that job for a reason. You should have told the boss to go to hell."

"I was frightened," Marie said. "I didn't want to lose my job."

"You didn't *think*," her brother said.

The man who had led the men at the kilns off the job was fired. His name was Oscar Zimmerman.

• • •

"You like baseball?" Harry Moth asked Marie on a rainy day in April.

"Better than football."

"The Tigers are home this weekend. You interested?"

"Sure."

They went to see the Tigers.

"You like jazz?" Harry Moth asked Marie.

"Sure."

Harry took her to a jazz club.

"You like Italian food?" Harry asked.

"Who doesn't?"

Harry took Marie to a place called Caruso's, on Emmet Street, between a funeral parlor and a travel agency with a photo of the Matterhorn in the window. Harry wore a brown suit. Marie wore a red dress and a necklace with pale blue stones on it. Her face was bright beneath her halo of frizzy white hair.

"Marie?"

"Yes."

"There's something I've got to tell you."

"What's that?"

"I don't know how you'll take it."

"Try me."

"It's about me."

"I'm listening, Harry."

"I've done some things I didn't tell you about."

"What kind of things?"

Marie waited. Harry's eyes looked mournful.

"You ever heard of the Mafia, Marie?"

•   •   •

In Cleveland in 1924, one of the women who worked painting milk cans with Marie was Oscar Zimmerman's sister. At a picnic one Saturday, a month after Oscar lost his job, Marie was introduced to him.

He was twenty-five years old, a big man with blue eyes and wheat-colored hair. He was carrying a book called *Progress and Poverty*, by a man named Henry George. Marie asked to see it. She squinted at the first page through glasses she had worn for the past five or six years.

"Something wrong with your eyes?" Oscar asked.

"I don't see so good," Marie said.

"So well," Oscar said. "Maybe you need new glasses."

Oscar told Marie about Henry George. Marie told Oscar about Charlotte Brontë. She had taken *Jane Eyre* out of the library.

"I don't read novels," Oscar said.

"Why not?"

"A man needs to read economics. Economics and history."

Oscar asked Marie about her schooling. Marie explained that she'd had to leave school at twelve, to make money for her family.

Her parents liked America, Marie said, but they were puzzled by native-born Americans. Most of the foreign-born families were Roman Catholic. Most of the American-born families were Protestant. Foreign-born families belonged to fraternal societies that took care of widows and children when trouble came. People born in America rarely belonged to fraternal societies. They relied on charity or public relief. At any rate, that was the way it seemed to Marie's parents.

Marie told Oscar about the coal miners' strike in Iowa in 1920, when she was eleven. The coal operators had cut wages when the war ended. In Wicksville, the town where Marie's family lived, foreign-born families supported the strike. The mines remained closed. In other towns, American-born men went to work as scabs. Not all of them, but many.

During World War I, Marie told Oscar, many white southerners had moved to Iowa to work in the mines. They hated the immigrants. There was a lot of name-calling, Marie said. American-born people called the immigrants "hunkies" and "flatheads." Foreign-born people called the natives "johnnybulls." The coal operators liked seeing the workers fight among themselves.

The Ku Klux Klan had a newspaper, *The Iowa Fiery Cross*,

that was sold in many towns. Night riders in white robes and hoods often rode into Wicksville. They fired pistols and shotguns into the air. They burned a cross in front of the Catholic church. They burned a cross on the slag pile in front of the mine.

The night riders burned down barns and haystacks. They destroyed crops. They slaughtered livestock. Marie remembered the fires in the night, and smoke rising from the ruins in daylight.

At the picnic in 1924, Oscar Zimmerman listened to Marie with an intense expression on his face. His eyes never moved away. The picnic went on, but Oscar and Marie had formed a separate circle.

Her father kept a loaded rifle near his bed, Marie said. He made it clear that he intended to shoot first, ask questions later. No one bothered him.

The union leaders decided that they had to get the scabs out of the mines. The miners met in Wicksville. Every man had a rifle or a shotgun. After the meeting, Marie's mother begged her father to stay home. "Think about the children," she said.

"If I don't fight this fight now," Marie's father said, "my children will have to fight it later. I'd rather fight it myself."

The union miners went to a nearby town where scabs were working the mine. They found the mine guarded by southern white women and teenagers. Everyone had some kind of gun. The union leaders put their guns on the ground. They walked up to the women with their hands empty.

"Our children are hungry," Marie's father said. "If your men join us, our children won't go hungry and neither will yours."

The women let the union leaders go into the mine. After a while, the leaders came out of the mine with the men who had been working as scabs. Nobody was angry. In a caravan of broken-down jalopies, everyone went to the next town. Those scabs also came out of the mine. A larger caravan went on to the next town.

After three days, the company decided to settle the strike. Marie's father and his friends came home in their jalopies.

"So you won?" Oscar Zimmerman said to Marie, at the picnic where she told him the story. The sun in the light of late afternoon gave his face a honey-gold glow. Looking at Marie with his face in the sunlight, Oscar took a bite of hot dog and slowly chewed it. "You know why you won?"

"Sure," Marie said. "We stuck together."

• • •

"You mean you're dating the godfather?"

"Not the godfather. More like a cousin."

Marie is visiting her friend Hannah Wexler, in 6-C. She's sitting at the dining table outside Hannah's kitchen, with a cookbook open in front of her. In the kitchen, Hannah, who likes to try new dishes, is making couscous. She is a trim and energetic woman, a few years younger than Marie, with hair nearly as white.

"What now?" Hannah says.

Marie consults the cookbook. "Two cups sliced turnips."

"He's retired?" Hannah says.

"Yes."

"So—what did he do, before he retired?"

"A little of this, a little of that."

"Tell me, Marie."

"Credit-card rip-offs, bookmaking, hijacking."

"Hijacking?"

"Not airplanes. Airplane cargo."

"Really!"

"You'd be amazed, Harry says, how easy it is to steal cargo from the freight terminals at the airport."

"Hmm. What now, Marie?"

"One and one half cups sliced carrots."

Hannah is a widow whose husband was a reporter active in the newspaper writers' union. Marie met her four years ago, at the swimming pool in the Flynn City Health Club, on Michigan Street.

"Of course," Marie says, "they've got inside information. The unions that load and unload those planes—those are mob-run unions."

"What about airport security?"

"Harry's got lots of friends in airport security."

"What about the cops?"

"Harry's got even more friends who are cops."

Hannah looks at Marie with a chopping knife in her hand.

"Three quarters of a cup chopped onions," Marie says.

"You think he ever killed anybody?" Hannah says.

"I'm afraid to ask."

• • •

"Harry, may I ask you a personal question."

"Sure, Marie."

"Did you ever . . . hurt anyone? In your business, I mean."

"You mean, did I ever kill anyone?"

"Yes. I guess that's what I mean."

Marie feels ridiculous. The look on Harry's face suggests that the question is not welcome. He says, "You sure you want to ask me that, Marie?"

"I'm sure, Harry."

"Why do you want to know, Marie?"

"Well, Harry, we've been seeing a lot of one another."

"It's a very personal question."

"I know, Harry."

"I'm going to tell you the truth, Marie."

"Okay, Harry."

"The truth is, I don't want to answer that question."

Harry looks uncomfortable. His big hands rest in his lap,

one on top of the other. Whatever they may have done once, now they're just the hands of an old man.

"Marie?"

"Yes, Harry."

"In my line of work, people get killed. No big deal. You know what I mean?"

"I guess so, Harry."

"What I mean is, it comes with the territory."

• • •

Marie makes Harry nervous. One thing he knows for sure: she's no bimbo. Harry knows how to handle bimbos. But this woman is different. With this woman, Harry likes to talk. They have coffee together almost every afternoon, in her apartment or his.

When he took her home after the Tigers game, Harry shook Marie's hand at the door. When he took her home after the jazz club, Harry shook her hand again. When he took her home after dinner at Caruso's, ditto.

Piano wire—that's what Harry used when he killed Bruno Petricelli. Bruno was trying to pocket more than his fair share of the bookmaking operation he ran on Fairmont Street. Harry was sent to collect. Bruno paid up, but he kept cheating. It all happened a long time ago—1947. Harry hasn't killed anyone since he wrapped piano wire around Bruno Petricelli's neck in 1947.

"Would you like to go to Italy?" Harry asks.

It's a mild day in May, three months after his heart attack.

"Italy! Are you kidding?"

"Why should I kid?"

"Harry, I don't have that kind of money."

"It's on me. You'd like Italy, Marie."

"I'm sure I would. But Harry—"

"What?"

"It's not as if we're lovers."

"We're friends, aren't we?"

"Of course, Harry."

"Well."

"Well what?"

"Think about it. You don't have to decide today."

Marie thought about it. She decided not to decide.

•   •   •

"Acid."

Jack Davenport sits facing Marie on the sofa in Hannah Wexler's living room. He's a stocky man in his mid-sixties, wearing a rumpled suit and a white shirt. Pink whales spout on his tie. His face is broad, with a full jaw. His nose looks like the nose of George Washington on the dollar bill. His eyes are hidden by dark glasses.

"A bucketful of acid, right in the face," Jack Davenport says, with a grimace.

"I'm sorry," Marie says. "I don't know what else to say."

"Not much anyone can say," Jack Davenport says.

Marie looks at him. Jack Davenport looks in her direction, but he cannot see exactly where she is, so his face points a little to her left.

He is telling Marie the story of how he lost his eyesight. In the 1950s, he was a columnist for a newspaper in Detroit. His big subject was mob control of labor unions—how the mob took over unions, looted their pension funds, stole union elections, organized rackets, beat up or killed dissidents.

Marie listens with a serious expression on her face. If Jack Davenport could see her, he would see that she is falling in love with him.

In his newspaper column in 1956, Jack says, he wrote a series of attacks on Local 44 of the International Union of Operating Engineers, based in Detroit. He also criticized Jimmy Hoffa, who was then moving to take over national control of the teamsters.

One night, Jack went to a sandwich place near the newspaper building for a late snack. When he came out, a figure stepped out of the shadows with a bucket in his hands, walked up to Jack, and flung acid from the bucket straight into Jack's face.

"Did they ever catch the guy who did it?" Marie asks.

"The guy who did it wound up in a gutter with his brains decorating the sidewalk," Jack says.

"How about the guy who gave the orders?"

"The guy who gave the order is retired now. He lives in Arizona, in a house with tennis courts and a pool."

"Crime never pays."

"His granddaughter goes to Harvard."

• • •

"Harry, you shit! You fucking shit! You damned fucking nogood shit!"

Harry Moth is thinking about the end of his second marriage. He is thinking about the day in 1938 when Linda, his wife, found out about Casey, his girlfriend.

"I'll tear out her eyes, Harry. You tell her I'll tear her fucking eyeballs out."

A guy like me needs a girlfriend, Linda. You should have understood that.

Harry, back in 1938, was wearing a dark suit with a silver pinstripe and a white shirt open at the collar, with his tie pulled violently askew. His hair was black and shiny. Linda, yelling, was in a gold silk nightgown.

You should have seen yourself, Linda, in that slinky gold thing, with your eyeballs big and bulging. You looked terrific. I'll give you that.

Harry turned his back on her. He walked upstairs. He pulled a suitcase out of the closet. He threw the suitcase onto the bed. He pulled open a drawer in his dresser and started throwing clothes into the suitcase.

"You leaving, Harry? Is that it? You're leaving?"

"I'm leaving."

"What about the kids, Harry?"

"Fuck the kids."

"Great! That's just great, Harry."

"Shut up, Linda."

"You're true blue, Harry. You're Mr. Terrific."

A noise at the doorway caught their attention. Michael, their six-year-old, and Roberta, their four-year-old, were standing there in their pajamas. Roberta was holding a small brown teddy bear.

"Tell them yourself, Harry. Kids, Daddy has something to tell you."

Slinky Linda in her gold nightgown looked at handsome Harry in his charcoal suit, standing in front of the open suitcase. Harry looked back at her, for the first time ever, with pure hatred in his eyes.

• • •

Roses. Harry Moth has sent Marie red roses.

Alas, poor Harry.

"Harry, there's something I want to tell you."

They're sitting with coffee at the table in Marie's dining nook, on an afternoon near the end of June. Outside, the sky is a dazzling blue.

"Harry, we can't go to Italy."

"That's okay."

"I've met someone, Harry. I've met a man."

"You mean—a man you like?"

"Yes, Harry."

Harry Moth is a big man with a big face that looks as unhappy, at this moment, as a man's face can look. His chin quivers. He bites his lip.

"I'm sorry, Harry."

"Yeah. Me, too."

"I hope we'll still be friends."

"I love you, Marie."

It was the first time he had said it.

"I know, Harry. I'm sorry."

"If you ever change your mind—"

"Thank you, Harry." Marie reaches out and touches his hand. It is a quick touch, and then her hand moves away. Harry watches it go. The way her hand moves away is a dagger in his heart.

• • •

The faces change in Jefferson House, though slowly. Mrs. Buggle, in 9-A, moved to Florida. The Yoshitakas, in 3-G, now have a baby girl. Mrs. Deutsch, in 5-D, moved into the Flynn City Geriatric Center. Mr. Cates, a bachelor who works for a telemarketing company, moved into 5-D. Mr. Bashkavich, in 11-E, was arrested on charges that he had used a monitoring device to steal cellular telephone numbers from motorists traveling on the expressway between Flynn City and Detroit.

Marie Zimmerman has been content in her marriage to Jack Davenport. They share a love of books and an interest in ideas. They listen together to National Public Radio and to recordings that are decades old—Broadway shows from the forties and fifties, jazz from the same era, old albums by Pete Seeger and Paul Robeson. For two or three hours every day, Marie reads out loud to Jack. They like Dickens and Dreiser. At present Marie is reading the autobiography of Clarence Darrow, a book that both of them read many years ago, and *Our Mutual Friend*, a book that is new to both of them.

Jack Davenport has gained ten pounds since Marie started cooking for him. The Hungarian specialties that Marie learned from her mother—beef goulash, goose liver, chicken paprikash—Jack finds irresistible. He has always been an angry, impatient man, but Marie soothes him. Sometimes at night, lying in bed with Marie's hand in his, listening to an old *I Love Lucy* show while Marie watches, he feels so lucky he thinks his heart will burst.

Harry Moth has remained friendly with Marie and has developed a friendship with Jack. Harry has never understood why a woman as attractive as Marie would saddle herself with a blind man, but he accepts that the heart moves in mysterious ways. Harry himself had a second heart attack, in September 1984, while standing in line to buy a sandwich at Katz's Deli on Winter Street. The attack was not major, but it weakened Harry more than the first one. He has lost weight, he walks more slowly now, and he cannot climb a flight of stairs without pausing to catch his breath.

Harry likes Jack Davenport, and Jack has come to like Harry, though at first Jack was bothered by Harry's past. "Your pals did *this* to me," Jack said once, pointing his thumb toward his dark glasses. Harry could not deny it. "Those unions you care about so much are full of crooks," Harry said. Jack replied that he knew as much about crooked unions as any man in America. In the calm that descended at the end of one argument, they realized that they saw the world in much the same way—as a racket. Jack was interested in cleaning up the mess, and Harry was interested in getting a piece of the action.

At this point, somehow, what matters most is that both of them love the same woman, both of them find it necessary to nap after lunch, both of them have prostate problems, and both of them would rather talk about things that happened forty years ago than things that happened yesterday.

• • •

Blueberry pancakes.

Sunlight fills the dining nook in Marie's apartment. Marie is making blueberry pancakes for Jack Davenport and Harry Moth. Harry is setting the table. Jack takes a seat and bends to put his blind man's walking stick on the floor, next to his chair, where no one will trip over it.

"Jack, tell Harry about your speech," Marie calls from the kitchen.

"You're making a speech?" Harry asks.

"Memorial Day. You remember what happened on Memorial Day, fifty years ago?"

"1937?"

"Yeah. 1937."

"Joe Louis fought Max Schmeling?"

"Good guess, Harry, but that's not it."

"I don't know, Jack. You're making a speech about something that happened fifty years ago?"

"The Memorial Day Massacre. You ever heard of that, Harry?"

Marie brings out blueberry pancakes on a platter.

"I don't think so," Harry says.

"On Memorial Day, 1937," Jack says, "cops killed ten people demonstrating outside a steel factory in South Chicago. Republic Steel. That was the Memorial Day Massacre."

"You want syrup, Jack?" Harry asks.

"I'll pour it. I know how much I like."

Jack pours syrup on his pancakes. Marie sits down opposite him, on the chair closest to the kitchen.

"Somebody caught the whole thing on newsreel," Jack says. "Cops beating up women, men trying to crawl away, spitting up blood, cops firing into their backs."

"Jack, you want more coffee?" Harry asks.

"Please."

"For a while the newsreel was suppressed," Marie says to Harry. "The big shots were afraid people might riot if they saw it."

"The Memorial Day Massacre," Harry says, shaking his head from side to side. "I don't remember it."

"That's the trouble with this country," Jack says. "Nobody remembers anything."

"The cops were just doing what the companies wanted," Marie says. "The companies called the tune, as usual."

"Who's got the syrup?" Jack asks.

Harry passes him the syrup.

"So what's this about a speech?" Harry says to Jack.

"At the community college. They've got a history teacher there who thinks his students should know some labor history."

"Memorial Day, 1937, I was in jail," Harry says. "They'd caught me fencing a load of stolen toasters."

"You missed a hell of a year," Jack says. "Nineteen thirty-seven—that was a year a lot of shit hit the fan."

"You gentlemen still hungry?" Marie asks. "I could make another batch."

"Count me in," Harry says.

"Me, too," Jack says.

Marie goes into the kitchen. Out of the corner of one eye, Harry can see her at the stove. She pours batter into the frying pan. He hears the hiss as the batter hits the pan.

Jack says, "Besides the Memorial Day Massacre, 1937 was the year they had the famous sit-down strike at GM, and GM recognized the UAW, and Chrysler recognized the UAW, and U.S. Steel recognized the steelworkers, and company thugs at Ford beat the shit out of Walter Reuther and his pals at the Battle of the Overpass."

"I'll come to that speech," Harry says to Jack. "You can teach me some history."

Harry sees Marie in the kitchen. With the bowl of batter still in her hand, she has turned to face the dining nook. She looks puzzled. Jack cannot see the look on Marie's face, but Harry will remember that look for the rest of his life.

"Jack?" Marie says.

Her hand opens, and the bowl drops onto the floor with a crash. The bowl rolls an inch or two on the floor, but does not break. Batter pours out of the bowl.

The look on Marie's face is the look of someone taken by surprise. She turns toward the refrigerator, lifts one hand toward her chest, and topples. Her head hits the side of the cabinet under the sink. Harry moves as fast as he can, but she's dead when he gets to her, her eyes wide open. On her lips there's a trace of blueberries.

• • •

"We ought to call that guy who wrote *The Odd Couple*," Jack Davenport says. "He could do a sequel."

A year has passed since Marie's death, and ten months since Harry Moth moved into Jack Davenport's apartment.

What to do with Jack? That was the big question in the days after Marie died. With his first wife, who died in 1977, Jack had two children. A son, Paul, was killed in Korea. A daughter, Robin, lives in an adult home for the mentally retarded, in Detroit.

Marie's daughter Grace, who lives in Philadelphia, said that Jack could come live with her, but Jack said no. To Harry he said, "I've lived here all my life. Why should I go to Philadelphia to die?"

Harry said, "Maybe I could help."

At first, Harry just went over to help Jack with his meals. Then, one morning about six weeks after Marie died, Jack passed out on his way to the bathroom. That was when they realized he had circulation problems.

"You shouldn't be alone," Harry said. "How about if I move in with you?"

"Are you crazy?"

"What if I am?"

So Harry moved in with Jack.

Their days are peaceful. They listen together to the radio

and to records they have collected over the years—Broadway shows from the forties and fifties, jazz from the same era, old albums by Frank Sinatra and Peggy Lee. For an hour or two every day, Harry reads out loud to Jack. He especially likes true crime books, which Jack also enjoys. If Jack wants to listen to Dickens or Dreiser, he gets a recording.

As a cook, Harry specializes in hamburger, pot roast, and meat loaf. Though both men have heart conditions, they've decided to eat whatever they please. Once Harry tried to make chicken paprikash, but it didn't come out right, and both men got depressed, thinking about Marie. They'll probably never eat goose liver again, or stuffed cabbage with sauerkraut, or the crepes called palacinky, rolled around apricot preserves or chestnut puree.

In the bedroom, Harry has separated the twin beds that were shoved together when Marie was alive. Harry will watch any kind of garbage on TV, whereas Jack is more selective. Sometimes at night, lying in bed, listening to music with headphones over his ears while Harry watches some god-awful police show, Jack remembers how he would hold hands with Marie while she watched her *I Love Lucy* reruns, and he feels sad.

During the day, in good weather, they often go to Hogg Creek Park, six blocks from Jefferson House. They sit on a bench in a sunny spot and listen to the thud of the ball on the basketball court and the squeals of kids on the swings or the jungle gym. Harry looks at the young mothers and wishes he were young. Jack tilts back his head and enjoys the sun.

At some point they get hungry, and Harry buys hot dogs from the vendor at the corner, or pretzels, or ice cream. Harry likes cones, and Jack prefers cups, which he's less likely to spill. Jack likes chocolate. Harry likes vanilla.

Both of them know that someday one of them will die suddenly, or be diagnosed as having some terrible illness, but for now, they're doing all right. To people who have recently moved into Jefferson House, they are simply Mr. Moth and Mr. Davenport, the nice elderly couple in 4-M. They are seen walking in and out of the building, with Mr. Davenport carrying his blind man's walking stick and Mr. Moth gently guiding Mr. Davenport by the elbow. They are seen sitting together in the park, or walking together to or from the park, or having a meal together at Bykofsky's Diner, on 4th Street. They are heard having conversations about people who mattered a long time ago.

Harry will say, "I met Al Capone once. In a barbershop in St. Louis."

Jack will say, "I met Hank Greenberg once. Remember the year he hit fifty-eight?"

Harry will say, "I saw Rita Hayworth once. Getting out of a taxicab in New York."

Jack will say, "I saw Judy Garland once."

Harry will say, "I love blueberry pancakes. But I haven't ordered them since—you know."

Jack will say, "Yeah. Me neither."

No doubt most of the newcomers in Jefferson House believe that they are gay, but no one snickers or whispers behind their backs, or treats them unkindly. They move slowly, and sometimes their slowness irritates or inconveniences younger people, but no one tries to hurry them. No one worries about them, or wonders about them, or thinks about them. Everyone can see that they're a pair of harmless old men, taking care of one another, living day by day, waiting for the end.

A Doctor's Story

Dr. Buchner sits on a white bench in a well-kept garden in the town of Dimmsdorf, on the grounds of the nursing home where he has lived for the past four years, since the heart attack that nearly killed him in 1980. A long stretch of grass shines in the sunlight. He stares at the line of trees in the distance. With his high forehead, his firm chin, and his sprinkling of silver-white hair, he is still a fine-looking man. But his chest, abdomen, and thighs have shrunk. His hands tremble. His eyes water. You would not think, looking at him, that he has ever done anything loathsome.

• • •

"Medicine?" Dr. Buchner's grandson says. "Yes. Of course I've thought about it."

"It's a fine profession," Dr. Buchner says, looking at the boy from the chair by the window in his room at the nursing home. It is a heavy chair with crimson upholstery. Through the window behind his grandfather, the grandson can see a stretch of lawn with white benches and, farther down, a wavy line of dark blue—the river.

"You should not let my experience deter you, Karl. You know, I'm sure, that our family has a long tradition."

This is an understatement, the grandson thinks. Not only is Dr. Buchner a physician, but so were his father, his grandfather, and his great-grandfather. Dr. Buchner himself was born in 1904 in Munich, received his medical degree in 1931, and married, that same summer, a much-desired beauty of that time, Dora Fetscher, the daughter of the renowned Dr. Otto Fetscher, a professor of biochemistry at Heidelberg. Dr. Buchner's daughter Anna (Karl's mother) is a pediatrician with a thriving practice, and her sister Klara earned a Ph.D. in biochemistry, married an American physician, and now heads the laboratory of biochemical and molecular virology at a prominent university in the United States.

"When I think about becoming a physician," Karl says, "I'm not sure whether I'm fulfilling a destiny I've chosen or one that tradition has imposed upon me. Also, I'm not sure that I have the temperament for it, or the ego."

"I understand perfectly," his grandfather says. "You're not alone. Everyone in the family struggles with the same doubts. And everyone, or almost everyone, overcomes them in the end."

   • • •

Loathsome? Is that the right word?

Yes, Dr. Buchner thinks. That is the right word.

"What exactly do you want to know?" he asks his grandson.

"Everything. I want to understand."

"And you think that I understand?"

The boy hesitates. Dr. Buchner thinks of him as a boy, though he is twenty-one, about to enter his final year as an undergraduate at the university. A tall youth, thin, with long hands and dark-hued, reddish-brown hair—the image of Dr. Buchner himself at the same age, though not quite as handsome. Karl says, "At least you can tell me what happened. That's a start."

"All right. But not today. I'm tired, Karl." Dr. Buchner sighs. "And I must think. It all happened so long ago."

   • • •

It takes the old man a week to gather his thoughts. Then he summons his grandson. They sit in Dr. Buchner's room at the nursing home. Rain streaks the window. The radiator clanks and rattles. From the flesh of the old man comes an odor the boy must force himself to ignore.

"I decided on a career in psychiatry," Dr. Buchner begins,

"because I had realized that I could not distinguish myself as a research scientist. If I could not distinguish myself, I thought, then I would enter a field where I would not embarrass myself."

"What made you think you couldn't distinguish yourself?"

"I had compared myself with people who excelled in basic science. I disliked laboratory work. I disliked test tubes and microscopes. I was—how shall I put it?—I was *sensitive*. I was not sure I had the temperament for medicine. In a family of scientists, I read poetry. I felt that I had, just a little, the soul of a poet."

The old man pauses. His grandson says nothing.

"The soul, but not the talent," the old man says modestly, his face wrinkling into dozens of lines. "Young Germans, even scientists, tend to be romantic. I was one of these romantics. Instead of peering at microorganisms or mixing chemical compounds, I thought I might explore the hidden side of human personality. So I took my degree in psychiatry."

"And then?"

And then, Dr. Buchner tells his grandson, he received an invitation to join the staff of the asylum at Ebbinburg. So he went in 1934 with his wife and infant daughter to that pleasant, red-roofed town renowned for its chocolates, nestled among hills in a part of Germany that seemed closer to medieval times than it did to the modern world.

• • •

"Dr. Buchner, I presume?"

With those words Dr. Buchner was greeted on his first day by the asylum's director, Dr. Hans Gruchmann, a hearty, broad-shouldered giant, six feet six inches tall. "Welcome! Welcome!" the older man boomed, stepping forward to shake hands and pounding the young physician on the back for good measure. To be greeted by Dr. Gruchmann was an experience a man did not forget, even fifty years later.

The work was difficult, Dr. Buchner tells his grandson. "Asylums are full of unhappy people. Difficult people. Miserable, wretched, suffering people." But this was the life Dr. Buchner had chosen. He plunged in, wanting to do his best, to do what he could. The old man's face darkens. "And then, almost before I began, something happened that changed everything."

A law—that was what happened. Dr. Buchner recalls sitting with the medical staff in the conference room on the summer day when Dr. Gruchmann informed them about the new statute. The Law for the Prevention of Hereditarily Diseased Progeny authorized the compulsory sterilization of individuals suffering from a number of diseases, including congenital feeble-mindedness, schizophrenia, hereditary blindness or deafness, hereditary epilepsy, Huntington's chorea, and various physical malformations.

"Was there any protest?" Dr. Buchner's grandson asks.

"Karl. My dear boy."

"I thought some people might have protested."

"No. We did not protest."

The law, Dr. Buchner explains, addressed an issue that had vexed German physicians for many years. An issue that was often described, in a phrase that might seem cruel or unfair, as . . .

"Life unworthy of life?"

"Precisely!" The old man slaps his open hands on his thighs. "Life unworthy of life. That was the issue. That was the very phrase we used."

• • •

In a general way, Karl knows much that his grandfather is telling him, but he wants a knowledge that transcends what he has learned from court transcripts and other documents. He wants to hear what his grandfather says, to see the expressions that pass across his face, to hear how his voice rises or falls, to observe his gestures. He is not quite sure how he feels or ought to feel about the subject they are discussing. He is not quite sure what he thinks or ought to think. He only knows that the subject grips him and will not let go.

In any case, even without hearing about it from his grandfather, Karl is familiar with the tract entitled "Permission for the Destruction of Life Unworthy of Life," published in 1920 by a professor of psychiatry and his coauthor, one of Germany's leading specialists in constitutional law. Karl has studied the tract, knowing how much it influenced the events that followed. The authors ask: "Is there human life which has so far forfeited the character of something entitled to enjoy the protection of the law, that its prolongation represents a perpetual loss of value, both for its bearer and for society as a whole?" Are there not lives—for instance, the lives of incurable idiots—which are "not merely worthless, but actually existences of negative value"? Are there not people whom we must recognize as a "travesty of real human beings" and lives that we must recognize as "absolutely pointless"—lives that place "a terrible, heavy burden upon their relatives and society as a whole" and whose termination "would not create even the smallest gap—except perhaps in the feelings of their mothers or loyal nurses"?

Though he feels some discomfort when he considers these questions, Karl recognizes that the issues the authors raise are reasonable. A state cannot function without calculating the costs and benefits of the activities it undertakes. The authors estimate an average annual cost of thirteen hundred reichsmarks for the care of every idiot maintained in an asylum. Assuming a life expectancy of fifty years, they conclude that the care of the nation's idiots represents "a massive capital in the form of foodstuffs, clothing and heating, which is being subtracted from the national product for entirely unproductive purposes." These "ballast existences" are a burden that threatens the health of the nation. Individuals of higher value—that is, higher productivity—cannot bear this burden forever. In its own defense, the nation must throw the human ballast overboard. Future generations, the authors say, will condemn the "over-cxaggcrated notions of humanity and over-estimation of the value of existence" that weakened the fatherland. A nation that promiscuously indulges its compassionate impulses runs the risk, as another author memorably put it, of "caring itself to death."

• • •

"There was once a woman who had three daughters, the eldest of whom was called One-Eye, because she had only one eye in the middle of her forehead, and the second, Two-Eyes, because she had two eyes like other folks, and the youngest, Three-Eyes, because she had three eyes; and the third eye was also in the center of her forehead. However, as Two-Eyes saw just as other human beings did, her sisters and her mother could not endure her."

Klaus Buchner has lived a long life, and no matter how unpleasant the memories that his grandson provokes, he also has many pleasant memories, which fill most of his hours. Half dozing in his bedroom at the Dimmsdorf Geriatric Center, or sitting with legs outstretched in the downstairs lounge full of flowers, or on a bench in the garden on a sun-drenched morning, he allows his mind to wander through the past, among sccncs and people it pleases him to remember.

How Dr. Buchner loved the stories his mother had read to him in his childhood, out of a thick volume with gilt-edged pages and a cover the color of burgundy wine. How soothingly his mother's voice had flowed over him; how gracefully her neck had curved as she bent over the book. On her breath, how sweet the smell of an apple or cherry tart or, now and then after dinner, the smell of plum brandy. How much

Dr. Buchner missed her, even now. His heart warmed when he remembered what it seemed he could not possibly remember–the sound of her voice, the touch of her hand smoothing his hair, the pressure of her lips on his forehead when she had finished reading.

And the stories, with their elves and goblins and stepmothers, with their frightened children lost in the woods, the stories as old as the forests of Germany, as old as its rivers, valleys, and mountains—how he had loved these stories even when they terrified him. "The Elves and the Shoemaker," "The Wolf and the Seven Little Kids," "The Bremen Town Musicians," "The Golden Goose," "Hansel and Gretel," "The Fisherman and His Wife," "Sleeping Beauty," "Rumpelstiltskin," "Snow-White and Rose-Red," "The Iron Stove," "The Queen Bee," "The Hut in the Forest," "The Frog Prince." How Dr. Buchner's heart swelled, even now, when he recalled the spell they had cast.

"Two-Eyes lived a long time in happiness. Once two poor women came to her in her castle and begged for alms. She looked in their faces and recognized her sisters, One-Eye and Three-Eyes, who had fallen into such poverty that they had to wander about and beg their bread from door to door. Two-Eyes, however, made them welcome and was kind to them and took care of them, so that they both with all their hearts repented the evil that they had done their sister in their youth."

• • •

Tuesday is sauerbraten day at the Dimmsdorf Geriatric Center.

"What I wouldn't give for *good* sauerbraten," Helena Ruttke says, lifting a bite of overcooked meat drenched in grayish-brown gravy.

"Ah!" Dr. Buchner says. "What I wouldn't give for good anything."

"That bratwurst was good the other day," Max Overhamm says. "When was that?"

"Saturday."

"Ox tongue," Dr. Buchner says. "I like a good ox tongue salad, or ox tongue soup."

The conversation goes on, moving from main courses to dessert.

"Marzipan cherry cake," Helena Ruttke says. "That is what I would like."

"I prefer Black Forest cake," Max Overhamm says. "A big piece of cake."

"Give me a good piece of strudel," Dr. Buchner says. "Apple strudel, made with the freshest apples. And a cup of good Viennese coffee. Yes! That is what I would like."

"Viennese coffee. Yes!" Helena Ruttke says, taking a deep breath, as if filling her nostrils with the smell. "A cup of good Viennese coffee!"

"I ask nothing more," Dr. Buchner says. "I would die content."

•   •   •

The food at the asylum?

"Not good," Dr. Buchner says to his grandson. "The food was not good, and there was not much of it. Turnips. Potatoes. A little meat now and then."

They are talking about the asylum in the 1930s, about the lives of the inmates, about the quality of life. Again, Karl is hearing much that he already knows, thanks to his own research. He knows that at Ebbinburg, the asylum population increased by 50 percent, without any increase in staffing, after asylum officials abandoned as outmoded the notion of optimum capacity. He knows that expenditures per patient went down 25 percent from 1933 to 1935. This reduction, Dr. Gruchmann noted in one annual report, resulted in a total saving of over three hundred thousand reichsmarks —a sum "made available to hereditarily healthy people." Everyone on the staff agreed that "the principal task we face is to manage the asylum in such a way that the outgoings of the National Socialist state on the propagation of unsuitable national comrades will be reduced to an absolute minimum."

Sterilization was one way to reduce future expenditures. "A simple surgical procedure," Dr. Buchner comments, looking at his grandson. Then his eyes turn away. He adds, "Though not, alas, one that always avoided complications."

At Ebbinburg in 1935 alone three hundred fifty patients were sterilized. Of these, two women died as a result of the operation, with one, aged forty, bleeding to death when a physician botched an effort to combine sterilization with a caesarean abortion. Two other patients experienced serious complications, and two committed suicide after the operation. One, a woman named Emma Brandt, choked herself to death by swallowing a six-inch spoon. The second, a woman named Maria Lublin, killed herself by swallowing feathers from a feather mattress.

"Grandfather," Karl says, "do you remember a woman named Emma Brandt?"

"Branch?"

"Brandt. Emma Brandt."

"No. I do not remember."

"Maria Lublin?"

His grandfather lifts his eyes, straining to remember. He shakes his head.

"Should I remember?"

• • •

"Bend forward. Yes, that's good. Now your knees. Bend your knees. A little more. Yes, that's it. Good. Now. Head up. Good. Ready?"

The year was 1911, Klaus Buchner was seven, and his father was teaching him to ski. Dr. Buchner remembers the brightness of the sun on the snow, the feel of the ski mask on his face, the struggle to stand upright on skis, the pleasure of receiving instruction from the man he admired most in the world—his tall, dark-eyed, full-bearded father. He remembers his father's reddish-brown beard, exactly the color of the beard Dr. Buchner grew in the early 1930s when he worked in the asylum at Ebbinburg.

The family had gone to Garmisch-Partenkirchen, the most famous resort in the German Alps, roughly twenty kilometers south of Oberammergau. They stayed at the celebrated Hotel Schneefernhaus, with its immense skiing areas. Klaus loved everything about the trip—the lodgings, the food, the sun, the snow, the cable cars, the mountains, the dazzling views. Something inside him that still has not died woke when he saw the snow on those mountains.

In his room at the Dimmsdorf Geriatric Center, the memory of those distant winters warms Dr. Buchner. All his life, he has loved winter sports. Skiing, skating, sledding, tobogganing, hiking, rock climbing, mountain climbing—since childhood, these activities have brought him joy. His eyes close, and the image of the Zugspitze, the highest peak in the German Alps, towering above Garmisch-Partenkirchen, comes before him. How, Dr. Buchner wonders, could the soul know itself without mountains?

• • •

"A dizzy spell. These things happen, Karl. I'm better now."

"I don't want to tire you, Grandfather."

"No, no. You've brought something to read to me? Read."

In his research, Karl has come upon a film called *Opfer der Vergangenheit*—*Victim of the Past*. The film was produced on Hitler's orders in 1936 and shown afterwards on a compulsory basis to large audiences in German movie theaters. Its purpose was to make the case for sterilization. Karl has obtained a transcript. He reads his grandfather one paragraph spoken by the film's narrator:

"'Sterilization is a simple surgical operation. It is a

humane method designed to spare the nation endless misery. The innocent should never suffer on account of the sins of the past. However, every honest and proud person will understand if we prevent these sins from becoming an endless chain. In the last seventy years our population has increased by 50 percent, while over the same period the number of hereditarily ill has risen by 450 percent. If this development continues, in fifty years there would be one hereditarily ill person for every four healthy people. An endless column of horror would march into the nation. Limitless despair would come upon a valuable population which would march toward its doom with giant steps. The Law for the Prevention of Hereditarily Diseased Progeny is not interference in divine law, but rather the restoration of a natural order which mankind has disrupted because of a false sense of humanity.'"

Karl looks at his grandfather. "A false sense of humanity?"

"The narrator is speaking from a eugenic perspective," Dr. Buchner says. "Eugenics, Karl, is the science that seeks to improve the quality of the human race through the scientific selection of genetically superior parents. In this film, the narrator criticizes the false sense of humanity that leads a society to permit people to breed even though the state suspects they will transmit genetic deficiencies to their children."

The old man pauses. Karl does not speak. The old man wets his lips and continues, "In any case, Karl, sterilization is not a perfect solution. Would you like to know about some of the difficulties that arose?"

One difficulty, the old man says, is that it is not easy to determine which illnesses, malformations, or deficiencies call for sterilization. For instance, what about the child of a blind mother with impaired vision because of childhood cataracts? What about dwarfs, people with harelips or cleft palates, people suffering from multiple sclerosis or muscular

existences." He estimates that thirty thousand institutional-
ized idiots cost the Reich 45 million reichsmarks a year, and
that the total expenditure on the mentally ill in Germany
comes to 150 million reichsmarks. He notes that killing these
people would substantially reduce the burden on the tax-
payer. He concludes that "every measure is permissible which
appears cheap and effective in the struggle against the less
valuable."

"Yes, Grandfather. I read the essay. In its own terms—that
is, in terms of a calculation of costs and benefits—I don't
think anyone could answer it."

"But you reject those terms?"

"I think we must. Otherwise, we turn our hospitals into
death camps."

The old man nods gravely. But then he says, in the tone
of someone conducting an examination in the Socratic
mode: "You think, Karl, that people who work should carry
on their backs, in effect, people who do not work—who cannot or will not?"

"People who cannot. Yes."

"And people who are unfit? You think the rest of us should
carry them?"

"To some extent."

"At any price?"

"No. Not at any price. Some limit must be set."

"Ah!" The old man's face brightens. "What limit?"

"I don't know."

"But you admit that some price is too high, that at some
point society must take a stand in favor of people who work,
as opposed to people who live without working?"

"Yes."

"Then we agree. Our only disagreement, perhaps, is
where that point is to be found. But that is a matter reasonable people can discuss," Dr. Buchner says. "It is a matter of

dystrophy, or families that have produced several generations of alcoholics?

"Are those all genetic problems?" Karl asks.

"Of course not. Nevertheless, sterilization was ordered in these and other cases. Then, too, it is difficult to draw lines. Who can draw a clear line between congenital feeble-mindedness and common stupidity?"

The old man pauses to give Karl time to consider the problems that might confront a state that went too far in attempting to eradicate human stupidity.

"In any case, Karl, sterilization does not address the full problem. It reduces the number of useless individuals that will burden society in the future, but it does not rid society of useless lives in the present."

• • •

Step one: sterilization.

Step two: extermination.

The grandson and his grandfather are discussing step two. In the garden of the Dimmsdorf Geriatric Center, among bright white and red blossoms, they talk about the extermination of mentally ill individuals, the extermination of terminally ill individuals, the extermination of crippled and incurably ill children.

"All of this was done for economic reasons?" Karl asks.

"For economic reasons and for eugenic reasons. In the National Socialist state, physicians were asked to become the executors of the eugenic will of the nation. You read the essay I recommended?"

Karl's grandfather has suggested that he read a lecture entitled "The Eradication of the Less Valuable from Society" delivered in 1932 by a psychiatrist named Berthold Kihn. The lecture provides a straightforward economic analysis. Kihn discusses the burden that hard-pressed German taxpayers must bear to care for individuals whom he calls "b locating a point or, if you prefer, drawing a line. It is not a matter of principle."

• • •

Butterflies.

A blizzard of butterflies, black and orange and silver and gold, white and yellow and bronze and blue, a blizzard of brilliant colors rising all around the newlyweds as they turned a corner in Rome, in dazzling sunlight, after visiting the house where the poet Keats died.

The year was 1931. Remembering the scene, Dr. Buchner smiles—an old man on a white bench in a well-tended garden, more than fifty years later. How much Klaus and Dora had loved their honeymoon in Italy, and how well he remembers it. They saw so much beauty, and so different from the beauty of Germany—the paintings of Tintoretto and Titian in Venice; Brunelleschi's dome in Florence; the Baptistery in Florence with its bands of green, white, and pink marble; Ghiberti's sculpted, gilt-paneled doors; the work of Michelangelo and Raphael in Rome. Yet, after all that dizzying immersion in beauty, what Dr. Buchner remembers most vividly is that bright storm of butterflies, beating their wings around the newlyweds as they turned a corner on a sun-drenched day in Rome, after visiting the room where a great poet died.

• • •

Dr. Buchner says, "Would you like to know how they were killed, these useless people?"

They are talking about Aktion T-4. That is the code name that was given to the extermination of mentally or physically disabled people in the "euthanasia" program that Hitler launched by secret order in 1939. Aktion T-4 mainly involved the murder of disabled adults, Dr. Buchner notes, but the program also included the murder of children.

The discussion stirs memories that Dr. Buchner does not share with his grandson. Dr. Buchner remembers the arrival of the workmen who converted a part of the asylum's cellar into a gas chamber and crematorium. The workmen attached a row of showerheads to the ceiling. They installed a gas pipe a couple of feet off the floor. They drilled holes in the pipe. The pipe was connected to gas cylinders outside the room and hidden beneath benches, so that the room itself appeared to be an ordinary shower. Airtight doors were built, and a ventilator was installed. Miniature railroad tracks were built to make it easier to transport corpses from the gas chamber to the crematorium.

In the killings that followed, carbon monoxide gas was released by a doctor standing in an alcove adjacent to the shower room. Karl knows that his grandfather took his turn performing this duty. He would like to ask his grandfather what he was thinking, what he was feeling, as he watched the asphyxiation of patients entrusted to his care. But he cannot find any way to phrase the question.

Dr. Buchner tells his grandson about signing the forms that authorized the deaths of inmates under his care. It was not work that he relished, but he felt he was making a necessary contribution to German society. Growing up, in Dr. Buchner's view, was a process of learning to perform unpleasant tasks. Soldiers did not wish to kill, but they killed for the sake of a greater good. In a small way, Dr. Buchner says, he considered himself a soldier. No one has ever become a physician without learning to perform unpleasant tasks.

"Tell me about the incentives," Karl says.

"Incentives?"

"The rewards. For working efficiently."

Yes, Dr. Buchner says, the state used rewards to encourage efficiency. Physicians at the asylum were paid on a piece-work basis: one hundred reichsmarks if they processed five hundred forms per month; two hundred reichsmarks if they processed up to two thousand forms; three hundred reichsmarks if they processed up to thirty-five hundred; four hundred reichsmarks if they processed anything over four thousand. Once he grew accustomed to the work, Dr. Buchner moved swiftly through the forms, at a pace of one every four or five minutes. He had seen no reason to delay. "Incentive compensation to speed the work of mass murder"—the phrase used to great effect by the prosecutor at Dr. Buchner's trial in 1954—seemed to Dr. Buchner to miss the point, which was—

"Which was what?" Karl asks when his grandfather hesitates.

"Which was that we were fulfilling a duty imposed upon us—a duty to the health and future of the nation. You must understand, Karl, that I did not consider myself a man of superior moral insight. The wisest men in the nation, I thought, had considered these issues. Who was I to dispute them? Physicians are said to be arrogant—gods in white coats—but I was not arrogant. I would have thought it preposterous to suggest that I possessed superior wisdom. I did not consider myself a member of a master race. I *deferred*. I let wiser heads make important decisions."

• • •

"Daddy! Daddy! Look!"

Fatherhood was a joy to Dr. Buchner. How happy he was, with his beautiful wife and his two healthy, laughing daughters. In his hours away from the asylum, how he loved to romp with his children in the garden behind their red-roofed house, to roll on the grass with them, to hear them squeal when he lifted them high off the ground, to hold and hug them, to read them the tales of the Brothers Grimm that he'd loved as a child, to share their excitement and enthusiasm as they discovered the world.

"Look, Daddy!"

"What, Anna?"

"A caterpillar. See, Daddy? There! Should I step on it?"

Lifting her little pink foot in its little white sock in its little white shoe.

"Step on it? Why would you want to step on it, Anna?"

"It's ugly."

"That's no reason, Anna. We don't kill things."

"But Daddy. *Why?* It's just an ugly old caterpillar."

"Someday it will be a butterfly."

"But Daddy!"

"A beautiful butterfly."

Stomp! Down came the foot in the little white shoe.

Or did it? Dr. Buchner cannot recall. He recalls the smile on his daughter's face as she weighed the alternatives, he recalls the lifted foot, but he cannot recall whether the queen was kind or cruel. In any case, the little girls he'd cuddled and spoiled had grown up to be beautiful and brilliant, one a physician, the other a scientist, both of them splendid. Good genes, no doubt, but also a good upbringing.

• • •

Work and worth. Work as the measure of worth.

Outside, thunder cracks and roars. Rain smashes down. The sky is an ugly gray gash.

Dr. Buchner says to his grandson, "Work was the measure."

"Those who could work were spared?"

"Often. Yes."

"And those who could not work? They were allowed to starve? Or gassed?"

"Yes."

"Those who could not work were considered worthless?"

Dr. Buchner shrugs. Karl says, "But if someone is too old to work, or too sick, or too weak? Every man and woman in every nursing home, every soldier in every veterans' hospital, every idiot, every cripple, every invalid, everyone who has stopped working, no matter what the reason—aren't they all burdens on those who work? Aren't they all ballast existences?"

"I suppose they are."

"Why should any of them live?" Karl went on, the thoughts that had been pressing and building inside him rushing out at last. "Why should anyone live here, now, in this nursing home, or in any other nursing home? Haven't all of you been worthless from the minute you stopped working? From an economic perspective, in terms of current value, in terms of costs and benefits, aren't all of you simply dead weight?"

•   •   •

Karl often thinks about German justice.

After the war, Dr. Buchner eluded prosecution for several years. But in a trial in 1954, he was convicted on charges relating to the performance of his medical duties under the National Socialist programs that authorized the sterilization and, later, the extermination of mentally and physically disabled individuals on grounds of racial or genetic undesirability, or simply on the grounds that it cost too much for a nation at war to take care of them.

Dr. Buchner was implicated in nine hundred deaths. For reasons that the judge who imposed sentence might be able to explain, though not in a way that is likely to satisfy the most scrupulous sense of justice, Karl's grandfather was sentenced to serve four years in prison—that is, one year more than the statutory minimum for the murder of one person.

In an odd way, Karl finds the sentence the judge imposed on his grandfather more difficult to understand than anything his grandfather did. Like his grandfather, Karl knows he possesses no special moral insights. He is content to let wiser heads think for him in any situation that involves issues of difficult policy. He detests the arrogance he sees in many physicians. Yet, as a consequence of the modesty that he considers a virtue, a modesty that he sees in both his grandfather and himself, Karl understands perfectly the spirit that led his grandfather to say, with an emphasis that approached vehemence, "I *deferred.*"

• • •

The iron cage.

"In Baxter's view," Max Weber wrote, "the care for external goods should only lie on the shoulders of the saint 'like a light cloak, which can be thrown aside at any moment.' But fate decreed that the cloak should become an iron cage. . . . No one knows who will live in this cage in the future, or whether at the end of this tremendous development entirely new prophets will arise, or there will be a great rebirth of old ideas and ideals, or, if neither, mechanized petrification, embellished with a sort of convulsive self-importance. For of the last stage of this cultural development, it might well be truly said: 'Specialists without spirit, sensualists without heart; this nullity imagines that it has attained a level of civilization never before achieved.'"

Professor Wiskemann, in his course on classics of modern sociological thought at the university, asked Karl and his classmates to ponder the metaphor of the iron cage that Max Weber elaborated so carefully in the final paragraphs of *The Protestant Ethic and the Spirit of Capitalism.* Some people, Professor Wiskemann told his students, manage to convince themselves that Weber glorifies the spirit of capitalism. Have they read these paragraphs? How do they interpret the phrase "mechanized petrification, embellished with a sort of convulsive self-importance"? What do they make of Weber's final judgment, adapted from a passage in Goethe: *"Specialists without spirit, sensualists without heart . . ."*? Professor Wiskemann repeated every word, slowly, forcing the class to feel the weight of the judgment. "Are these the words of a man who is pleased to find himself living in a civilization shaped and dominated by the spirit of capitalism?"

To blame capitalism for Nazi horrors seems absurd, but what is the spirit of capitalism, Karl wonders, if not the spirit embodied in the set of statistical tables discovered by the Allies in a steel filing cabinet in June 1945? These tables calculated the exact economic consequences of "disinfecting" the 70,273 people killed in Aktion T-4. Assuming an average life expectancy of ten years, the total amount saved was estimated to be 885,439,800 reichsmarks. Tables, charts, and graphs illustrated the benefits in terms of foodstuffs such as marmalade, eggs, and potatoes. For example, assuming that each patient consumed 700 grams of marmalade per month, and assuming that a kilo of marmalade cost 1.2 reichsmarks, the extermination of 70,273 useless individuals would yield a ten-year savings of 7,083,504 reichsmarks. To this were added a savings of 1,054,080 reichsmarks on cheese, 20,857,026 reichsmarks on bread, 36,429,588 reichsmarks on meat, and so on, down to the last toothbrush.

This nullity imagines that it has attained a level of civilization never before achieved.

• • •

"You must eat, Dr. Buchner."

"I have no appetite."

"Is there any treat we can get you? Some cake? Some sweet?"

"Nothing."

"Dr. Buchner, *please*."

"Nothing, I tell you. I shall eat when I feel better."

"You must keep up your strength, Dr. Buchner."

"Very well. A piece of strudel. Get me a little piece of strudel."

"Good, Dr. Buchner. You must eat. You must stay strong."

• • •

German apple cake is served at the party that celebrates Dr. Buchner's eightieth birthday. Also a Black Forest cake, pastries, fresh fruit, coffee, tea, and champagne. The residents of the Dimmsdorf Geriatric Center lift their wine-glasses to toast him on this milestone. Dr. Buchner makes gracious remarks in response, his hands trembling as he speaks. Throughout the party, a piece of apple cake sits on the plate at his side, but he takes no more than two bites. Now and then he looks down at the cake, wishing he wanted it, but he wants nothing. It is as if he has forgotten how to be hungry.

• • •

Three days before he died, Dr. Buchner fell into a sleep so deep nothing could stir him. He lay flat on his back, breathing steadily, with his chin lifted, his eyes closed, his lips slightly parted.

When he opened his eyes, he found himself on a mountain in bright sunshine, walking a few steps behind another climber. Dr. Buchner climbed easily, on strong legs. He felt young. The day was beautiful, with a sky as bright and blue as any he had ever seen. On a ledge in the sunshine, his fellow climber paused and looked back at him.

"Dr. Gruchmann! How good to see you," Dr. Buchner said.

"Come," Dr. Gruchmann said with a wave of his hand. "I have something to show you."

They continued upwards along the winding path until they reached an opening in the side of the mountain. Dr. Buchner followed Dr. Gruchmann into a cave lit by flickering torches, and then through a series of tunnels into a cavern where they stopped on a ledge that overlooked a pit full of groaning people. There were thousands of people in the pit, moaning wretchedly, scratching at sores, trying to move on deformed limbs.

"Who are they?" Dr. Buchner asked.

"These are the souls unworthy of life," Dr. Gruchmann said.

In the pit, Dr. Buchner saw people with all manner of deformities—hunchbacks, dwarfs, cripples, people obviously retarded, idiots with staring eyes, madmen with raving eyes, malformed children, old people, people unable to clean the filth from their bodies.

"These people are condemned?" Dr. Buchner asked.

"This is life unworthy of life," Dr. Gruchmann said.

"God has made this judgment?"

"We have made this judgment."

Dr. Gruchmann motioned for Dr. Buchner to follow him out of the cavern. They walked through another series of tunnels that terminated in a stone corridor like the corridors in an asylum where Dr. Buchner had worked as a medical student. Three doors were visible in the corridor. The first door led into a room full of children. A group of them near the entrance gazed at Dr. Buchner and Dr. Gruchmann.

"Hello," Dr. Buchner said.

"We cannot work," said a twisted boy in a wheelchair.

"We are worthless," said a girl with an idiot's stare.

"We are unworthy," said a boy with a withered arm.

Dr. Buchner followed Dr. Gruchmann out of the room, back into the corridor. The second door led into a room in what seemed to be a hospital ward. The room was full of men in soldiers' and sailors' uniforms. Most of the men were on crutches or in wheelchairs. Many had lost arms or legs; others were bandaged, with arm, leg, or head injuries.

"We cannot work," said a legless soldier in a wheelchair.

"We are worthless," said a soldier who had lost one arm.

"We are unworthy," said a soldier who had lost half his face.

Dr. Buchner followed Dr. Gruchmann out of the room, back into the corridor. The third door led into a shower room, with showerheads in the ceiling, benches, airtight doors, and a ventilator. Old people, including many whom

Dr. Buchner knew from the Dimmsdorf Geriatric Center, were standing naked in the shower room.

"We cannot work," Dr. Buchner's grandmother said.

"We are worthless," Dr. Buchner's father said.

"We are unworthy," Dr. Buchner's mother said.

"Mother?" Dr. Buchner said with a puzzled expression on his face.

All the old people spoke, as if in a chorus, in voices full of sorrow:

"We cannot work."

"We are worthless."

"We are unworthy."

Dr. Buchner pressed his hands over his ears and looked for Dr. Gruchmann. But his guide had disappeared, and the door leading out of the shower room was locked. The doorknob rattled in Dr. Buchner's hands as he struggled to turn it. At his back, from the showerheads in the ceiling, he heard a hissing sound. The same sound came from the pipe beneath the benches. After one final effort that came to nothing, Dr. Buchner let go of the knob. All the strength seemed to rush out of him. He turned to find his parents.

• • •

A year has passed since the death of Dr. Buchner. Now the doctor's daughter and his grandson are having lunch together at a restaurant in Dimmsdorf, on the day that would have been the doctor's eighty-first birthday. Karl has just begun his first year of medical school. He is wearing gray slacks, a navy jacket, a white shirt, and a pink tie with a pattern of pale gray stars on it. His mother—a tall woman with the fair skin, straight nose, strong chin, and reddish-brown hair that runs in the family—is wearing a simple white dress with a red belt. Her hair recently has begun to be streaked with strands of silver.

"He never wanted to be a burden," Karl's mother says. "He told me many times."

Dr. Buchner had spent the last three days of his life on a respirator, after the stroke that put him in a coma. Then he had died without regaining consciousness. His death had freed his daughters from having to decide whether to pull the plug on the respirator.

"Did I ever tell you about the dental work?" Karl asks.

"No. What dental work?"

"Employees in Aktion T-4 were eligible for cut-rate dental work, which used gold taken from the mouths of the victims. There were jars of rotten, gold-filled teeth in the offices where secretaries typed their reports."

"Charming," Karl's mother says. After a while she adds, "I'm glad you had those talks with him. I never could. Did he ever say anything that made you think he was ashamed about it, or tormented, or troubled?"

"Not tormented," Karl says. "But I'm sure he was troubled. He hadn't imagined, when he studied medicine, that anyone would ever ask him to sterilize or kill his patients."

"You know," Anna says, "he was a good doctor."

"After the war, you mean?"

"Yes. He was kind. Many people have told me so."

Karl does not comment.

"I don't say that it makes much difference," his mother says.

"I can tell you something else that troubled him."

"What's that?"

"The fake death certificates. The fake letters of condolence to the families, with made-up details about the cause of death. The urns that supposedly contained the ashes of the deceased. The whole elaborate system that was set up to make the family think that the person in the asylum had died a natural death. When, at the same time, the doctors were sending brains of special scientific interest to the university clinics in Frankfurt and Würzburg."

"Ah, well," Karl's mother says. "We're not the only ones

who'd rather not face what our parents did in those days. If only we could know that we would behave differently."

"There's a new book about German medicine in that period," Karl says.

"Oh. Have you read it?"

"I haven't had time. But I looked to see what it said about Grandfather."

"And? What did it say?"

"Nothing. I guess he wasn't important enough."

Karl's mother clears her throat, shielding her mouth, but does not speak.

"He might have spent years on that respirator," Karl says.

"No," his mother says.

"You'd have pulled the plug?"

"With my own hands."

Karl stirs his coffee. "A mercy killing? For Grandfather?"

"Not a mercy killing. A letting go."

"Because his life wasn't worth anything anymore?"

"Because his life was *over*, Karl."

"Not because he'd become a burden? Not because he'd become an inconvenience?"

"I'm not talking about convenience, Karl."

"I know. 'A letting go.' That's a nice way of putting it."

"But that's what it is. Don't you see?"

"Once we start letting go, I'm afraid we'll find it difficult to stop."

"Oh, Karl! One step on a slippery slope is not the end of the world. I think we can trust most physicians to keep their balance. In any case, you get too worked up. We've learned from the past. We've set up safeguards. We won't make the same mistakes. Different ones maybe, but not the same ones."

Karl remembers the woman who killed herself by swallowing a six-inch spoon; the woman who killed herself by swallowing feathers from a feather mattress; the physicians who sterilized, gassed, or starved their patients; the jars of teeth; the fake letters of condolence.

"Doctors," he says with a grimace. "God have mercy."

His mother lifts her cup. "God have mercy. I'll drink to that."

The Reckoning

Cynthia, the hired cook, was in the kitchen when Howard Burns came downstairs. Howard opened the refrigerator, bent to see what was in the fruit bin, and straightened with a ripe peach in his hand.

"Well, Cynthia, it's almost over now," he said.

"Is it?"

"This time tomorrow, we'll have a decision."

"About time. That's my opinion, if you don't mind my saying so."

Cynthia was a Negro woman—she never called herself black—who performed her role in a manner that seemed to derive from *Gone with the Wind*. Howard bit his peach, chewed, and swallowed. He took a napkin and wiped the juice from his lips.

"It is time. It is indeed," he said. "How long have you worked here, Cynthia?"

"Here at Arcadia, or at the president's house?"

"Both."

"Arcadia, twenty-nine years. President's house, nineteen."

"I guess you've seen about everything."

Cynthia smiled a big smile. "Not a thing! Nineteen years in this house, and I never seen a thing!"

Howard smiled back at her. "You're a wise woman, Cynthia. Someday let's sit down together, and talk about all the things we haven't seen."

"What about you, Mr. Burns? How long you been here."

"Seven years, Cynthia. Since the beginning—almost."

What he meant was: since the beginning, almost, of Simon Hubble's presidency. Cynthia understood.

"I bet you could tell some tales," she said.

"Not me, Cynthia. I'm like you: See no evil."

Seven years as special assistant to a man whom investigators had recently exposed as perhaps the most shameless crook in American higher education. Thinking about this state of affairs, Howard strolled out of the kitchen, through the richly furnished dining room where Arcadia's president entertained his most important guests, through the stuffily furnished living room that reminded Howard of rooms in the novels of Edith Wharton, through a garden room, and out the back door of the mansion. He descended a broad stone staircase and headed in bright sunshine down the path that led to the president's pool.

Even on this, the day before everyone expected a committee of the state legislature to recommend the removal of Simon Hubble as president of Arcadia College, a crowd had gathered at the pool. Jason, the Hubbles' sixteen-year-old son, was in the water, with two teenage friends, while two other friends, a sturdy-looking boy in black swim trunks and a pale-skinned blonde in a pink bikini, were sunbathing on lounge chairs.

The oldest child, twenty-five-year-old Robert, had flown in from Chicago for the weekend, with his pregnant wife, Mary. Mary was lying on her back, in a navy swimsuit, while Robert lay on his stomach, his skin turning from rose to gold. The Hubbles' middle child, twenty-two-year-old Jennifer, had shown her distaste for the situation by remaining in Berkeley.

A tall woman with silver hair was reading in a lounge chair in the shade near the deep end of the pool. Howard walked over and eased himself down onto the chair next to her.

"Where's the great man?" he asked.

"The great man has holed himself up in the library, with two lawyers and a bottle of Scotch."

"Sounds like a smart move to me."

The president's wife went on reading—a book about Scott and Zelda Fitzgerald. She was in her mid-fifties, lean and fit, with a face that had lost almost every trace of softness, if it had ever had any. After a minute or so she said, "Could you do me a favor, Howard?"

"I'll try."

"Go over there"—she motioned with her chin—"fix yourself a drink, and fix me another gin and tonic."

"My pleasure."

Howard went to the table at the other side of the pool, prepared two drinks, and came back. "Mm. Thanks," Julia Hubble said after she took a long sip.

Howard liked Julia, which was appropriate, since they'd had an affair several years ago. Julia had started it, Julia had dictated its terms, and Julia had ended it, after six sweet and nerve-wracking weeks, when she became involved with Frank Singer, the chairman of Arcadia's art history department. What mattered in the long run was that she had ended it gently, with the result that she and Howard remained on good terms.

A heavyset woman in a plain gray dress and black shoes appeared at the top of the path that led down to the pool. Walking slowly and with obvious difficulty, assisted by a cane, she began to make her way towards them. Howard jumped to his feet, trotted up the path, took her free hand, and helped her with the descent.

"Hello, Claudia," Julia said to her mother-in-law. "How was your nap?"

"What a day!" the old woman said, ignoring the question. "What a vile day!"

"Yes. Well, we've done all we can do," Julia said.

"Did you see the papers?"

"You shouldn't read them, Claudia. You know they just upset you."

"See if you could ignore the papers, if it were your son being crucified."

"Would you like a drink, Mrs. Hubble?" Howard asked.

"Thank you, Howard. I certainly would. Scotch on the rocks, please."

Howard went over to fix Claudia a drink. When he came back, people were talking about movies. Howard took a seat on a chaise a few feet away, lay back, closed his eyes, and let the sun beat down on him.

It was hard to believe, Howard thought, considering the sordidness that now stood revealed, that he had once prided himself on working for Simon Hubble. Yet he had. Even Stuart Cliff, the leader of the opposition on the faculty, acknowledged that Hubble had impressed him at the start. "Simon's a dynamo," Cliff said, "but then, Napoleon was a dynamo." At any rate, no one denied that Simon had sought to shake up sleepy Arcadia, to lift academic standards, to address persistent budgetary problems, to attract more competent students, and to recruit outstanding scholars.

What seemed clear, now, was that he also had sought to line his own pockets. Brazen—that was the word people used when they spoke about Simon Hubble. Brazen and arrogant. The evidence that had come out over the past three months would have caused any ordinary man to flee with his tail between his legs. But Simon Hubble was not ordinary. Even his enemies conceded that much.

It wasn't any one revelation, Howard thought now, but the cumulative force of multiple revelations, that had brought Simon down. Over the past few months, the newspaper articles had struck like gunshots. Details—in the end, Howard thought, details were what had doomed Simon. Not the fact that the board had bought a car for him, but the fact that it had bought him a Mercedes. Not the fact that the board paid him a high salary, but the fact that it paid him the third-highest salary of any college president in the country. Not the fact that the college had spent $2 million on a condominium for Simon, but the fact that the trustees had given him the option of buying it for $750,000.

The public might know little about art and nothing about science, but the public knew a sweetheart deal when it saw one. When the newspapers reported that expenditures to furnish Simon's condominium included fifty thousand dollars for a terrace electrified to melt snow, forty-nine hundred dollars for two glass-topped tables imported from Venice, and sixteen hundred dollars for gold-toned towel racks and soap dishes, and when that revelation was followed by the news that Simon and his allies on the board of trustees routinely entertained themselves with four-hundred-dollar bottles of wine, paid for by Arcadia, Howard had known that even a man as combative as Simon Hubble must lose the fight in the end.

At the side of the pool, without quite realizing it, Howard had dozed off. When he woke, it was because he sensed some commotion. What woke him, in fact, was the booming voice of Simon Hubble. "Pygmies, fools, and imbeciles!" Simon was saying. "All my life, I've had to deal with pygmies, fools, and imbeciles!" At that moment, Howard's eyes flickered open, and Simon, missing nothing, immediately drew him into the conversation: "Isn't that right, Howard?"

"Right, boss."

Simon was wearing pale-gray slacks and a yellow short-sleeved polo shirt. He was a short, muscular man with the build of a football tackle of the 1940s—a man who might have made a living shoveling coal, Howard thought, if he hadn't been a gifted scholar and an effective—some people said ferocious—academic administrator.

Simon began to turn away from Howard, but then he turned back, with a puzzled look on his face: "Why are you here, Howard?"

Howard asked why he shouldn't be here.

"You're dozing on the deck of the Titanic. Tell me the truth, Howard. Have you lined up a new job yet?"

The truth was that Howard, anticipating that Simon's successor would not take long to roll out the guillotine, had lined up a job with a public relations firm in Chicago.

"I'm going down with the ship, boss," Howard said.

"I'm surrounded by pygmies, fools, imbeciles, and *liars!*" Simon smiled with what seemed to be genuine merriment. "I appreciate the sentiment, Howard. Good luck with the new job, whatever it is."

Without opening his lips, Howard smiled a faintly affectionate smile.

"Who the hell knows?" Simon said, turning away from Howard. "Maybe we'll win." No one in the group nibbled that bait, though Simon gave them a chance. With a shrug he said, "*Nah!* No way. The pygmies want me dead."

Then he was off again, explaining himself, justifying himself, blasting everyone who opposed him, railing against his "enemies," as if his enemies had compelled him to drink those four-hundred-dollar bottles of wine, to electrify that terrace, to negotiate those sweetheart deals, to drive a Mercedes, to purchase sixteen hundred dollars' worth of gold-toned bathroom fixtures.

Somehow, in the midst of his tirade, Simon noticed that sixteen-year-old Jason had joined the group that was listening to him, along with two of Jason's friends, the boy in black swimming trunks and the girl in the pink bikini.

"I guess it's pretty hard for you," Simon said to Jason, "having everybody convinced your old man's a crook?"

"Not so hard," Jason said, unpersuasively.

"Yeah. Well. Keep your chin up." Frowning, Simon began to turn away.

"Dad?"

"Yes."

"It's true, isn't it? I mean: everything they say you did, you did it, didn't you?"

The boy hadn't used the word crook, but he'd called his father a crook. Howard understood that, and so did everyone else who had heard.

Simon turned back to face his son. "Is that what you think?" he said.

"It's in all the papers."

"You can't believe everything you read in the papers. Don't you know that yet?"

"You mean it's lies?"

"I mean—" Simon hesitated, as if not sure how to frame his response. At last he said, "I only took what I deserved."

"You mean you were entitled?"

"I mean I *earned* it."

Jason did not respond, though he looked unhappy. Simon said, "Jason, do you want your father to be a fool?"

Jason still did not respond, and after a few seconds, Simon said, "Did I take? You bet. Did I give value for what I took? You bet! Who else could've done what I've done with this place?"

"I guess it's hard for me to understand," Jason said. Then, gathering courage: "Is it okay to take what you want, just because you're in a position to take it?"

"It's okay to take what you *deserve*. A man's entitled to take what he deserves."

Howard felt sorry for Jason. In the face of the father's booming self-confidence, who wouldn't shrink?

Jason said, softly, "What if you wind up looking . . . the way you look."

"The way I look? How do I look?"

Jason ignored the question. With something desperate in his voice, as if he yearned to hear some magic words that would make the whole messy subject go away, he said, "Anyway, Dad, I don't understand why you thought so *much* was coming to you."

Simon explained. Being a college president was a tough job. You needed energy, you needed vision, and you needed stamina. You needed all that and more, Simon said, because a college president was forced to deal constantly with fools, imbeciles, and pygmies. To be a good college president, you had to be a fighter.

Jason stood frowning in the sun. Simon was standing with his back to the light, and the glare in Jason's face made the boy squint. Howard looked at him while he looked at his father. *A fighter, but not a crook,* the look on the boy's face said. In the years that followed, when Howard remembered Simon and Jason Hubble, that moment in the sunlight was the one he remembered.

• • •

"Mr. Burns?"

"Pardon?"

"Excuse me, but I thought I recognized you. I'm Jason Hubble—Simon Hubble's son. Are you Howard—?"

"Jason!"

Twenty years had passed. Howard Burns was now a man near sixty, with silver hair and eyes that had faded to a dusty brown. He was wearing a business suit, a white shirt, and a red-and-navy tie. Jason Hubble was in his mid-thirties, a dark-haired, slender man in blue jeans and a cheap T-shirt. Something in the way he was dressed, a suggestion of shabbiness, told Howard that he was, at best, down on his luck.

"Jason! Good to see you! How are you?"

They had met in a waiting area at O'Hare Airport, outside Chicago. They shook hands and sat down next to one another.

"Fine. Just fine," Jason said. "How are you, sir."

"Call me Howard, *please*. I'm fine. What are you doing these days, Jason?"

"I'm—uh—well, I'm sort of between jobs."

"Oh?"

"Yes. I had a job with a computer company, but I was downsized. You know how it is."

"Yes. I'm sorry."

"How about you, Mr. Burns?"

"Howard."

"Howard."

"Well, you know, Jason, I'm a p. r. man. I work for Senator Finch now, in Indiana."

"Really? That's great!"

"Not so great, actually. But it pays the bills."

"My father died, you know."

At the mention of his father's death, Jason looked mournful. Howard was glad of that.

"Yes. I saw it in the papers. I'm sorry, Jason."

"He never really got back on his feet. After Arcadia."

"No? I lost touch with him."

"He couldn't get a university job—that is, not running a university. But he finally found a little college that would let him teach. In Iowa."

"I see."

"It depressed him—you know what an ego he had—and he started drinking. That's what killed him in the end. Liver disease."

"How about your mom, Jason?"

"She's in a nursing home now. Alzheimer's."

"I'm sorry."

Julia Hubble, with Alzheimer's! Howard was stunned, almost to the point of wooziness, by the thought that a woman whom he remembered as a lover was old enough to have Alzheimer's. He recalled her long, sharp face, the way her lips curled when she heard something that amused her, the way her eyes glittered when she said something mean or got something she wanted.

"But she's young," Howard said.

"Only sixty-six," Jason said. "It happens."

"I guess."

"Remember my brother Bob?" Jason said. "He's an investment banker, in New York. He's got the whole shebang—yacht, townhouse on Park Avenue, Jaguar."

Bastard! Howard thought. What he said, with a smile, was "Good for him!"

"He's like my dad. No holds barred."

"How about your sister?"

"Jennifer?" Jason's face darkened. "She's got—problems. You know, she took it badly, the whole business with my father. They had awful fights, didn't talk for a couple of years. Not that it's fair to blame him."

Why not? Howard thought, but he merely shrugged.

"Anyway," Jason said, "she got a degree in nursing, didn't like it, tried to get into medical school, couldn't make it, got involved with some guy who turned out to be bad news, and now she's living in Rhode Island, in some kind of commune."

"I didn't think we had those anymore."

"I guess you could say it's a cult. It's kind of scary."

Howard did not say anything for a while.

"Mr.—uh, Howard?"

"Yes."

"I didn't quite tell the truth. About the downsizing."

"Oh?"

"The truth is, I got fired because I had a breakdown."

"I'm sorry, Jason."

"I'm like Jennifer, in a way. Not too stable."

"I guess it was tough, all that stuff with your father."

"I don't think you should blame him."

"I'm not blaming him. I'm just saying it was tough."

"Yeah. It was tough."

Looking at Jason as a man, Howard recalled the boy at the pool, twenty years ago, confronting his father. Almost every day, in one newspaper or another, Howard read about some scam, some scandal, some violation of trust or honor, some brazen sleaziness, that reminded him of Simon Hubble. Corporate executives in pharmaceutical companies covering up evidence that a new drug produced dangerous side effects. People selling babies to parents desperate to adopt. A beloved niece fleecing her ninety-year-old aunt out of $15 million in art. A father who refuses to pay child support for his daughter—and then seeks a share of the estate after she is killed in an auto accident. A judge's decision in child support or custody battles depending on the woman's response to his request for sexual favors. In every case, Howard thought as he looked at Jason, the untold story was the story of a blasted family. Where were the newspaper articles about the husbands and wives, the parents and children, who were caught up in these scandals?

"You know," Howard said, "your father had his good points, too."

"I know."

"He did some great things at Arcadia, some important things, but he got greedy. Believe me, it happens all the time."

"It's different when it's your father," Jason said. "A kid doesn't just want a father he can love. He wants a father he can respect."

"Yes. That's true."

"It knocked me for a loop," Jason said. "There he was, the great educator, the *leader*. But he was just a crook."

The sadness in Jason's eyes told Howard that the world had demanded a reckoning for Simon Hubble's actions. The sins of the father had come back to haunt and damage his son.

"I hope you don't hate him," Howard said to Jason. "A son shouldn't hate his father."

The airport was full of noise and bustle, but Howard and Jason paid no attention. Jason seemed to be struggling to reply.

"No," he said at last, with a weary look. Then, with a twist of his mouth that was almost a grimace: "No. I don't hate him. I just hate the way I feel when I think about him."

Afterword

No publication is as poignant as that of a posthumous first volume of fiction. With Peter Baida's *A Nurse's Story and Others,* this sense is further compounded by the fact that the author died within months of the title story winning first prize in the O. Henry Short Story Awards.

No fiction writer would have dared to invent such a heart-breaking coincidence, and yet it happened just this way. Instead of the O. Henry Award being a true happily-ever-after ending with more stories, more awards, more recognition, Peter, who had suffered from hemophilia all his life and had endured any number of complications stemming from that disease, ultimately could not overcome the final, devastating illness he battled for five long months in the hospital, before his death at the age of forty-nine on December 10, 1999.

Rather than allow life's heavy-handed irony to overshadow Peter's work, however, I prefer to let it serve, instead, as a lens that helps illumine Peter's literary achievement. On the most obvious level, given Peter's own history of illness, it is no acci-dent that many of his stories are set against a medical back-drop. More subtly, these stories reveal that what Peter learned from his travels in the world of illness was a compas-sion for the vulnerable. And it is this understanding, one that goes beyond empathy, that suffuses his work.

In story after story, Peter focuses on the lives of ordinary people struggling with extraordinary ethical choices. With the true storyteller's breathtaking economy of language, Peter cuts straight to the core: Can even the most devoted nurse, or parent, or child, ensure his or her loved one a "good" death? More to the point, how do you measure whether it was a "good" life? What is the legacy each of us will leave behind, through our work and through our deeds? Peter dramatizes these questions through the individual quandaries his characters face, sometimes on the job—as potential whistle-blowers, union-builders, or union-busters—and always in the life-and-death medical dilemmas very few of us will manage to escape.

For the most part, Peter's characters see themselves (whether they actually turn out to be what they say is up to the reader to decide) as basically decent, middle- and working-class stiffs who suddenly find themselves smack-dab in the middle of some unusual, uncomfortable, even unspeakable circumstance. Being merely human, without exception these characters make it clear that they would have preferred to decline the honor of having life deal them such a difficult hand. Yet play that hand they must—and it is not until the game of life itself is complete that they can begin to measure just how high, and how far-reaching, were the moral stakes for which they played.

As the title of the collection's concluding story so aptly puts it, there is always a "reckoning," and its impact endures for generations. And now, with Peter's death, comes the summing up of his life, and his work. He lived the way he wrote, with a straightforward grace, precision, and insight—and, yes, a dark, inescapable irony—that everyone who knew and loved him will miss. But Peter's voice, in all its fullness, is here in his stories to be read and cherished—the writer's legacy he would have wished.

—*Diane Cole*